The Long Walk

Slavery to Freedom

Kentucky slaves who suffer the indignities of bondage,
seek freedom on the Underground Railroad

Historical Novel

Judith C. Owens-Lalude

Anike Press
Worldwide Publisher
Henderson, Nevada US

The Long Walk: Slavery to Freedom
© Copyright 2012, Judith C. Owens-Lalude, Louisville, Kentucky
Second Edition, published 2019, AnikePress, Henderson, Nevada

Anike Press
Worldwide Publisher
Henderson, Nevada, USA

Orders AnikePress
        jcamille@AnikePress.com
        http://AnikePress.com

ISBN   978-0-9972613-4-9

LCCN 2018915225

The Long Walk: Slavery to Freedom
includes:
        Acknowledgements from scholars
        Supportive institutions
        Suggested readings
        Discussion questions

Book cover design by Judith C. Owens-Lalude
Cover illustration by Sean Pike Gardner

To contact the author or receive information about programs
connected with the novel:
jcamille@AnikePress.com
http://jcamilleculturalacademy.com

This book was written in honor of my ancestors, who were noble Africans not seeking to be enslaved; my loving, stand-by-my-side-always husband, A. O'tayo Lalude, M.D.; my two wonderful sons, A. Adesina Lalude and Akinwande A. Lalude, whose endorsement was invaluable. My dream of telling my story would not have been realized if it were not for the tenacious and loving support of my family and friends.

ACKNOWLEDGEMENTS

Note: The Long Walk: From Slavery to Freedom is the title of the first person interpretive program of Clarissa, a character from the book titled:
The Long Walk: Slavery to Freedom.

California State Polytechnic University Pomona, Pomona, California, scheduled *The Long Walk: Slavery to Freedom* program on several occasions, establishing a partnership that has led to a college program for students interested in studying the Underground Railroad in Kentucky and its border states.

Carnegie Center for Arts and History, New Albany, Indiana, granted the opportunity to present an interpretive program, *The Long Walk: From Slavery to Freedom,* to the families of their community, friends, and students when recognition and support was needed.

Family, Friends, and Second Friday Critique Group became a much-needed fulcrum, never giving up on me, even when I doubted myself and wanted to quit.

j. camille cultural academy staff members and partners diligently worked on my behalf, enabling me to write and continue with the academy activities.

Jefferson County Public Schools, Louisville, Kentucky, recognized the significance of *The Long Walk: Slavery to Freedom,* for their students as an introduction to an antebellum Kentucky story written, told, and dramatized by the great-granddaughter of African Americans enslaved in Spencer County, Kentucky.

Kentucky Center for the Arts, Louisville, Kentucky, accepted the interpretive program and teacher's guide developed for *The Long Walk: From Slavery to Freedom.* It is part of the Kentucky Arts Education Showcase.

Kentucky Foundation for Women, Louisville, Kentucky, awarded me an Artist Enrichment Grant that enabled me to enhance *The Long Walk: Slavery to Freedom,* while reaching out to women, children, and families, bringing to life the history of Africans and African Americans enslaved in Northern Kentucky before the Civil War.

Lorraine Monroe Leadership Institute, New York, New York, was the first organization to recognize *The Long Walk: Slavery to Freedom* and the impact that it might have on school history and social studies curricula for students in elementary and middle schools. Their support was a significant springboard for my Kentucky history programs.

Lyles Station, Princeton, Indiana, extended an invitation to perform *The Long Walk: Slavery to Freedom,* a storytelling of the enslavement of African Americans in North Central Kentucky during the 1850s.

National Underground Railroad Freedom Center, Cincinnati, Ohio, extended an invitation to perform the interpretative program that is a part of *The Long Walk: Slavery to Freedom.*

Nelson and Spencer Counties community members and historical societies provided information about my ancestors and their enslavement and enslavers who lived in Fairfield and Goodwin Spring, Kentucky, during the 1850s.

Society of Children's Book Writers and Illustrators answered questions and critiqued writings intended for *The Long Walk: Slavery to Freedom*. That support afforded the courage needed to uphold a writing dream.

Women Who Write, Louisville, Kentucky, insisted that I publish my manuscript and then stood behind my work–encouraging me to pursue my dream and never waffling in their support.

Table of Contents

Preface

In 1619 the Dutch ship *Man-of-War,* commanded by Captain Jope, sailed to Jamestown, Virginia. On board were twenty West African natives who had been stolen from a Spanish vessel and held as cargo. While at sea, Captain Jope ran out of rations and needed to restock his ship.[1] When the vessel docked in Virginia, Africans stumbled down the planks to a new and strange world. They were exchanged for provisions such as blankets, food, fabric, sugar, and rum, and then held in indentured servitude, working undesirable jobs while being treated harshly and paid very little, or not at all.

After approximately forty years, the European settlers began to realize the booming profits that resulted from the cheap labor of the Africans, and began to buy and sell them. That is when African enslavement in the American colonies grew to a profound level of greed.

In Louisville, Kentucky, during the 1800s, the buying and selling of slaves was legal:

> The Louisville slave markets were located in the heart of the downtown area. The Arterburn Slave Pens . . . were located on the east side of First Street between Jefferson and Market; it had pens and a jail yard . . . Matthew Garrison, also a notorious dealer, had pens on the east side of Second Street between Market and Main. Garrison employed a "runner," William W. Wilson, who was paid $20 for every African American person he brought to Garrison. Free men and women from both north and south of the Ohio River were sometimes taken back into slavery this way.

After the enslaved Africans were auctioned in the Jefferson County courtyard, some were dragged to the levee to be loaded onto boats waiting on the Ohio River, ready to haul them away along with the baled cotton, sugar cane, hemp ropes, fabric, and tobacco. They were sent down the Ohio River to the Mississippi River into the Deep South to work on plantations–the one thing every slave feared. Other enslaved Negroes were trotted to Tennessee. Brought by twos, the men and boys were fastened by their ankles to about fifty feet of chain. They led the march and the women followed them. Women and children who were unable to walk were packed into wagons, and rode at the rear of the line. The order of the march was always the same.[3]

Once men, women, and children were purchased, it was not unusual for them to be whipped, overworked, and denied adequate food, sleep, decent clothing, and family privacy, making life hellish for the enslaved Africans. Slave trade continued in Kentucky until 1865. Those turbulent years of enslavement never squelched the desires of the enslaved to be free.

The Long Walk: Slavery to Freedom is an historical fiction that celebrates those heroes and heroines of the nineteenth century who may be unnamed but are not forgotten by a people grateful for their courage. The characters are fictional, and the names were selected from those that were common in the mid-1800s. The quilt in the story is a fictional device created solely for the purpose of the storytelling.

1. Hugh Thomas, *The Slave Trade: The Story of the Atlantic Slave Trade: 1440–1870* (New York: Simon & Schuster, 1997).
2. Pamela Peters, *The Underground Railroad in Floyd, Indiana* (Jefferson, North Carolina: McFarland & Co., 1940).
3. Isaac Johnson, *Slavery Days in Old Kentucky*. Ogdensburg (New York: Republican & Journal C. Print, 1994).

The Long Walk: Slavery to Freedom
Readers of all ages can relate to this profoundly moving story of overcoming obstacles. *The Long Walk: Slavery to Freedom* is not only compelling history, it's fascinating reading, too!

Dr. Lonnetta M. Taylor-Gaines
New York and Florida
Educational Consultant and Author
Fia and the Butterfly: Seven Stories for Character

The Long Walk
Slavery to Freedom

Under Effie's Roof

1

Frightful Journey

The woman leaned against the rear of the auction block. Her small boy squatted at her feet bundled in the quilt that had been handed down, woman to woman, in her family. Befuddled, she studied the surface of the block. It was polished by damp feet, marred by shackles, stained with blood, and punctuated with dark bits of flesh. The woman closed her eyes. Recollections of her family being sold raced through her mind: her man, Jake, burdened with age and worn out; her big boy, Toby, with the butterfly birthmark on the back of his neck; and the twin gals, Mary and Molly, wrapped together and bonded as one. Grieved, the woman shifted her focus to Ben Mullins, her new owner. He was tall and slim, wearing goatskin gloves and a wide-brim hat that camouflaged the stubbles on his face.

Ben moved between the unsold slaves as if he danced a peg-legged waltz without a partner. He shielded his ears against their deafening moans and cupped a hankie beneath his nose to impede the stench of human filth. He stumbled until he stood at the edge of the pathetic group.

"Enough's enough," he said gruffly.

Ben Mullins collected his stock and led them across the courthouse yard to the ox and cart that he had parked at the bend of the Louisville Turnpike. A sense of ease emerged as the mayhem of the auction dissipated and was gobbled up in the hush of a single but grievous voice.

Mullins loaded his stock into the back of the cart, pitched scabrous horse blankets on top of them, same as he did for his hounds on frigid nights. The woman gasped, nearly losing her breath. She swiftly shifted her nostrils above the stench of the blankets and threw her shawl over the boy's head.

It was January 16, 1846, Louisville, Kentucky. Mullins stood next to the oxcart, lost in a daydream that twisted his gut. He scanned the heaviness of the late evening sky, trying to determine the threat of a fresh snowfall. He kicked his muddy boots against the wheel, knocking off the slop. He mumbled to himself, "Glad that damn snow stopped falling." Mullins pulled the burdensome weight of his body up and dropped it onto the hard, cold, but welcoming bench of the oxcart. Anxiety curved his shoulders as he reached for the reins. The shirt he wore beneath his coat tightened across his back when he leaned forward. With both elbows on his knees, he sorted the leather strips between his fingers. Mullins struggled to untangle the rambling thoughts that invaded his mind: his new stock, workdays ahead, and the reception that he might receive on his return home. He stared into the darkness as he monitored the length of turnpike leading south.

"Hike," he hollered and snapped the straps against the ox's rear. The cart jerked and headed toward Spencer County, Kentucky. The animal clopped along as dusk plummeted into darkness.

Holding on to her son, the woman cringed as she spied the slave pen where she and her family huddled together for the last time. The sights of it caused her head to throb. Her stomach twisted into a tight knot that forced a sour taste into her throat. The pen vanished just as her family had. Gone. Gone for what she knew would be forever. The woman swallowed and tucked her head beneath the covers. She wiped away tears for herself and the other poor souls being left behind to be auctioned, beaten, put on a steamer, or walked to Tennessee.

The woman turned her face away from the wind, peppered with ice and slicing beneath the blankets, intensifying the dense fear of the unknown that weighed her down. She squashed the covers against her chin. Without thought, her arms reached for her boy and coiled around his slight being. She tugged him under the cover into her sunken bosom. Only her eyes showed.

The woman cowered beneath the tree limbs that sparred above her head while the bottom of the wagon jabbed splinters into her hands and forearms. Blood oozed from the pinhole wounds. She grimaced, wedged part of the filthy quilt she had clutched, for what seemed a lifetime, beneath her boy's head. The rest was poked between their bodies and the coarse blankets thrown at them. None of the covers provided the warmth that the hearth, left behind in Virginia, had when she and her family were snatched from their slight happiness—too many days ago to tally.

"I miss ya pa, little man, and dem twins dreadfully," she murmured to her boy, whose head was pillowed on her arm. He was too depleted from the journey going west to be sold and too near death to respond with a spoken word. The gloom from his shallow eyes scrutinized her sorrowful face. The woman drew her cold, frail fingers down the prickly rope that kept the boy's britches up. She grappled to remember the number of times she had tightened the cord around his waist or looped the tail of the crude, homespun shirt around his vulnerable body.

"You gotta keep livin'. Dat be our only hope."

The woman laced her fingers with the boy's. She closed her eyes. She prayed aloud, and then louder, "Oh, Lawd! Watch over my boy and me. Give me back my man and my chillen."

Her devotions grew to a crescendo that pierced Ben Mullins' eardrums and hung on to every nerve ending. He yanked the headstall straps. The cart lurched and slipped into a furrow. Reeling with anger, Ben Mullins bunched his muffler around his neck and tugged his hat down over the helix of his ears. When he jumped down from the wagon, his footsteps squeaked on the snow. The boy's eyes shifted, following the sound of them.

Mullins snatched the blankets off the wench and her boy. "Gal!" She flinched. "Since you're keeping up that ruckus, I got something for you to snivel about."

He slammed his bullwhip down on the woman's flank with a powerful whop. She screeched out with pain. The boy drew himself into a pill-bug roll. Mullins turned like he hadn't done a thing and remounted the wagon. He flailed the reins, slapping the ox once more to move on. The animal snorted and tugged at its load, but the wagon resisted.

"Gal, get down. We're stuck!"

Mullins jumped from the wagon. The woman sat straight up. She looked down on her boy and told him in less than a whisper, "Be still. Don't move." His eyelids drooped against her words. She lowered her legs until the balls of her feet touched the frozen ground.

Without waiting for the woman to be sure-footed, Ben Mullins yelled, "Put your grimy paws up there. Push when I say push."

The woman positioned her hands on the wagon. With unsteady legs, she tilted toward it; her skirt mopped the ground. Mullins braced himself against the coarse frame of the cart and took in a hefty breath. "Push!" he yelled. She did, but her toes caught the tail of her skirt hem and dragged her facedown into the muddy slush. When she struggled to stand on her feet, Mullins tightened his fist and walloped her, knocking her into a ditch. The woman palmed the side of her face. She was too stunned to sob. When she raised her head, the boy's frightful eyes peered at her from between the wagon slats. She scrambled back up the incline close to where Mullins stood rocked back on his heels with his arms folded across his chest, staring through his evil-to-the-core silted eyes.

"Wench, you done caused me trouble."

Mullins lowered his arms and drew his elbows against his rigid body. He tightened his fist once more and then released his fingers for a backhand to the woman's lean shoulder. The blow sent her head over heels again into the ditch. Her toes grappled at the sloppy ground as she clambered back up the hill. Impatient, Mullins dragged her by her arm over the rise and thrusted her behind the cart.

"Push when I say push."

As the woman stuffed the hem of her skirt, weighted with the sting of icy slush, into her waistband, she and Mullins leaned against the cart. "Push!" he hollered. The wheel rocked until it lunged from the rut back onto the road.

"Get in that cart!"

Mullins climbed on the cart, adjusted his coat, and took charge of the reins. As the woman attempted to lug her upper body into the oxcart, it rolled away, leaving her lower half dangling off the rear and holding on to a sideboard. She cried out for help, but Mullins either didn't hear or didn't care. He yelled at the ox, urging it into a full stride. The cart dipped, jerked, and dropped into a crater. The woman's legs shot up into a kangaroo kick. Her body slammed against the rear of the cart with a sharp blow to her upper back. The boy landed on top of her.

"Ma! Ma!" he cried.

Breathing laboriously, the woman embraced him to silence his whimpers. She butted her lips against his ear. "Take care, boy. I's here, but I's weary. I knows you is too. Ya gotta live." She stroked her boy's bony cheek. "We be gittin' victuals soon . . . I pray." The woman paused. "You done seen two harvests and some. You gotta see more." She lay on her side, bent her knees, and scooped the boy into her fold. She gently smoothed down hairs that wired from his brows.

"You's all I got now." Dovelike, she tucked the covers around him and placed her head next to his. The two lay still as death before its soul is summoned by its creator.

2

Mammy's Cabin

The oxcart wobbled its way south to Goodwin Spring in Spencer County, moving closer to Ben Mullins' farm. The ox's hooves began to mimic the gurgling creek in the gully below that followed the road. It wasn't long before the springhouse at the edge of his property appeared as if it were leaning toward him. Feeling greeted by the structure, Mullins reared up off his seat. He slowed the cart before turning onto the graveled lane that sowed its way to the house. The wheels raked up a barrage of pebbles, crashing them against the floorboards, making a clatter so frightful the woman bore down on her boy.

Ben's spine straightened with pride as his eyes strained to scan the 600-acre property sprawled beneath the moonlight. He didn't need to continue gripping the reins; the ox knew to follow the handle of the three-tined pitchfork lane that separated identical hewed log cabins sitting back off the alley, five on each side, well manicured and evenly spaced. The slave quarters offered Mullins and his visitors a clear view of his Kentucky wealth. The center lane wove its way to the front steps of the big house while the right tine led off to the carriage house and on to the barn, and the left one passed the loom house and kitchen. Mullins couldn't see the entire grounds or all the outbuildings separated by lush swaths of land. It didn't matter. He knew every corner of the farm without seeing it all.

Effie's cabin was the last one on the left just before the bend at the base of the tine. She was the eldest female slave and the most beloved that Mullins owned. Her plump, round face was the color of polished walnut shells, set with soft almond eyes that glistened from beneath a crown of dull, cottony hair. The glow of Effie's face stole most hearts. Everyone who knew her, knew about the red oak tree she adored. It stood a far piece from the back of her cabin and was better than fifty feet tall. Its summer foliage was so broad it could easily protect a hundred hot souls from the midday heat. Effie wanted to be buried under it when her time came. She made sure that everyone was aware of her desire.

On up ahead was the loom house. It was the first structure on the straight of the north tine. Further on was the kitchen. It was a small brick outbuilding just to the rear of the big house and yard door. The ox slowed its pace to a stop in front of Effie's cabin where Mullins often visited before continuing on to the big house.

Ben sprang from the bench with the zest of a child eager to see his mother after being separated for some time. He knocked at Effie's door, the only barrier in the slave quarters that he respected. When it opened, the woman was sure that she was encountering an angel who wore a soft white apron fluttering like cream flowing from a milk can. That angelic figure greeted Mullins graciously.

"Evenin', Massa."

Her voice was more musical than Miss Bessie's harp. She was the wife of the man who owned the woman and her boy before they were auctioned off.

"Glad to be back and be done with my work, Mammy."

That's what he had called Effie since she had nursed him from the time he was a young boy in knickers and long stockings. He had continued calling her Mammy even after putting on his first pair of manly britches.

"It was a grueling three weeks. I got a couple of new ones for you. Margaret's going to like them. That is," he paused, smiled at Effie, and then respectfully lowered his eyes, "after you've taken care of them."

His mood shifted as he thrust his head back, aiming it at the new gal and her boy. He yanked the woman, who attempted to stand, but instead tumbled into his arms. With a swipe of his hand, he brushed her away like filth clinging to his coat. The woman floundered but remained on her feet. She lifted her trembling boy and the quilt from the wagon to the ground. The child hunkered down and clamped his arms around her. Swaddled in the quilt, he rested his head against her leg. He shuddered from the wetness of his clothes and the breeze that licked at him.

A stray puppy raised his leg above the toe of Mullins' boot. "You stuuupid beast! You just pissed on my boot. Git! Git, before I kick your hide back to the barn."

The hound wiggle-waggled over to the boy.

"Stu, stu," the boy puffed, repeating part of what he had heard Mullins say. The puppy slurped the words from the boy's mouth. The boy didn't realize he was naming the dog.

Mullins flipped his thumb at the child. "That's hers. Doubt he'll make it through the night. Seems awful sickly to me. Not much bigger than that puppy."

Effie reached out to the woman and the boy. They stretched their necks, wanting to feel the warmth from the brightness of the firelight spilling from the opened door.

"Come on in here, honeychile. I gits you close to dat fire." Effie's heavenly voice seemed to surface from afar.

The woman didn't move. She studied Effie. Not sure of what she was encountering, she leaned away from the scene.

The woman's blue lips quivered. "Cain't rightly move. I's painin' so. Got no feelin' in my hands and feet."

"Get!" Mullins snorted.

He jabbed the butt of his bullwhip into the woman's back, pressed it firmly against her flank, and twisted it, making sure that she knew he was her master. The boy tumbled over into the affection of the puppy that nuzzled him.

"She's got the stench of sweat and fear all over her. She's going to need a powerful scrubbing with plenty lye soap. That one there, he stinks of death and old piss. Don't know whatcha gonna to do about him. He hasn't made a sound since we left Louisville."

Mullins tucked his whip under his arm. He rummaged through his breast pocket before plucking out a red hemp pouch tied at the neck with an indigo cord. He carefully took Effie's hand and placed the bundle in her palm that was coarse from decades of hard labor. He rolled his fingers around her hand and gently squeezing it.

"Mammy, you take care to not waste this. You know it's hard to come by these days." He spoke with the adoration he typically reserved for highbrow white folks.

Effie beamed and tucked the gift inside her sleeve. "I knows what dis here is, Massa," she said, still smiling.

Mullins tipped his hat to Mammy and then nabbed the puppy. He tossed it into the rear of the cart and walked past the woman and her boy, so close he could have stepped on them. He didn't. Instead, he ignored them, mounted the cart, and flung the reins in his usual way.

"Hike," he hollered.

The wheels of the cart sent up a gush of slush that drenched the woman and the boy. Without looking back, Mullins loosened his hold on the headstall. The ox moved between the frosted trees silhouetted by silvery of moonlight. They defined the alley that led to the twin gardens before continuing on to the big house. Their glistening branches reached across the lane, touching the branches that reached back. They were the poplar trees that Margaret, his wife of seven years, loved most. She always spoke excitedly about the spring blooms, which looked like yellow tulips and had a floral fragrance that sweetened the air. She was delighted, too, in the fall when the green leaves transformed into a bristling golden-yellow foliage.

Mullins rested his body against the bench and centered his attention on the cart as it negotiated the dips in the carriage lane. His stare followed the road and onto to the big house. He nervously patted the gnarly bench next to his thigh. He wondered if Margaret would be waiting up for him. He hadn't taken a runner on this trip to send back messages letting the family know when to expect him.

Gazing into space, Mullins mumbled, "I got you everything you wanted in one woman. A gal that can cook, do laundry, sew, and run a loom. Plus, she's got that boy. He's young enough, if bred right, he'll make plenty of good-looking pickaninnies, adding nicely to the estate."

Mullins chuckled when he imagined Margaret's eyes capturing the slight beauty of the new slave woman.

That is, after she's been cleaned up, fattened up, and given decent clothing. But, I worry about that boy. He's sickly . . . real sickly. Didn't cry once. That's unusual for a chap as young as him. I pray Mammy can get him up and running around the quarters with the other little darkies and get that gal working in a few days. Mammy's always done wonders with those poorly hands, bringing them back from the dead when others thought they were gone for good.

Ben Mullins glanced straight off to his right. Up ahead, he saw the small shed that the hands built, at her request, to warehouse her whatnots: crib, toys, furniture, pots, pans, and a host of other goods. Things she couldn't live without but seldom saw. It was on the

South side of the property and wasn't much larger than a slave's cabin, but it had no windows or a chimney. It was vented at the overhang of the roof, allowing fresh air in to keep down the mold. Inside there was a deep hole with a rope pulley for the overflow of the orchard fruits that needed to be cooled. The field hands and help gathered in front of the structure when they made candles and lye soap, shucked corn, prepared meat for the smokehouse, stuffed sausages, did woodworking, and celebrated a crop's yield. The door was kept locked, forestalling the temptations for theft.

Further up, a corncrib and a smokehouse were anchored on solid foundations of precisely laid stones. Not far from them was a second knee-high stone wall that snaked across the southeastern part of the property. It retained a slight hill that sloped toward the alley, separating the slave cabins from the upper grounds. As Mullins drew nearer to the big house, he spotted a corner of the barn amid the trees. It set back a good piece from the main house. When he stood on the balcony at the rear of big house, he could clearly see the barn, but he couldn't see the second stone wall that rippled behind it, crossing the northeastern section of the plantation. It was the boundary between his land and that of Isaac Leyland, the people's doctor, a farmer, and his lifetime friend.

The cart passing between the oval gardens startled Sam, Ben's coachman and fiddler. He was a small aging man with thin limbs; smooth, ebony skin; kinky salt-and-pepper hair; and wrinkled hands always ready to fiddle a tune. He was half-hidden between the hitching post and the huntboard. It was used outside in the summer and spring when the hunters rode up on horseback to retrieve cool drinks and snacks. Sam stood next to it, hidden in the shadows. He stared wide-eyed into the night, ready to skedaddle if it were a no-good stranger approaching the house.

"Dat you, Massa?" His voice crackled.

"It's me, Sam."

"Thought so, Massa."

Mullins handed the reins to Sam. "Go tell Big Bo to fix this wheel and check the others. Tend to this animal. No need to tether him. I won't be going back out this evening. That gal that I brought from Louisville gave me a heap of trouble. And this damn cart got stuck in the mud." Mullins kicked at the faulty wheel. "Took some work to wrestle it out of an unyielding rut. It wobbled coming up the lane. Take that pup back to where he belongs."

Mullins adjusted his coat. He gave the huntboard a fleeting look. He was too fatigued to question its being left out in the night air. Mullins tugged a bag from behind the bench seat, slung it across his back, and retrieved a small bundle from beneath the seat. He tucked the fancy package under his armpit. Dragging each foot across the boot scraper, he peeled off the ugliness of his trip along with the mud. When done, he stepped back and glanced at the house as if being introduced to it for the first time. Troubled by the thought of what might be waiting for him on the other side of the door, Ben climbed the steps. Feeling the burden of his trip, he reached for the handle that sprang away from him.

Ann Marie threw her arms around his legs. "You're home, Papa."

"I am."

Mullins lifted up his five-year-old daughter who engulfed him in hugs and kisses. Just as he drew his fingers through Ann Marie's soft, golden curls, Margaret's voice penetrated the sweet moment.

"About time you got back. You've been gone long enough."

Mullins put Ann Marie down. "Go to bed. I'll visit you when I come up. Bought something for you on my trip."

His daughter rushed up the stairs, spun around on the lip of the landing and called to her papa, "Don't forget. I'll be waiting for you. I won't as much as doze 'til I see what you have for me."

Margaret clutched Ben's forearm and angrily stared into his sea-green eyes. After parting the aura between him and Ann Marie and nabbing his attention, she made her declaration, "The servants and the field hands have been acting up something awful since the day you left. First, it was Mammy not wanting to do as she was told. Then, Big Bo letting the pigs out of the pen. They trampled on the chicken wire, ruining the fence around the henhouse. The chickens were clucking, making such a fuss that they could be heard from the front of the house."

Margaret's shoulders drooped. Sadness surfaced on her face. She looked at Ben, who had straightened up to ensure her that he was taking proper notice of her concerns. She stepped closer to him.

"I was so perplexed, I dressed in my warmest riding habit and sent Sam for a horse. I wanted to ride along the river, even though the weather was poorly. I felt that I needed an outing to calm me so that I could properly collect my thoughts. He took so long bringing the animal, I was too flustered to ride. I laid my riding crop across his back in good fashion and sent him and the horse back to the barn. And Lily . . . she had decided that she was going to weave as slowly as possible just because she had lost that pickaninny of hers at birth last week."

"Lily lost her . . ."

"She did. And it was a buck. A poorly looking one at that. But you listen to me, Ben Mullins. Each time she sews or fixes something for me, I have trouble with it. You remember, Ben, not long ago when I strolled across the lawn, the stitches of my crinoline cage broke. The ruffling came away from the hoop and trailed me through the garden. I was humiliated! I told you right then to get rid of her and to get me a new seamstress. Then, the wench could stay down at that loom house and never come back to this one."

Ben's face flushed as he prepared to belt out a gut-load of laughter.

"Don't you dare, Ben Mullins!"

"Sorry for your troubles, Margaret."

Ben sympathetically patted her arm. When he turned to walk away, Margaret twisted his sleeve. Tightening her hold on him, she gritted her teeth and pulled Ben into her anger–so close, the damp, musty, woolen shirt that he wore beneath his coat gave off vapors that offended her nose.

"I'm not done." She shook the curls that escaped from her mop cap. "You need to listen to me, Ben Mullins. Petunia burned the breakfast this morning. When I told her she had, she told me, 'I ain't burn nothin'.' Have you ever heard such sass from one of them? I had to take a hand to her. I told her to leave those biscuits right where they were. I wanted you to see them. That gal's got too little beauty and not enough grace to be considered house help. Surely her mother was an impudent field Negress. I don't understand why you insist on keeping her. I have warned you time and again that you need to sell her and all of the other hands down the river. Get some fresh stock for the house and better hands for the field. That would instantly improve things around here."

"Margaret, if you keep that up, you're going to badly hurt one of those hands. I haven't forgotten about Sara. How you hurt her and sold her to the traders that came through here. She was one of my best, a prime Negress. Now Lily's done lost what I had hoped would eventually be additional help for you and maybe add to our earnings."

Ben shook his head in disbelief and then looked at Margaret once more.

"I got you this new one. I suggest you take care with her and think before you ask me to sell any of them. Who'll tend to you, Ann Marie, the house, the fields, and the animal stock . . . not to mention that spring's coming? Every healthy darkie we have will be needed for the plowing, sowing, planting, and hoeing. I don't have money to be buying more hands and don't want to be hiring any either. Best you think and then take care before you act."

"Ben . . . "

"Hold your tongue, woman. I've got good news for you."

"About time."

"This new gal has a young one. She's still in her childbearing years and can cook, sew, run a loom, and do laundry. I don't want you to see them right now. That gal's a bit sickly and sorry to look at. Her pickaninny's near death. Might not make it through the night. Mammy's taking care of them. Paid a good price for the two. Didn't know the boy was so bad off. But I feel they're going to be good for you. That is, if Mammy gets that boy up on his feet."

"I hope you know what you're talking about, Ben Mullins." Margaret released his arm, exhausted from her rage.

"Tell Ann Marie I'll be up soon," Ben said.

"What's that in your hand?"

"Something for my sweet girl."

"Humph."

Margaret held her tongue, determined not to give Ben the satisfaction of asking him what was tied in the floral wrapping. "We'll finish this talk later," she said.

Margaret braced her foot on the first step leading to the second floor. She hesitated. Not looking back at Ben, she told him, "Don't be late coming up. It's been difficult getting your daughter to bed. She sensed you'd be coming home today. I don't know how she does it."

His wife didn't wait for a reply. She hiked up the front of her skirt and continued climbing the stairs in a fashion that let Ben know the depth of her annoyance.

Mullins followed the light that beckoned from the fireplace warming the sitting room. He placed the small bundle on the mantel and loosened his belt. He let his travel bag and coat fall to the floor.

After he did, he dropped the gun holster on top of the heap. His foot eased the pile away from the flames. Ben dragged an oversized, wingback chair nearer to the fireplace. He let his body descended into its curves. Wiggling the toe of his booted right foot, he nudged off the left one and then toed off the right one. Hanging his arms over the armrests of the chair, he sighed and stretched his long legs to warm his cold, damp feet. There was no need for him to look around, he knew that Petunia was lingering in the shadows, resting against the wall with her head lowered, ready to serve. She knew not to move close to Ben or Margaret when they chatted seriously, not even to offer food or drink.

"Bring yourself here, so I can see you."

Petunia moseyed toward Ben, slow as she could. She stopped short of arm distance, not wanting him to touch her.

"Massa," she said.

"You look awful! Miss Margaret tells me you've been troublesome. Burned her food."

"Dem biscuits. I tells Missus, I's sorry."

"Fetch me some drinking water. Go tell Big Bo and Sam to bring the huntboard in out of the night air. Then go let Mammy tend that eye of yours. Take along those biscuits and some clabbered milk for those new ones I just purchased.

3

Effie's Gentle Hands

Effie wrapped an arm around the woman.

"Come on in here, honeychile. I gits dat youngun. You take yourself some of dem baby steps. We gots time."

The woman leaned left, and then right, dragging her feet and groaning with each step. She followed Effie, who had scooped up the boy and the quilt from the slush. His head dangled over her sleeved arm. The woman stumbled into the cabin behind the two of them.

"I gits you close to dat fire, little fella. Warm you up some. I gives your ma some of dis here hard candy with a sip of dem spirits," Effie told the boy, who didn't seem to hear her words.

The woman stood behind a wooden rocker with bedding draped over the back of it. She loosened the tight hold on her shoulders and thanked God for the fire and the warm, earthen floor that thawed her painful feet.

The yellow barbs from the flames caused a slight smile, dimpling the woman's cheeks. For a quick second, her mind raced back to the cozy cabin in Virginia where she bundled on the floor with her family just before they were herded off to be sold. She drew in a heavy breath, nearly choking when her arm skimmed the bedding. The touch of it overwhelmed her with a desire to be wrapped in the bedding with her baby at her bosom.

The sight of a crinkled tin plate and bent spoon made her aware of the cramp in her belly. She gripped her midriff and sucked in her lips. The woman's mind struggled to decipher the journey that had brought her to the spot where she stood.

"What's gonna become of us?" she asked and slowly rotated her head to explore the cabin more.

A pile of roughly cut firewood was stacked in the corner near the fireplace. Opposite it was a corn-shuck pallet and a three-legged stool. A rickety bucket with a dark, sweat-worn handle perched on another stool. A hooked-neck gourd protruded from beyond its rim. Before continuing her contemplation, the woman shifted her weight from one sore foot to the other. Chipped bowls, encrusted with that day's meal, were scattered about like bait leading to a trap. Against the wall, behind the woman, was a rope bed with a turnkey used to tighten its ropes. A heap of laundry was piled near the bed, but it was the sweet aroma of the hay bunched at the foot of the bed that brought the woman to a standstill. She wanted desperately to lie down but was scared to move close to it.

"What's gonna happen to me and my boy?"

"Don't worry your head about dat right now. I be takin' care of you and dat chile." Effie nodded to the woman, reassuring her that her young one was safe. "Dis here . . . boy or girl?" Effie asked, knowing that talk moved thoughts away from the core of pain.

"Boy," the woman said.

Clarissa wanted to grip the rocker, but not touch the clean bedding with her filthy hands. Instead, she struggled to steady her legs.

"What you call dis here fella?"

"George Henry."

"And you? What name dey give you?"

"Clarissa," she said. Her eyes went back to the hay.

"Go head. Sit yourself down dere."

The woman staggered to the mound of dry grass. She smelled its freshness as she rutted for a position that allowed her pains to ease some. When she had done her best, she straightened her skirt, prepared to receive her boy. Effie placed him in the bowl of his ma's lap. He rolled into Clarissa's midsection. Not able to hold on, he fell away from her embrace.

A tapping sound outside prompted Effie to pick up the bucket. She opened the door. A boy about eight years old, wearing a loose-fitting jacket and stumbling inside a pair of ill fitting boots, stood there. His head was clustered with tight, seal-brown curls. His skin was a sleek, dark cinnamon that glimmered in the firelight. Effie handed him the bucket.

"Fill dis halfway wid water. Be quick," she told him.

Effie shut the door behind the boy and turned back to Clarissa. "That's Little Bo. He be livin' wid me now. Just come down from the big house. He was up dere helpin' the Missus sort and count her silver. Massa knowed you here and sent him on. Soon as he bring dat water back, I takes care of you.

Miss Margaret, dat's the missus. She got a heap of meanness tied up inside her. Sold dat boy's ma away before he knowed he had one. Said she didn't like the way Sara be actin'. Never seemed to be likin' nothin' dat gal done—not her cookin', not her washin', not her sewin'. Sara be a sweet little thing dat was quiet and never makin' no trouble." Effie paused and shook her head. "Missus kin fire off swift as a rattler. Gotta stay on her good side as best you can. Don't sass. Walk soft. Other things you gotta learn as dey come to you. Rest now. I takes dat quilt. Wash it good and hang it to dry."

When Effie reached for it, Clarissa drew back. Effie put a gentle hand on the gal's shoulder. "It be okay, chile. I takes particular care wid it."

The woman let the quilt slip from her lap. Mammy draped Clarissa and George Henry with the bedding from the rocker. Its warmth drew out a flood of emotions. The woman sobbed; fresh tears soaked her face.

Effie pulled the hemp bag from her sleeve. When she tilted it, a blueberry-sized lump of sugary crystal rolled into her palm.

"Put dis here in your mouth. Hold on to it."

Effie got down on the floor and stretched out on her belly. She rummaged underneath the bed for a stash kept in a wooden box. She collected an amber-colored medicine bottle from it.

"Sip dis here. You gotta stop dat cryin', chile. If you don't, you gonna be too fretful to tend to dat boy."

Another scratch at the door prompted the woman to look up.

"Dat be Little Bo comin' back from the well."

Before she could reach for the bucket of water, the door was pushed from her grip. It was Petunia. She trailed in behind the boy.

"Evenin', Miss Effie."

Effie took Petunia by the arm and then glanced at Little Bo.

"Sit dat pail down over dere, near dat woman," she said, handing the bucket back to him.

"Petunia. Come on in here, chile. Why ain't you up at the big house?"

Petunia adjusted the cashmere scarf slipping from her head to her shoulders.

"What you shakin' so for?" Effie asked as she stepped back to allow her in. "What be troublin' you so, gal? You cain't rightly hold your head up."

"Massa done sent me. Wants you to fix on dis here eye. Dese victuals be for dem."

Petunia thrusted her bottom lip toward the woman and child.

"Close dat door. Come close."

Effie ushered Petunia toward the fire. The silken jewel tones in her scarf shimmered in the firelight.

"Dis here eye's bad. Done swell big as a plum and blue-black as one." Effie angled Petunia's head. "Be mighty bloody, too. My! Oh, my! You gonna need some tendin' to, chile."

Effie shifted Petunia's shoulders so that she could see the new arrivals.

"Dat's Clarissa and her boy, George Henry. You already knowed Massa done brung dem down from Louisville. After I settle dem some, I takes care of dat eye. Put some hot water in dis here bucket and den warm dat bread and milk you done brung."

Petunia put the food down. She tied the scarf around her waist at her back to keep it away from the flames. Using a strip of rumpled leather, she cautiously gripped the handle of a pot of boiling water that hung next to simmering corncobs. She poured just enough of the water into the bucket to warm the well water.

Effie took the slumbering boy and warm quilt from his ma's arms and placed her load on the bed. The boy blinked, but he stayed exactly as she put him, not moving a limb.

"I takes care of you now," she said to Clarissa.

Effie dipped a rag into the tepid water and bathed the woman from her waist up. She gingerly glided her hand over the cuts and bruises, trying not to provoke the hurts any more than they had been aroused already. Effie noted the woman's back before she smeared black liniment across the exposed shoulders.

"Why dey got to always be hurtin' us?"

The salve melted on the woman's feverish flesh, leaving a dark glossy coating behind. Clarissa laid her head on Effie's shoulder. Effie stroked the weary woman who moaned from her inner and outer wounds.

"I sees too much of dis. Rest yourself, chile." Effie patted the woman's head and then turned to Petunia. "Dem victuals ready?" she asked her, while pulling a fresh, blue, homespun shirt over the woman's head. "Dis be yours now. You be feelin' better soon."

Petunia placed a broken bowl on the hearth floor and drenched it with scalding water, washing off the grime. She placed two of the scorched biscuits in its slight arc and drizzled them with warmish milk. She angled the molasses jar above the quick bread. A blob of blackstrap molasses oozed over the rim of the jar and melted onto the warm sour-milk-soaked biscuits. Using the bent-handled spoon, Petunia mashed the bread and milk together. Soon, it was a caramel-colored mush. She handed the bowl and spoon to the woman.

"Use dis here. You kin scoop and eat." Petunia crimped the woman's hand around the spoon and brushed the corner of the boy's mouth with her fingertips. "He don't seem to be wantin' to open dat mouth of his. Wiggle your fingertips 'tween dem lips of his. Git dat boy to take some of dat. He be awful puny lookin', 'bout near death. You gotta try harder, gal."

"Come here, Petunia. You done said a 'nough. Don't upset dat woman. The missus gonna be ringin' for you soon. Sit yourself here."

Effie's hand smoothed the bed next to her. Petunia hesitated before she sat down. She pinched up the sides of her apron and fanned them out, sway dancing and licking her dry lips. When she was ready to speak, her words got trapped behind her tongue. Petunia let loose of the apron and took in a rush of air through her nose.

"Dat . . . dat woman. She be talkin' 'bout sellin' us down the river," she blurted.

"Hush, gal. Don't worry 'bout dat. We ain't goin' nowhere, at least, not no time soon."

"But look what she done to poor little Sara."

"Massa gotta git ready for dat spring season. He say he gonna plant extra fields. He don't got no time to be showin' no new darkies what to do and how not to be makin' trouble. And Big Bo . . . he already gittin' dem tools ready. Massa be havin' his head in dem books. He's been cipherin' dem numbers. Rest dem worries for now."

Effie straightened her apron. "Lay dat head of yours down here," she said, patting her lap. "Little Bo, git dat food pail."

Little Bo dragged the small bucket from underneath the head of the bed and pushed it toward Effie's feet. Effie reached for a slice of bacon that rested on top of dried beef and smoked pork rinds. She positioned it over Petunia's eye.

"Dis here eye done swell shut."

Effie snapped several wet rags, cooling them before layering them over the greasy fat.

"Hold dis here steady."

4

Lily's Gift

Consumed with loneliness and fear, Clarissa folded her body over George Henry's. Effie lifted Clarissa's chin.

"I been sold away from my family and my family from me. You here now. Ain't no turnin' back. Gotta make the best of what you got here. If not, you rots from dat anger gnawin' at ya innards. Cain't promise you nothin'. But I tells you, if you don't look back, dem things don't hurt so much."

"I knows what you be tellin' me, but I's full of worry. My boy be peerin' at death. He don't even blink his eyes. Dat devil tryin' to steal my boy away from me. George Henry, he be all I got now."

"Don't you fret, chile. I fix dat boy of yours corn water and molasses. Most babies be likin' dat."

Effie filled a drinking gourd with pot liquor from the boiling cobs. She plunged two fingers into the molasses jar and then into the gourd.

"Try a little of dis here, chile."

The boy buried his face under his ma's arm.

"What I gonna do? He be fadin' away. Gonna lose him 'fore dat rooster crows."

"Keep him close. I be back. Eat dem biscuits and sweet milk."

Effie drew a blanket across her back and stepped into the howling winds that snaked around her legs and underneath her skirt, chilling her body from ankle to hip. She drew her cloak tighter and shuffled to the end of the alley where she knocked as she opened Lily's door. Lily was sitting in the spotlight of the fire, curved over a white satin nightgown that she was hemming for Miss Margaret.

"Put dat sewin' down. Come wid me. We be needin' your milk. Gotta a little one dat might not see tomorrow."

Lily was a quiet, petite, milk-coffee quadroon with an extra dose of cow's milk in her color. Her eyes were a perfect hazel tone and her hair a pleasing tawny that hung over her shoulders. She had a beauty that held fast to her heart-shaped face and wide lips that stopped smiling the day she lost her near full-term baby boy just days ago.

"Come on, chile. Gotta hurry."

Lily set her basket aside. She lovingly adjusted the covers over Sally, her slumbering daughter. Lily grabbed her cloak and followed Effie. Their wraps flapped in unison as they stepped together swiftly moving up the alley until they were startled by Hycus, Ben Mullins' despicable overseer. He stepped out of a dark shadow. His whiskey drinking was evident, along with stale tobacco smoke and horse sweat that coated him. The nighttime breeze forced obnoxious odors from his body up into Effie's nostrils, leaving a strong taste in her mouth that she wanted to spit out but didn't, fearing she would be knocked to the ground or maybe worse.

Hycus stood before the women with his feet parted, blocking their way. When he cleared his throat, his pointy Adam's apple rose above the bandana tied around his neck. The rag was streaked with dirt and several days of perspiration. It choked his neck the way Effie wanted to, clutching on and sending him to the devil's pen. Hycus bounced his whiskey-red eyes from Effie to Lily, and then back to Effie.

"What's brung you two out on dis cold night? Looks to me like you darkies gettin' ready to run."

Feeling antsy and ready to do harm, Hycus gripped the cat-o'-nine-tails that itched his hand. His smirk rolled into an open-mouthed laughter that exposed the few tobacco-stained teeth that remained in his head. A rough, beefy-red scar wormed down his left cheek.

"Where you gals goin'?"

Steam winged off his odorous breath and over Effie's head as she swung her arms open with a defiant attitude. She moved in front of Lily, pushing her to the rear and forcing Hycus to look down into her face. She elevated her chest, spoke directly into his dank mouth, and warned him to hold his tongue.

"Massa Ben done brung me two new hands from Louisville, wants dem nurtured. Den, he sent Petunia to me to git her eye doctored. I needs help and come fa Lily. Best ya step aside, or ya be havin' Massa to deal wid."

Hycus nervously adjusted his stance. He tapped the tails against his trousers, anxious to raise them against Effie. Her stern stare wouldn't release him, so he withdrew his thought of striking her or Lily.

"What's he done brung dis time?" he asked, peering beyond Effie, gawking at Lily, who clutched Effie's blanket, wanting to slither beneath it.

Holding on to the corners of her blanket, Effie fisted her hands and propped them on the solid curves of her hips.

"A gal and her sickly boy dat might not see a new day," Effie said. Her full voice drew Hycus' wandering eyes from Lily back to her. He lessened his grip on the whip. The tips of the braided cords fell toward the ground.

"Best you move on. I got a mind to use dis here on dem hides of yours."

Hycus snapped the whip but took care not to strike Effie, who didn't flinch. Bad news from her could mean trouble for him. He had already lost pay for beating a field hand so badly he couldn't plow or work for weeks. Effie didn't move until Hycus faded into darkness. Then she hooked Lily by the arm.

"Come on, chile."

"Dat man . . . his ugly face scare me. He done lay his hands and dat whip on me too many times. Most for no-good reasons."

"Hush, chile. Dem wrong ears might be hearin' your words, den we both be gittin' a whuppin'."

"Miss Effie, my heart be racin' terribly fast. Kin hardly put one foot 'fore da other." Lily's voice trembled on the cold breeze that blew her cloak and lifted her skirt and petticoats.

"Take a deep breath. Keep yourself hobblin', or dat fool'll come back. Den he'll let loose dat evilness of his on our rumps 'til dey raw."

Effie opened the cabin door to a soft crackling fire. Clarissa was swaying and humming to her boy who was cuddled in her lap. Petunia slept on Effie's bed with the fatback still in place. Little Bo had curled up on his pallet next to the fire. He was buried beneath a red woolen blanket patched with scraps from tattered rags.

"You talk to dat wee one. I looks after Petunia."

Lily squatted in front of Clarissa and positioned her face near to George Henry's as if he didn't reek of piss and baby sickness.

"Hello, little fella."

"He's George Henry. Dat's his ma, Clarissa," Effie said.

Lily stroked the boy's head and murmured, "We talks later, little George Henry," she told him.

Lily removed her wrap. Her swollen breast leaked, dampening her shirt. Seeing it, Effie moved close to her and put an arm around her shoulder.

"I knows dat tightness in your breast be pinin' for dem lips of your baby boy dat you done lost. I know you be wantin' his sucklin'. Dis here little one be needin' you now. Sure hope it be in your heart to help him."

Effie left Lily with her thoughts and tears. She turned back to Petunia.

"Let me see dat eye," she said to her. Effie lifted the rags and bacon. "Swellin' done gone down some. Best you hurry back 'fore Missus knows you gone. Keep dem fixin's on your eye long as you can." Effie guided Petunia's hand back to the bacon fixings. "Keep hold of dis here."

Effie covered Petunia's head and face with the woolen scarf until only her good eye showed. Effie opened the door to the cold. She bid Petunia a cautious "so long" and watched as Petunia stepped into the dark, frigid air. Effie sighed deeply before turning her attention back to the others.

"Clarissa, dis here's Lily. She just lost her baby some days ago. She still got milk. She gonna try and feed dat boy of yours."

"How old?" Lily asked, her hands still at the fire as she assessed the boy's weakness from the corner of her eye. She contemplated the feel of his lips tugging at her firm nipples that dripped with the feeding intended for her baby boy.

"Born two harvests ago. Not sure what day," Clarissa said.

"My! My! So feeble. He be the same age as my little Sally and be half her size."

After warming her hands, Lily gently slid them beneath the boy's clammy back and scooped him from Clarissa's hold.

"He 'bout gone," Clarissa whimpered.

Lily grinned when she noticed the sweet-whiskey remedy that wafted from Clarissa. She took George Henry to the hearth to rock him. She feathered the boy's brow, arranging the fine hairs away from his eyes. She raised him to her cheek. He was cold and lifeless.

"Hello, little fella. You be safe now," she whispered into his ear and lowered him to her bust.

Lily peered heartbroken into George Henry's sunken face and adjusted his skeletal body to fit into the curves of her arms. She timidly put the nipple of her breast to his parched lips. He reached up, touching her warm tight breast with his tiny chilled fingers. He struggled to gaze at her, but his weakness forced him to close his eyes. He crossed his feet at the ankles and turned into Lily's softness. His face was tranquil as a slight hint of a smile emerged when he clamped down on her nipple, sucking warm milk from her generous breast.

The smacking sound prompted a burst of laughter from Effie and giggles from Clarissa that filled the cabin with glee. Effie lifted her skirt to her knees, threw back her head, and kicked up her heels. Then she spread her arms and reached toward the rafters. She danced a juba with such gaiety that dust rose from the earthen floor. Turning and twirling, Effie shouted from the pit of her gut, "Thank you, Lawd Jesus and all dem saints up above." And then she belted a blissful tune:

> *Oh, Peter, go ring dem bells*
> *Peter, go ring dem bells*
> *Peter, go ring dem bells*
> *I heard from heav'n today*

Clarissa's back yielded to the cozy hay. Tears tumbled down her fatigued cheeks. Calmness wafted over her just moments before slumber buried her.

"My work be done here, Miss Effie," Lily whispered.

Lily laid George Henry, fast asleep, on Effie's bed. Effie could tell from the blush on Lily's face that she was pleased with what she had done for the boy.

"You got a way wid dem babies, Lily. Dey all loves you. Sure glad you had dat milk."

"I's glad too, Miss Effie. Ain't much more we got to offer in dis here life."

"Git your wrap. I be holdin' the door for you."

Lily reluctantly eased into the alley. She gripped her cloak against the wind, drew her head down between her shoulders, and peered sheepishly at Effie.

"Go on. Nothin' gonna bother you tonight. God be with you. Walk close to dem cabins. I keep an eye out for Hycus. Don't say a word to nobody 'bout tonight. Go on now. I be a listenin' for you, chile."

Effie watched after Lily until the cold became unbearable. She closed the door quietly and rested against it. She lowered her eyelids to concentrate on the nighttime sounds until she was sure that Lily was safe and back in her cabin. Effie imagined that Lily was adjusting Sally's covers and wishing that George Henry was her lost baby boy that had suckled at her breast.

A Hellish Life

5

1848

Summer came early with a dryness that strangled Mother Earth. She coughed up a constant swirl of dust, making any kind of farming an absolute misery, especially for the field hands. She also provoked Hycus, causing him to raise his cat-o'-nine-tails more often. The souls in the fields moaned and wept as he lashed lean tissue from their backs. Flesh and clotted blood mingled with plowed dust that was muddied with dripping sweat.

At night, the wounds kept the slaves from a peaceful sleep, making each day in the fields rougher than the one before. Effie spent hours into the night nursing and reassuring each tattered soul.

"Take care, chile. Dat next life promises to be a sho'nuf good one," she'd tell them.

When daybreak tinted the skies with a dim gray light infused with a slight orange glow, Clarissa twisted her dark, wavy hair up into a flour-sack scarf and tied on a fresh apron. Her routine had been the same since that first night she arrived at the farm and started to work about a year and a half ago. She was a pitiful soul then, just off the auction block. But, this morning her eyes gazed at Effie stretched out on the slacking rope bed. The deeper-than-usual furrows of her wrinkles crisscrossed the finer lines in her face and then dipped into crevices encircling her eyes and framing her mouth, exposing the harshness that had been a part of Effie's life.

No matter how deep dem wrinkles be, I sees dat kindness in your old face, Miss Effie. You be givin' me comfort when I be needin' it.

Clarissa moved nearer. Her apron clung to the bedside as she lowered herself to Effie's head. Effie lay still. Her color was ebbing, nearly translucent.

"You needs me to tighten dem ropes for you?" Clarissa whispered into her ear.

"I be at peace. You go on, chile. Don't you be late," Effie said, not raising her eyelids to the day.

Clarissa rested her head next to Effie's on the sweaty, dark rise of the pillow. She stretched her arm across Effie's chest, inhaling the scent of sweaty rose water and healing oils she had used to bathed Effie with the night before.

"I hates Massa Ben and his missus worse den deadly snake venom. Dat man's done hurt me too many times, Miss Effie. Some days I kin hardly walk from where he done come from behind me when I's walkin' back to the quarters wore out from bein' worked so hard. He put dem big dirty hands of his on my shoulder, knocks me to the ground, and shove my skirt over my head. Den he jump on me like I's an animal. When he done took from me what don't belong to him, he go on. I's still on the ground painin', wishin' I's dead. I's so full of hate for him, I cain't think right. I wants to kill him for every baby he done made inside me and I done had to kill. I don't be wantin' nothin' wid his likeness growin' inside me."

Clarissa gritted her teeth. She buried her tearful face deeper in Effie's pillow.

"Miss Effie, I ain't gonna give birth to no pickaninny dat belong to dat man. I dies first."

The frown lines tightened across Effie's upper face. Still not opening her eyes, she sank further into despair before asking, "You wid chile again, Clarissa?"

Clarissa jerked her head back, "Ain't. Ain't gonna be. Every time he knock me to the ground, I gonna git up and drink dat potion. Don't care how sick it be makin' me."

Effie's eyes opened. "Dat be a pain we been totin' since dey took us off dat boat to pleasure demselves and suckle dere babies when dey wouldn't let us suckle our own. Take care, gal. Don't git hurt tryin' to fight what's bigger den you."

"Miss Effie." Clarissa's head sprang up. She looked at Effie with absolute seriousness. "Dey might take my body, but dey ain't takin' my soul. Dat, I die fightin' for. I gonna be free. You see."

"You gotta let dem bad feelin's go, chile. Like I done told you, over and over, dey ain't gonna do you no good. Just slow you down."

"But I wants to be done wid dem! I hears dem songs dey be singing in dem fields. Dey say, 'Let my people go.' Miss Effie, I ain't waitin' for no lettin' go. I gonna be gittin' on."

"Your day gonna come, chile. You gots to be patient. Bad timin' kin take a life quick as it kin give one."

Cock-a-doodle-doo.

"Dat be the rooster. Missus be lookin' for me. I left ashcakes in the fire and fatback on the hearth. When you ready, dey be ready for you and George Henry. Don't have no molasses. Bo be goin' on to the barn. He be eatin' wid his pa."

Clarissa adjusted Effie's covers and kissed her slackened cheek.

"You comfortable, Miss Effie?"

"I be so, chile. Me and George Henry . . . we gots work to do. You go on."

Clarissa fixed George Henry's cover, too. Bo was so twisted in his bedding that she let him be. She drew a light cloak around her neck and back.

Clarissa's beauty had grown evident. She didn't need gadgets to hold up her skirt winged by the curves of her hips. Her face was flushed and her cheeks were plump and tawny. Pure white encircled her dark alluring eyes.

To not make a sound, Clarissa slowly pulled the splintered door behind her and moved swiftly under the fading moon. The slave cabins shrank behind her as the kitchen loomed up ahead. Clarissa moved about the grounds with ease and did her jobs well. During the morning walks to the kitchen, she planned her day ahead and sorted through the pestering thoughts that cluttered her mind.

I's tired of my boy always sleepin' when I leave dat cabin and seldom awake when I gits back. I miss nuzzlin' wid him. But I's mighty pleased dat Miss Effie be lookin' after him. George Henry be growin' nicely. He gonna be seein' more of dem harvests. Dat is, if the bad parts of life don't chew on him too hard. He and Sally be turnin' four and some   . . . be nearly the same size. Dey be spendin' dere days playin' in the alley and bouncin' about the quarters wid dere pretendin'. Sometimes dey enjoy a game of hide and seek wid each other. "Cain't part you two pups," I always tells dem.

Little Bo be nigh 'bout ten. We calls him plain Bo now. He runs errands for Massa and helps his pa. "The best blacksmith around dese parts," I hear Massa tell Dr. Isaac and the other neighbors dat come around, chattin' 'bout the harvest and dem 'portant city folks.

Clarissa knew that after she left the cabin, Miss Effie would get George Henry up and fed. Bo would leave for the blacksmith shop to sort nails, clean tools, and help his pa set up for the workday.

Clarissa stood under the trellis that arched from one garden to the other. She absorbed the beauty of the floral sculptures and the essence of the climbing roses twisting their way up, in, and out of the lacework. At the peak of the arc, they crept down the other side to join the yellow buttercups, pink lilies, red geraniums, and white lily bells coating the ground below them. Clarissa felt a wisp of freedom each time she passed through the gardens. Many a morning she wished deeply that she could pick just one bloom to spruce up the kitchen or put a red rose in Miss Effie's hair, but she knew better. She frowned at the sun and veered left onto the pathway that led to the loom house and onto the kitchen. A monarch butterfly trailed behind her, before fluttering so close that its wing flicked a hair of her brow, taking her breath away.

The back door to the big house slammed shut, causing Clarissa to misstep. It was Ben Mullins. He adjusted the large-brimmed hat on his head that cast a shadow over most of his face, leaving only a slight bit of his chin that caught the sunlight. He pulled on a leather vest and slipped his holster onto his belt that had been notched to ease the stress caused by his added weight. When his head came up, his brows were nearly touching. He snatched a pair of gloves from his hip pocket.

"Mornin', Massa," Clarissa said.

Ben didn't answer. Instead, he examined the limp, well-aged leather gloves that he forced onto his hands and against the webs of his fingers before he tightened his fists to stretch them some. When he glanced up, Sam was bringing his horse from the barn.

"How you be doin' dis mornin', Massa?"

Ben frowned and looked away. Sam held on to the bit and offered his hand to hoist Ben up and into the saddle. Ben gripped the saddle horn, stepped into Sam's waiting hand and then threw his leg across the horse's back. He shoved his boot toes through the stirrups.

"Mornin', Massa," Clarissa hollered again, not wanting to chance Mullins rushing at her with the bullwhip for not giving him proper recognition.

Mullins raised his stare above her head and galloped toward the cornfields. Sam waved a hello to Clarissa and went on to the carriage house to tend the horses and buggies.

Down at the quarters Miss Effie and George Henry prepared for the morning.

"Gotta check dem little ones, George Henry. Dem sick ones, too. Give me a hand, boy," Miss Effie said.

George Henry fetched her walking stick that was fashioned from a tree branch, smoothed, and shaped to fit her hand. He reached for Effie's arm and tugged her to her feet.

"Lean on me, Miss Effie. I be strong now."

Effie balanced on the walking stick with one hand. With the other, she braced her weight on George Henry's shoulder. They didn't move until her feet and legs were ready to work as a team.

"Git dat turnkey and tighten dem bed ropes and den git dat medicine bag, bucket, and a brick of dat lye soap."

George Henry twisted each rope until it was taut. Then he fluffed the bedding, making it ready for Effie's rest when she returned from tending to the children and visiting the ailing.

"Come along. Come along. We gots work to do, boy. Tweet, twee-tweet," Effie's voice rang out like a bird's whistle.

The children, who ring-danced and played kickball in the alley halted their play and trailed Miss Effie to the coolness of a shade tree. George Henry drew water from the well while Miss Effie counted each head, assuring that none of her charges had fallen in the river or had been snatched by a wild animal.

The young ones gathered around her as she sat on the nippy ground, washing and wrapping scraped knees, salving bruised elbows, cleaning cut chins, tying a bit of rag around a stubbed toe or two, putting wet rags on puffy eyes, and drying a few tears.

Stu, the dog, scooted his body between George Henry and the medicine bag. He nudged George Henry's arm for attention. George

Henry scratched behind Stu's ear. Stu flipped over for a playful tummy rub.

"Leave dat dog be, boy. We gots work to do."

"Run along. Run along," Effie sang to the children. "Time to visit dem old ones."

Effie grunted in pain as George Henry tugged her stiffened body until she stood.

"I be your walkin' stick, Miss Effie."

Braced once more on his shoulder, Effie shuffled one puffy foot in front of the other as she made her way through the slave quarters.

"You's a strong one. Done growed big. Taller den most of dem babies dat come along 'bout your time."

Effie knocked on the doors of the infirm slaves. She simmered peach leaves to make tea that settled uneasy tummies, offered rock candy and whiskey to cut coughs, and left rattlesnake pieces and boiled cockroaches to draw out the fevers. When she stepped into the cabin where Turtle Jim, Sam, and Old Abe lived, George Henry followed her. He stood back and waited for his orders. Effie paid close attention to the old man. He was fragile with age and the eldest slave. He was slow and wrinkled but had the wisdom and wit of a young man. Turtle Jim was always confident beneath his oily, green straw hat and seldom left the cabin without it. Some said he was a hundred years old, plus some.

"How you be doin', Jim?"

He waved a hand from his bed. "Not so good. Not so bad. Lawd ain't ready for me yet, gal." He chuckled.

"George Henry, git dat little red sack from dat bag. Jim, you put dis here on your tongue. Hand me dat bottle, boy. Sip dis here."

"Dat be mighty good, Miss Effie. Be warmin' up dese innards of mine. You sho' know how to take care of folks." Jim's toothless smile was full and good-natured.

"Got some tea for you, too. I put dis here on the floor next to you. I be leavin' dis here potato on Sam's sleepin' hay. It be for his arthritis and dis here knotted string be for Old Abe. He be wantin' it to chase away dat rheumatism dat be slowin' him down when the day be endin'. It'll be here for dem when dey done finish up things at dat carriage house and whatever Massa might be havin' dem do."

Clarissa continued up the lane after Ben rode off. She entered the kitchen where the redolence of yesterday's boiling and frying met her. She started the day as usual: removed her wrap, hung it on a rusted nail, dipped her skirt-tail into a bucket of chilled water to keep the flames from licking the hairs off her legs, stacked logs in the hearth, and started the cooking fire. The morning was still and quiet except for her stirrings in the kitchen.

Clarissa bustled around, gathering mixing bowls from the shelf, taking down the wooden beating spoons, and collecting the rolling pin mounted above the hearth. She opened the flour-bin door and stood on tiptoe to peek inside. Seeing that it was half full, she placed a bowl beneath the sifter and turned the crank. After a soft white peak formed, she slid the bowl underneath the sugar jar and cranked its handle. As the sweet crystals dusted the mound of flour, they spit bits of rainbow colors against the inside of the bowl.

"Mornin'," Petunia said to Clarissa as she came through the door with fresh milk. She set it down on the workbench, picked up the empty egg basket, and waited for Clarissa to tell her what to do.

Clarissa's mouth opened to say something about the day ahead and how she had noticed the looks that the missus had given her lately, but she didn't. Instead, she kept quiet and told Petunia, pointing with the mixing spoon, "Git dem eggs and don't be long. We gotta get dat food on the table. No need upsettin' Missus 'cause we be late."

Clarissa chuckled at Petunia swinging the egg basket on her arm as if it were purse.

"I hurry," Petunia promised.

Clarissa added a spoon of soda to the flour and whisked it with the beating spoon. Then, she cut lard into the mixture and moistened it with sour milk. After sprinkling the sticky dough with a pinch of flour, she powdered her hands and the tabletop, kneaded the dough into a smooth ball, and gave it a hefty slap. Then, she rolled it into a flat smooth oval. With a biscuit cutter she sectioned off soft rounds. She danced each cut of dough palm-to-palm. On the fourth beat, she passed it to a well greased, three legged skillet and covered it with its heavy lid. While the biscuits baked, she fried sliced pork pieces, stacked them in the center of the platter, and then returned to the cooking fire. She slid sliced apples into hot bacon fat, spooned a generous dollop of pan-browned cinnamon-sugar over them, and stirred until they were caramelized.

"Dem hens didn't want to give up dem eggs dis morning," Petunia said, coming through the door cackling. "Had ta bop dat big, mean, black-and-white hen on her beak. Should 'a seen dat bird fly out of dat henhouse. Dat floppy red comb jiggle like jelly. She won't be peckin' dese here fingers of mine no more . . . least not for a while. Wish dat chicken could 'a been Hycus," Petunia snickered.

"Put dem eggs down here. Finish dat coffee."

Clarissa cracked, whipped, and scrambled the fresh, warm eggs in hot butter and rolled them onto the platter with the pork and apples. The biscuits were stacked in a basket, lined and covered with a white kitchen towel. The strawberry jam and butter dishes were already on the dining table.

"Git dat coffee and bread basket. Follow me. Don't aggravate the missus dis mornin'. Keep your eyes down and your mouth shut. Don't scrunch your face up at her like you just done to me. Watch dem sassin' hips. Dey gonna git you in a heap of trouble and git dat good eye of yours knocked out."

Clarissa tightened her shirt around her waist before picking up the platter. She walked with the sure footedness of a ballerina to maintain the balance of the full platter. Petunia rolled her eyes and swished her hips with more sass than before. Using a small bit of leather, she lifted the hot pot of coffee and hooked the handle of the breadbasket with her other arm. They entered the side door of the big house and went directly to the butler's pantry. It was a small room off the rear hall to the right and across from the opening to the dining room. They entered and set the food down on the tabletop before serving it. Petunia filled the silver service pot with coffee.

Chatter from the dining room let Clarissa know that Ben had checked the fields and was back for breakfast. Since Clarissa was put in charge of the kitchen, Big Bo had extended his belt more than once; Lily had let Margaret's dresses out at the waist several times, and Little Miss Ann Marie frequently needed new clothes.

"Bring that platter. Set it here," Margaret said.

Clarissa did as she was instructed to while Petunia put the breadbasket on the table before she poured the coffee. Then, Petunia stood with her back plastered against the wall and subserviently curled her shoulders. She monitored her toes; her fingers fidgeted with threads dangling from a tear in her apron. Clarissa moved away from the table with a toe-to-heel movement until she bumped the sideboard, rattling the crystal teardrops on the candelabras. She stood stiffly and checked each face at the dining table before moving again. Not a soul looked up. She nabbed a piece of rock candy from the crystal dish, coughed, slapped her chest, and let the sweet topple down into her shirt.

Mullins rested his forearm on the table next to Margaret. The magnolia fragrance and the aroma of caramelized apples brought on a mischievous smile. Ben stared at Margaret with his pesky green eyes, remembering the night before when he had lured her close to him.

"Mr. Mullins, I suggest you shift your thoughts."

Ben nodded his head, disturbing the disheveled curls on the crown of his head as he let Margaret know that her message was received. Then, he abruptly shifted his attention to Ann Marie.

"She's nearly seven years old and growing nicely. She's shy and quiet . . . seldom causes trouble. Her complexion resembles that of the porcelain doll I bought for her on my trip to Louisville. Don't you think so, Margaret?"

"Think what?"

"Look at her. She's got those long, blond curls and big blue-green eyes, same as the doll. She's about as delicate as it is, too. Her beauty will generate proper attention. And I tell you, Margaret, she's blooming nicely. Our daughter's going to turn the heads of those young suitors when they come calling."

"Enough of that."

Margaret pouted at the thought of her own beauty fading behind her age and unwanted pounds. She lifted her chest and tilted her head.

"I want to order a new bonnet and gown from France. I'm never sure what Lily, that shameless wench, will design for me. I'd be glad for the opportunity to wear something European . . . new and fashionable."

"Since we had a fair crop this year, perhaps we should first buy a new huntboard. That's what we need. The old one is weather damaged. The wood's dull, deformed and splitting. Don't think Big Bo can wax and sand it anymore."

"Perhaps we should . . . "

"I have a hard day's work ahead, Margaret."

Ben leaned back in his chair and boasted about auditing the ledgers, hauling goods, feeding stock, plowing fields, and keeping Hycus in check.

6

Broken Platter and Good News

Ben pushed back his chair, dismissing Margaret with a rap on the dining table. He stood closer to Clarissa than social comfort allowed, stationing his body against the folds of Clarissa's apron. He swept his hand along her shoulder, stopping at the base of her neck.

"I'm not moving you or that pickaninny of yours. It's just as well you stay on with Mammy and Bo. I don't see a need for change." Ben said with his coffee breath bathing Clarissa's cheek.

"Yes, Massa," she said in a disgruntled tone and pivoted her hips to move away from Mullins' unwanted touch.

Clarissa's head was flooded with thoughts. She turned her eyes away from Mullins' stare. She scrunched her face to conceal her delight of the news that she and George Henry would be staying on with Effie. Clarissa feared that Mullins would send her to live in another cabin if he knew of her joy. The idea of being separated from George Henry and Effie had been a constant torment for her.

Ben adjusted his stance, putting his body against Clarissa, sealing the gap she created. His thigh muscles rippled against her leg. She quivered. Unable to inhale, she felt faint.

"Stop playing with your food!" Margaret snapped at Ann Marie.

The roughness of her voice pricked Ben's consciousness. He glanced over his shoulder. Pleased that Ann Marie enjoyed her breakfast, he smiled and then let her know, "Dr. Isaac's mare will birth her foal any day now . . ."

"Oh, Papa! Please take me to see it. I want to feed the new baby." Ann Marie squirmed and giggled with delight.

"Be ready when I call for you."

"Ben, what do you think . . . "

"I got to go, Margaret. The fields and workers need my attention. I've got unfinished business to take care of."

With her mouth ajar, Margaret sat in a state of puzzlement before she sprang up, muttering as she scurried at Ben's heels. He snatched his vest and his hat from the row of brass hooks that led to the rear door. On his way out he grabbed his holster and belt from the hall table below them. He ignored Margaret's voice and her footsteps that seemed to clamber up his back as he went out the door. She slammed it shut behind him, knocking the dust off his rear pockets.

Margaret withdrew to the dining room. She wanted to convince Ben that donning a fashionable bonnet and matching gown would arouse the envy of every females far and near. But he cut her short to discuss Ann Marie and Clarissa which ripped at her core.

Ann Marie stacked eggs and pork on a buttered biscuit. She topped it with jam that oozed from between its layers. The news of the coming foal teased her thoughts as she bit down on her creation. Cranberry-red goo drooled from the corners of her mouth. Ann Marie hooked the crushed fruit with her tongue and pulled it back into her mouth. The remnants somersaulted down the front of the crisp, white bib of her pinafore, landing in Robin's lap, leaving a spotty trail behind. Ann Marie dabbed the gooey mess, smearing it across her bib and the doll.

"Little Miss, go to your room. Clean yourself up and that doll, too. Then practice being a lady."

Ann Marie cuddled her doll, got down from her chair, and crumpled the soiled napkin next to her plate. She stomped up the stairs and deliberately banged the door to her room shut.

Margaret flinched and flipped back a clump of stray chestnut hair that had fallen over her ear. In an absentminded way, she ran her fingers along the grain lines in the dining table. Without a thought, she picked up the small silver valet set and began sweeping scattered table crumbs into the pan.

"I gits dat, Missus," Clarissa said and quickly took the tools from Margaret. When she did, Margaret drew her head back and extended her arms preacher style over the uneaten food and used plates.

"Clear this. Be quick!" Margaret said to Clarissa.

Margaret's voice thudded against Clarissa's chest, causing her to nearly drop the pan and brush. When she put them down and reached for the platter, Margaret pounded her fist on the dining table, sending a rumble beneath Clarissa's hands. Petunia, scared and wide-eyed, forced her back up the wall until she was on toenails. Hesitantly, she came back down to a flat-footed stance and nervously removed the valet tools from the table and placed them on the sideboard. With shaky hands, she collected the tableware and stacked it in the butler's pantry before taking it out to the kitchen.

Going out the side door, Petunia heard Margaret's bark at Clarissa: "Gal, you're foot-dragging and not getting the job done."

Margaret rested on her elbows and laced her fingers together. She lowered her chin on the back of them and focused straight ahead, looking blindly into space. Although Clarissa had been told to hurry, she moved cautiously to arrange the butter and jam dishes on the platter along with the smatterings of apples, pork, and eggs. When she turned to leave, Margaret poked Clarissa's elbow with a butter knife. Clarissa's arm contracted, sending her load spinning and crashing to the floor.

"Look what you have done! You clumsy gal! You have just broken my platter. There won't be any food rations for you this Friday, and probably the next one, and maybe the next. I'll see to that myself. That money will be used to replace my good dish you just destroyed."

Down on her knees, Clarissa created a pouch with the hem of her apron. She raked the food and the broken china pieces into it and sat back on her heels clutching the bundle, too frightened to move.

Margaret forced her chair back. She viciously knuckled Clarissa on the crown of her head. Clarissa groaned but didn't move for fear that Margaret might also twist her ear. Instead, Margaret stood up and left the room. Clarissa reeled back and forth, gathering the courage to leave the big house and return to the kitchen. She slowly exhaled the air trapped in her lungs and sighed. She tightened her grip on the heap in her lap and then hustled to the side door and out to the kitchen.

"Where dat wicked woman?" Petunia asked when Clarissa came through the kitchen door.

"Went to check on the Little Missus . . . maybe. Don't rightly know."

"Dat woman be ornery. Don't even want 'a git next to herself," Petunia said.

"She say I won't be gettin' no rations dis Friday and maybe the next."

"Don't worry yourself. Miss Effie knows how to git for all us Negroes when we be needin' it."

Clarissa dumped the contents of her apron onto the worktable and leaned against it. She drew her head down between her shoulders.

"Dat woman scares me. Don't know what she gonna do from one moment to the next," Clarissa said.

Petunia's hands fell lax in the soapy water. The dish she was washing slipped from her hold.

"You knows she be tryin' to kill me," Petunia said as she raised her gaze. "Look here at dis here eye of mine. Not much good to me now. Next time, dat woman gonna clobber me in dis here good eye. Den, I won't be seein' nothin'."

Petunia closed her eyes to imagine life without vision and quickly opened them. A salty wetness stood at the rims of her eyes ready to fall.

"Finish washin' dem plates and clean up dis here mess."

Clarissa pushed the broken pieces of the dish and food bits away from the edge of the workbench.

"I be back 'fore you know I's gone."

"Where you be goin' to?"

"Down to the quarters."

The corners of Clarissa's smile dimpled with pleasure. When she moved to leave, Petunia's wet, soapy hand caught her sleeve.

"What I gonna say if missus be askin' for you?"

"Keep your eyes down and your hands busy. Say I done gone to clean the outhouse where somebody done made a mess. She won't be wantin' to come lookin' for me dere. I be back 'fore you done wid dem plates."

Peering out the kitchen window facing the twin lawns, Petunia wrung her hands as Clarissa vanished between the gardens. A monarch butterfly fluttered around Clarissa's head. Its wing kissed her cheek with a softness nearly too slight to detect. When her eyes caught sight of the dark spots on the hind wings, it reminded her of Toby. Her feet faltered as the earth quaked beneath them.

George Henry stopped jumping the hopscotch squares. He watched the small figure that stumbled from beneath the trellis, under the glare of the bright sun. With Stu at his side, George Henry shielded his eyes. He squinted at the image moving down the lane and growing larger.

"Ma!" He raised his hand with a saluting-the-high-sun gesture. "Dat you?" he hollered.

"Sho nuf, chile."

A breeze whistled past Clarissa, funneling her words straight to George Henry. He tossed the hopscotch stones aside. Followed by Sally and Stu, he raced up the alley. Clarissa leaned with open arms and gathered the two of them in her embrace. Their weight knocked her to the ground. She kissed their soft, sweaty cheeks and smiled into their sun-buffed faces. The good buddies locked their arms around Clarissa's neck, pressing their faces against hers, cheek-to-cheek, nearly rolling her over.

"How you two be?" Clarissa asked, folding her legs underneath her skirt.

Stu clawed at Clarissa's shoulder and licked her ear.

"You too, Stu. Now get down, boy," she said, patting his back, encouraging him to sit.

"We's good, Ma. But I be missin' you. Missin' you big. Like dem corn stacks on shuckin' day."

"Me, too, Miss Clarissa."

"Dat be a mighty lot."

Clarissa got to her feet.

"I brung you and Sally somethin'."

With his mouth opened like a flytrap, George Henry eyeballed Clarissa's hand as it reached inside her shirt and rummaged around. Finally, after what seemed longer that it would take George Henry to jump all the hopscotch squares, Clarissa brought out a tightly closed fist.

"Whatcha got, Ma?"

"Just hold on dere. You be seein' soon enough, boy." Clarissa laughed and turned her fist over. She blew a magical breath across her clenched fingers. "Luba. Guba. Buba. Bee. I have somethin' for you to see."

Clarissa very, very slowly uncoiled each finger. George Henry's feet danced as his eyes bulged at the sight of what lay on the palm of his ma's hand. Not able to hold his tongue any longer, he asked, "Dat be candy, Ma?

"Is, boy."

"Can I have it?"

"Sho' can."

George Henry snatched the sweet and ran.

"Come on, Sally!"

When he stopped to wave, Clarissa was gone. She disappeared as if she had never been there. Still gazing over his shoulder, George Henry took hold of Sally's hand.

"Come on. Ma done brung us dis here hard candy."

"We gonna eat dat now, George Henry?"

"Sho nuf."

With their toes turned in, the two best friends sat on the stoop of Effie's cabin. Stu laid on his belly, back legs stretched, and head resting on his front paws. George Henry gloated as he sucked on the sweet rock.

"Dis here peppermint," he said.

Sally's eyes never left George Henry's mouth. She watched his lips and waited patiently for her turn to suck on the candy. George Henry's slurps grew louder and louder as he smoothed the gritty candy with his tongue. Sally was sure she tasted the peppermint that hadn't yet reached her lips.

"My turn, George Henry!"

George Henry sucked the peppery syrup from the candy bulb that he had steadied in his mouth. He poked out his tongue, gripped the lump with his fingers, and popped it into Sally's watering mouth. Her lips smacked a sweet tune. The two passed the candy until it was too small to pass again. That's when George Henry bit down on it and then gave half of the granules to Sally.

"Dat sho' was good, George Henry."

"Wish we had more of dat," he said and licked the stickiness from his finger tips and lips. The buddies kicked their heels against the step, laughed and grinned until they were giddy.

Later that evening, George Henry and Bo played a game of mud marbles on the earthen floor in the cabin. Effie sat on her rope bed with her grandmotherly eyes doting over the boys. They all glanced up when Clarissa entered the cabin with a bouncy step and spun into the web of firelight. Her good news fought to bolt from her innards. George Henry and Bo raced to hug her. Effie took particular notice of Clarissa's manners.

"You been in Massa Ben's moonshine, gal?"

"You know better, Miss Effie. Massa wants George Henry and me to stay on wid you." Clarissa's words sang out.

"I's plenty glad! I be wonderin' what gonna happen to you now dat I be gittin' ready to go on."

Clarissa dropped to her knees. She laid her head in Effie's lap and wrapped her arms around her.

"Don't talk dat way, Miss Effie. You cain't be goin' on . . . least no way soon. You know I takes care of you. Same as you done for George Henry and me when we was first brought here to you."

Effie reclined on her bed. She wiped the old worrying tears from her eyes and flashed a toothless grin. Still on her knees, Clarissa secured the covers around Effie's neck. George Henry was clapping his hands and dancing a fancy buck-and-wing. Bo was unable to move. He was sweating when it wasn't hot.

"Miss Clarissa, what he say 'bout me?" Bo asked.

"He ain't movin' you yet. You be stayin' on, too, for now."

Clarissa hugged Bo like a mother would her own child.

"But, I got some bad news, too. Not gonna be much food dese next few days. Maybe, the next few weeks. Missus gonna take my rations."

"Why so, gal?"

"Pay for dat platter she make me drop."

"Don't worry yourself. I always got somethin' for dem hard times."

Effie leaned out of bed and swished her hand underneath it. She thwacked at the sack of dried pork until she could grasp it.

"That's enough meat to make stew for eight to ten people. Maybe twelve if Petunia got hold to it." Clarissa laughed.

7

Clarissa's Hurt

An early frost marshaled in fall 1853. Days were cooler. Trees were heavy with foliage that glided down on breezes until the earth was blanketed with a golden carpet stained with rusty red leaves from the surrounding oak trees. Bouncy with a song in their hearts, the slaves scattered throughout the fields. They gripped tools and belted spirituals that seized at souls glad to not be burdened with the heat of the sun and weight of the whip.

The musical voices of the Negroes fluttered on the thick fog that swirled up from around their ankles. Hycus found himself soothed by rhythmic ballads commanding the hands and feet of the bent backs that plowed and hoed the fields.

"Go down, Moses; roll, Jordan, roll; walk together, children," they sang.

Hycus squirmed in his saddle, his face void of the usual frown. He was uncomfortable with the pleasantness of the day. His seldom-idle hand waxed the saddle horn where the bloodstained whip looped it. He rotated his head. No matter which part of the field he viewed, crops were misted with droplets flickering rainbow colors.

That night, the harvest moon shone like a brilliant pearl nesting in the midnight-blue sky. The field hands slept harmoniously, but not Clarissa. Beneath that same moon, she caterpillar crawled, cursing each pit in the lane, sobbing as she dragged her battered leg behind her until she reached Effie's cabin. There, at the foot of the stoop, her shoulders melted to the ground. Her sweat bled into the dirt. She collected what strength she had, heaved, and hoisted her body onto the stoop. She bumped the cabin door to jar it. She fell limp with part of her body in the cabin and part still on the stoop.

The scraping of the cabin door against the floor announced a presence. The moonlight sprayed ghostly shadows across the room.

"Bugaboo! Bugaboo! Fly away," George Henry cried.

He ducked beneath the covers. His heart pounded inside his chest like Big Bo's hammer against a horseshoe. When he peeked again, he saw Clarissa's head resting on the floor, barely inside the doorcase.

"Ma! Dat you?"

Clarissa whimpered for Effie, who sprang off her bed ropes like a spooked hen and bent-walked to the buckled body. George Henry crouched on his bed ready to leap when his call to his ma wasn't answered. Effie's hand warned him to stay put.

"I takes care of your ma, boy."

Effie caressed Clarissa. The coolness of her naked shoulders prompted Effie to gently lift Clarissa's chin, same as she did the first night she was brought to her.

"Honeychile, where your cloak and apron be? And your head wrap?"

Mystified by Clarissa's nose caked with grit, her cheeks streaked with filthy tears, and the putrid vomit that plastered her shirt to her breast, Effie asked, "What done happen to you, chile?"

"Missus . . . the missus . . ."

Effie leaned closer to hear Clarissa's faint voice.

"She's done hurt me. Hurt me bad."

"Lawd! Lawd! What she done now?"

Guided by the moonlight, Effie studied where Clarissa's hurts might be and listened attentively to her whimpers.

"She whacked me. Whacked me wid dat hot poker. 'You aren't movin' fast enough, gal,' she say over and over. Keep a whackin', 'til I cain't stand proper."

George Henry stretched himself, posturing to get off of his bed again.

"I helps you, Ma."

Effie raised her hand once more. This time she let him know to stay put. He backed down beneath his blanket. He drew his legs up and pulled his tow shirt down over his knees. His eyes remained on his ma.

Effie finger-combed gravel from the hair clinging to Clarissa's forehead. Then, she dabbed Clarissa's face with the tail of her gown. Effie stroked Clarissa's head. When she did, the gal winced and moaned with pain. Effie pulled back.

"I be hurtin' you? I's sorry, chile. Didn't mean to."

"Not you, Miss Effie. Dis here step be hurtin' my backside."

Clarissa tightened her muscles and adjusted her lower body that rested on the jagged stoop. Effie sensed that it wasn't time to move Clarissa and engaged her with more talk.

"What makes her hurt you so, chile?" she asked, bringing Clarissa back to her tale.

"Missus told me to have supper fixed 'fore Massa come in from dem fields. But she keep comin' to the kitchen addin' to my doin's. Once, Little Miss Ann Marie come wid her. Dat didn't keep her from bein' the devil dat be givin' me more to do. 'Gal, do dis. Do dat. Hurry up. Stop draggin' your feet,' she say. 'I tries Missus,' I tells her. Little Miss Ann Marie, wid her sweet self, clutchin' dat doll . . . "

"Doll?"

"Dat be the one her pa brung her from Louisville. It be the day he brung me here to you."

"What den, chile?"

"Little Miss Ann Marie look at her ma. She say, 'Mommy, you gave Clarissa too much to do. You sent Petunia fetching and Clarissa's got no help. She's fixed a tray of sandwiches with boiled corn and apple pie. And she was about to fry those sliced potatoes.' Missus looked at her gal. She drawed her face plumb to ugliness. She tell Little Miss Ann Marie dat she be too young to be understandin' such matters dat concerns the help. She send her to her room. Later, I hears Missus bangin' dat door for the Little Missus to come out, but she done lock it. She stay put. Didn't answer her ma's calls. Don't believe she come back down . . . not even for supper."

"And Massa. Where he be?"

"In the house. I knowed he was late goin' out to the fields after his noon meal. I hears the rear door bang shut. Sam was talkin' to him. Couldn't make out what he be sayin' 'cause dat horse be a neighin' and a cloppin' so. Massa went on to the fields. Left the missus wid the troubles."

Clarissa's body wasn't as tight as it had been. Her chest rose and fell like a bellow. Her arms gestured freely. Effie knew nothing was wrong with Clarissa's upper body and clamped her arm around her a bit tighter, taking note of Clarissa below the waistband of her skirt where raggedy threads held snug to her leg.

"When Missus hurt you?" Effie asked.

"After Massa come back in from dem fields dat evenin', he be kickin' up a mean fuss. He was screamin' somethin' awful. His words come from the yard between the house and kitchen right to my ears. He say, 'I'm tired. I'm hot. I'm sick of those lazy darkies. The grounds are still not plowed. Hycus is being unreasonable, thrashing the hands until they can't work. What good is that?'"

Looking up at Effie, Clarissa took in a thimble more of air before she said, "Den he come to da kitchen."

Effie's arms twitched at the thought of what Clarissa might say next.

"Massa looked around wid dem gropin' green eyes of his 'til he took note of me. Wid his thumbs in his belt, he come waddling toward me like a proud duck. 'Give me a drink of lemonade, gal,' he holler while he be standin' right up on me, spittin' in my face. He puts his no-good hands on me, in a no-good way, where dey got no business bein', makin' me uneasy. He snatch me. His belt buckle be pushin' against my belly. I feels vexed. Didn't know what to do. His body snatched up my breathin' air. I 'bout pass out. He be smotherin' me for sho'. When I looks up, Missus be standin' in the door. She don't come in. Don't say nothin' neither. Just turn and leave, gone on."

Deciding what to say next, Clarissa had closed her eyes. When she opened them, she looked fixedly into the darkness of night.

"'Massa,' I say. Den I steps back from his hands. Don't want dat nasty feel of him against me. When I move, he slam his fist down. I knowed den, he gonna hurt me. Dem eggs rock, dey falls, and dey breaks."

"Oh, Lawd . . . ," Effie said as a knot tightened in her chest, choking off her words.

"Dat's when he buck me wid his loud roar. 'You won't be eating supper tonight, gal. Unless it's those eggs on the floor that you just wasted.'"

"'Massa, I makes you lemonade. I be quick,' I tries to tell him. He don't say nothin'. Don't seem to be hearin' nothin' neither. Just give me dat look. Same as he did dat night he knock me in dat ditch when he bringin' me to you. Dat be dat first night. When he turn to leave, he say, 'I'm goin' to rest by the fire. I'll come for you later.'"

"Miss Effie, I's mighty scared. I shake so, my teeth clattered and didn't seem to be belongin' to me neither."

When George Henry glanced at his ma, she was clutched onto Effie's arm, angling her nose up to catch snippets of air. Heat from the pit of his stomach rushed to his face. He fretted about what would become of him and his ma?

George Henry was wrenched from his thoughts of losing his ma when Clarissa muttered, "When the yellin' was done and Massa was gone, Missus come runnin' wid dat hot poker above her head. She brung it down on my leg, again and again, tryin' to part my it from the rest of me. She be yellin' somethin'. I cain't say now what it was. I knowed it be somethin' bad dat be festering inside her head wantin' to come outta her mouth."

"What she do 'bout supper?"

"She throw dat poker at me den took up dat tray wid dem victuals on it. She went on back to the house. I couldn't move. I just lay dere in my misery 'til I rolls my body into the corner. Waits dere 'til I's sure Missus and Massa Ben done gone on up to bed. When dem candles go out, I crawls here on my belly."

Effie bundled Clarissa with all the love she had to give.

"I done heard enough, chile. Dat done took my breath away. Be forcin' my mind back to where it don't want 'a be goin', remindin' me of when Bo's ma, poor Sara, was troubled by Missus' madness. Let me git to fixin' on dat leg 'fore it be gettin' worse."

Effie slipped her hands beneath Clarissa's shoulders. Effie sucked in her lips as she managed the pain from the disgruntled muscles in her back and encouraged her cramped legs to be steady. She tugged at the dead weight.

Clarissa slapped the backside of her hand over her mouth and bit down on it until blood trickled from between her teeth.

"Bo, git up! You and George Henry come help me," Effie cried without loosen her grip on Clarissa.

Bo forced his hands underneath Clarissa's mid-back and hips. George Henry lifted her legs at the ankles. With a good hold, the three moved the body close to the fire. They let George Henry's ma down easy. Effie stoked the embers, increasing the light. She attempted to examine Clarissa's leg, but her shredded, blood-soaked skirt was embedded in the flesh.

"Oh, Lawd, chile. Dis here leg be worst den I thought. When dem people gonna stop hurtin' us?" Effie mumbled and then said to Bo, "Go fetch a bucket of water. George Henry, git dem rags from under my bed. Den lay yourself back down 'til I calls your name."

When Bo returned, Effie left Clarissa grimacing by the fire. She shuffled over to the bucket to steal a minute to think. Afterward, she dipped a large drinking gourd into the water, supporting its bowl in the palm of her hand, she drizzled its cool content over the battered leg. Grit and gravel sloshed off with the bloody water. Effie tried again to tease the skirt away from the gash. The stubborn blood-glued fabric didn't ease. She drenched the leg, again and again, until the fibers separated from the mangled flesh. Rage swelled inside Effie as she inspected the leg. She dabbed at her tears with the sleeve of her gown, knowing it wasn't the time to be emotional. There was work that had to be done. She smeared black salve over the raw flesh.

"Hurry, Bo! Bring dat bucket closer."

Effie submerged a fistful of rags, then wrung and layered them over the pulverized limb.

"Come, Bo. Fill dis bucket again wid more well water. Gonna be needin' it in the mornin'."

Doing as he was told, Bo rushed out and soon trotted back with a heavier bucket.

"I helps you put her in dat bed?"

"Naw. She got too much pain. Best we be leavin' her here by the fire."

After Effie covered Clarissa with a blanket, the woman slipped into a fitful slumber. George Henry spread his fingers and stretched his arm. He reached for his ma and patted her, same as she did him whenever he was hurting. She didn't know that she had been touched. George Henry pulled his hand back and rolled over into a sleep posture, but never enjoyed a full rest that night. When the rooster crowed, his sluggish eyes opened to a timid light from the glow of embers. His ma struggled to sit, but collapsed from the pain. George Henry scooted on his rear to his ma. The mingled smells of sweat and blood caused him a great deal of uneasiness.

"Don't cry, Ma."

With the feathery touch of his young, shaky fingertips, he rearranged a damp curl that clung to her eyebrow.

"Don't mean to be upsettin' you none, boy."

Effie came from her bed. She tucked the covers around Clarissa, blocking the brisk morning air.

"How you be feelin', chile?"

"Cain't move! Dis here leg done swelled a powerful lot. It be near the size of a young watermelon. Painin' me so, I cain't see. How I gonna work, Miss Effie?"

"Hush, chile. You here wid me now."

Effie's voice was firm, but she knew that Clarissa might not be safe. The thought of what Miss Margaret might demand from Clarissa tore at Effie's heart. She laid a consoling hand on Clarissa's sleep-dampened shoulder.

"Bo, git up. Lay in some wood. Stoke dat fire good. Den go git the wheelbarrow, fill it wid hay, and den bring it here."

Effie removed last night's wrappings from Clarissa's leg and washed her wounds. The clotted blood glistened a dark crimson red, dotted with the first signs of pus. Troubled by what she saw, Effie forced her head over her shoulder before coming back to her duty at hand. She shoved the soiled rags deep into the bucket, forcing up a rush of bloody plums. She shook the excess water from her hands and dried them on her gown. With a silky touch, her fingers glided over the battered leg.

"Dis here be fire-hot. Got a beastly fever. It be showin' signs of a bad burn and infection, too."

Effie fished a rag from the bucket and again bathed the wound that festered with the smell of blood and raw sickened flesh. After it was bathed, she fanned it, cooling the surface of the leg. She smeared on more salve and re-dressed it. Effie had done this so many times that the wrappings were smooth as plastered walls.

Not taking his eyes off his ma and still squatting next to her, George Henry rubbed his own leg. His hand hesitated when he heard a crackling crunch on the other side of the cabin door.

"Come on in here, boy," Effie called to Bo.

George Henry sprang to his feet. He quickly stepped back when Effie cried out as she attempted to lift his ma. A sharp pain had knifed its way up Effie's spine. Little Bo tucked Clarissa's legs into his armpits. With Effie holding on to Clarissa's torso, they lifted Clarissa's rear up off the floor.

"George Henry, help us some."

George Henry thought he had reached out to support his ma's bottom, but his hands hadn't moved. He rushed to shove them underneath her. Clarissa collapsed before they could lower her into the wheelbarrow.

"Lawd be wid you, chile. Don't you worry none," Effie said to Clarissa's deaf ears. "Let's go 'fore she be knowin' where she is."

Bo steered the wheelbarrow. Effie supported Clarissa's leg. George Henry ran along the side of them, keeping his protective eye on his ma. When they got to the big house, Miss Margaret was standing in the yard wearing her sea-blue morning robe and gown, trimmed with a delicate lace the color of natural pearls. The brocade slippers that she wore matched the color of the ensemble. Margaret's arms were folded across her chest. Her lips were arched and pulled downward, toward her chin, as she stared at Clarissa with a hatefulness that Satan's brother would flee.

"What's this?" she muttered.

Effie looked straight into Margaret's face, the only slave on the grounds who could. With a firm but respectful voice, she uttered, "This gal cain't stand. She cain't walk. Dat leg's done been hurt real bad."

Effie's tone let Margaret know that she had done something dreadful to Clarissa. Effie released Margaret from the bondage of her stare to loosen the rags and expose the horrid gash. Margaret's head jerked back. The color in her face drained. The blue veins behind her ears and down her neck twitched.

"She won't be of any use around here," Margaret said and backed away from the wheelbarrow to not spoil the elegance of her nightwear. "Take her on to the loom house. She'll work with Lily 'til she can stand. Then she can come back to the kitchen. Until then, Petunia will take care of the cooking."

Margaret clamped her lips shut, peered down her upturned nose, slung her finger from George Henry to Bo, and then pointed at Effie.

"You can take care of those two pickaninnies."

Dumbfounded by Margaret's words, George Henry drew his chin with parted lips. Effie always took care of him, his ma, Bo, the rest of the darkies, and the ailing white folks up at the big house that the city doctor couldn't cure.

A slight movement of Clarissa's head grabbed George Henry's attention. His ma didn't need to look up to know that Margaret glared down on her with all the hatred she had in her being.

"Gal," Margaret snatched her hankie back and forth, "don't get lazy sitting at that loom visiting and chatting with those other Negresses. If I catch you hem-hawing, I'll sell you down the river for sure and the others with you, regardless of what Mr. Mullins might say or think about my actions."

Margaret flicked her wrist, sending her slaves off without another word and then made an abrupt turn. She flipped the tail of her robe, turned her nose further up, squared her shoulders, and thundered up the steps into the house. The door slammed shut behind her. From the hall, she heard Ben's playful chatter.

"Tell me again . . ." Ben words dried up before he finished expressing his thought. He sipped his water and continued saying, "Sweet girl, how did you come to name her Robin?"

Ann Marie giggled. "You know, Papa. It was after the red-breasted birds that nest in the rafters outside my window. Look at her eyes. They're the color of the robin's eggs."

"Then that is surly the proper name for her."

Filled with delight, Ben smiled. Then he raised his head to the sound of footsteps coming from the hall.

"That you, Margaret?"

"It is." She said, straining to speak.

Before she entered the dining room, not sure that her ankles would support her weight, Margaret's fingers trembled as they adjusted the facings of her morning coat. With her flushed face turned away from Ben's stare, she hurried to the far side of the dining room. Peering out of the window, Margaret saw Clarissa and the others staggering down the lane to the loom house. Margaret loosened the tiebacks that held the drapes in place. The heavy fabric fell shut with a dusty, muffled sound that startled her.

"The sun troubling you, Margaret?"

"No! Just checking for tears." Margaret's voice trembled as she stole a quick glance at Ben. "The holidays are coming soon. I might need to send them down to the loom house for repairs."

Margaret's back kinked as she finger-brushed the drapes. The falling dust sent her into a sneezing and coughing fit.

Ben was mystified by Margaret's behavior and the haunted expression on her face. The day had just started and it was much too early for her to have had any unusual encounters with the hands.

"Is this the best time for what you're doing?"

"It is."

"Do you find them in suitable condition?"

"Where's Clarissa, Mommy?" Ann Marie asked before Margaret could answer Ben. "She always serves fruits and sweet cream when breakfast is late."

"That was her at the yard door. She wasn't feeling well and begged my permission to work at the loom house with Lily for a few days. Feeling generous, I told her that that would be fine."

"What about breakfast?" Ben asked.

The racket of an approaching horse-drawn carriage and a knock at the door disturbed the conversation.

"Continue with what you are doing. I'll see who that is," Ben said. He came back smiling. "That was Sam. Isaac's darkie is at the front of the house with a carriage to fetch Ann Marie and me. The horse has foaled."

Margaret continued with the drapes and didn't reply.

"Are you coming, sweet girl?"

"Oh, yes, Papa!"

Ben steadied Ann Marie's chair as she hopped down, clutching her doll.

"We'll be having our morning meal with Isaac and possibly lunch."

"Can I bring Robin with me, Papa?"

"If you like."

Out on the veranda, Ann Marie saw Clarissa in the wheelbarrow and the others standing around her.

"Daddy, look! Clarissa's hurt."

"Come along, sweet girl. Dr. Isaac's waiting for us."

Ben lifted Ann Marie and carried her down the steps to the waiting coach. Sam offered them a steadying hand as they climbed aboard. The two settled on the red velvety bench. Ann Marie searched Ben's face for an answer to what she had seen.

"All is fine. I'm sure she's not hurt or your mother would have said something more."

Ben was certain that his words held no truth. When he saw Margaret's ashen face, he knew there was something more that hadn't been said.

"Move on," Ben said to the coachman.

Ann Marie scooted close to Ben. She took his hand in hers. They didn't speak as the carriage rolled away from the house with only a slight rocking motion. Still clutching her doll, Ann Marie hopped up on her knees and peered through the carriage window next to her seat. She looked up ahead. Effie, George Henry, and Bo were gathered around Clarissa, rolling her along.

They wheeled Clarissa off the road as the coach passed them. Afterward, George Henry ran to the center of the alley. He looked at the coach and then at his ma. His throat burned, his mouth was dry, and he could hardly swallow. His clammy palms sweated inside his cold fists. The words, "Sell you down the river," nagged at him. His mother had told him often how his dad, twin sisters, and a big brother, whom she called Little Man, had been sold. Even though he didn't remember them, he missed them deeply and didn't want to be missing his ma, too.

"Miss Effie, if she sells my ma, what's gonna happen to me?"

"Hush, George Henry. You keep movin', Bo."

8

Loom House

The door of the loom house was ajar. The dozen or so steps leading to the second floor sent a tremor through Clarissa.

"Cain't git up dere, Miss Effie."

"Hush, chile. Don't you cry. I be figurin' on dat. You be still now."

Effie, with her face lifted, hollered for Lily. "You up dere?" The cool fall air lofted her words to the upper floor.

"Dat you, Miss Effie?" Lily's voice seeped from beneath the partially opened window and drifted down to the group below.

"Sure am."

"Come on up," Lily invited, raising the window to its fullest. "Whatcha got dere?"

"Clarissa done been hurt bad. She cain't stand. Cain't walk neither. Missus done sent her here to you. 'Won't be no good up at the big house,' she done told us."

Lily hurried down the steps. The air parachuted her skirt above her knees. It didn't settle until she was squatted next to the wheelbarrow. Lily kissed Clarissa's bloodstained hand and pressed it to her cheek.

"I's sorry for you, gal," Lily said.

Bo stood stiff-legged. His arms cramped as he managed to hold the wheelbarrow steady. He gawked at the two women, hesitant about what to do next.

"Put dat down. Go git ya pa," Effie told him.

Bo set his burden down, glad to be given another command. Dust trailed his heels as he bolted up the carriage lane, taking the path to the barn.

"Pa! Pa!" he yelled.

Big Bo squeezed the hammer handle. Blood rushed to his head. A frightful dizziness blinded him. He knew something dreadful had happened to his boy. When his son came through the door, he dropped his tool and stepped from behind the fire pit. His boy stood at the door with the sun at his back, panting, unable to speak. Big Bo snatched him up by his upper arms. Holding him eye-to-eye, he asked, "What be troublin' you, boy?"

"Miss . . . Miss Effie. She needs you. It be Miss Clarissa."

"Clarissa dead?"

"Naw. Naw, Pa. She ain't dead."

Big Bo put his breathless boy down. It took a while before he could bring himself back to the now. He prayed, thanking the Lord that Clarissa was still alive and that no harm had come to his boy. He followed his son a few steps before he swooped him up to his shoulders. The closeness of their bodies made him pine for the boy's ma, his Sara. Big Bo never knew where Sara ended up or if she was, dead or alive. The only solace he had was that she might hear his hammer from wherever she was. Those feelings and thoughts tormented him so, he couldn't focus on much when they surfaced. He drove them off with the pounding of his hammer.

Bo grinned and waved his arms for all to see him on his father's shoulders, but his smile faded when he saw the anxious faces that waited for their return.

"We be needin' you to git dis here gal up dere," Effie said to Big Bo, angling her chin with her hand arched over her brow, blocking the rays from the strong morning sun.

After Bo shimmied down his pa's back, Big Bo scooped up Clarissa like a heap of down. She buried her face in his hairy, sweat-dampened chest; grabbed his neck; and let out a piercing scream.

"Hold on, gal, I gits you up dere quick as a hiccup."

Lily's bare feet flopped on the steps as she rushed up behind them. She ducked beneath Big Bo's arm to collect the fabric cuttings and colorful yarn snippings left on the weaver's bench. She dusted them off the seat with a swift hand.

"Put her right dere," Lily patted the weaver's bench. "You gonna be fine. I takes care of you, honeychile."

Big Bo went back down the stairs, hoisted the wheelbarrow up to his massive shoulder, and proudly stroked his boy's head. Then, he gave a so-long glance to the others and started back up the lane. His back grew small before vanishing behind the big house. Effie, George Henry, and Little Bo strolled on back to the quarters, each mastering their own thoughts 'til Petunia appeared in front of them. She was on her way to the kitchen.

"How you doin', Miss Effie? And you, Little Bo? You, too, George Henry," Petunia said in her good-morning voice. She raised George Henry's sagging chin, put her face so close to his he smelled her warm breath mingled with hoecake and sweet coffee. "What be troublin' you, boy?"

"Miss Margaret done hurt my ma. Hurt her plenty bad, Miss Petunia. Ma cain't walk. Cain't stand neither."

"Oh, my! She gonna heal?" Petunia asked over the top of George Henry's head as she drew him to her heart. She searched Effie's face for reassurance.

"Gonna take some time. She be workin' a good while here in da loom house wid Lily. Miss Margaret say you take care of dat cookin' for now."

"Oh, Lawd! Dat woman gonna fill my days wid misery. She be da devil himself. What I gonna do, Miss Effie? Dat woman hate me. She be tryin' to git rid of me. Kill me, too."

"She ain't gonna kill you. Not just yet. She be needin' you. You pray. Do your best. Keep your eyes down and don't sass. Come wid us. I give you some victuals to take to Clarissa on your way to the big house."

"What I gonna tell Missus? She be frettin' if I's too late gittin' her mornin' meal."

"Don't worry. She busy tryin' to figure what she gonna tell Massa 'bout what she done to Clarissa. He still upset about you and Sara."

Back at the cabin, Effie cooked hoecakes and fatback. She fed George Henry and Little Bo. Then she bundled victuals for Clarissa. Effie dumped a bucket of apples on the floor and fished for unspoiled ones. George Henry's feet juba-danced around the fruit bobbing across the floor. Effie gave each boy an apple. They gobbled them up and slapped their hands together like knocking off playtime dirt. The rest of the apples would be dried for eating later or tied up in a drip cloth to make vinegar.

"How you git dem, Miss Effie?"

"I be gittin'," Effie said and plucked another one up off the floor. She placed it in the bundle with the hoecakes for Clarissa.

"Gotta go, Miss Effie. Hycus be gittin' dat whip after me," Little Bo said.

He grabbed the rest of his food and devoured it on his way to the barn. Petunia smiled as she watched him scamper off to the blacksmith's shop.

"Dat boy done growed good. He be gittin' up to a nice size. Dem big arm muscles of his be like his pa's," Petunia said.

"He kin swing dat hammer good as his pa now. And Big Bo be the best blacksmith around dese here parts. I done heard Massa say so to Dr. Isaac and dem other farmers dat be comin' to visit." Effie bragged as if Little Bo and his dad were her folks.

"Best I be takin' leave, or Missus be actin' like dem fancy drawers be bitin' where she be sittin'," Petunia said.

"Ha ha ha!" A welcome laugh rang out from Effie and Petunia.

"Dis here's for Clarissa. She ain't had nothin' to eat."

Effie placed a small red and white bandana bundle in Petunia's hand. Petunia welcomed the warmth of the food. Her fingers still ached from the early morning milking and churning.

Miss Effie's eyes shifted as she glared toward the floorboards, concentrating on the outside noises. She tarried a while longer before pulling out a wadded hanky from her bosom. She tugged the knot until it fell open. Effie pinched up a few seeds and then put the hanky away. She took Petunia's hand, turned it palm up, and placed the kernels on it.

"Crush des here. Put dem in the missus' mornin' coffee. Settle her down for a day or so. Hurry on, gal, before it be gittin' too late."

Petunia tied the seeds in the corner of her head wrap. She secured the knot among the creases of the scarf that rested above her ear. Clutching the food, she raced up the alley to the loom house and knocked at the door.

"It be me," she hollered.

Petunia took her time mounting the steps. Clarissa was sitting at the loom, pumping the treadles with her good foot, finishing the mustard-colored, linsey-woolsey cloth that Lily had started. When finished, it will be a coverlet for Ben Mullins' daybed.

"How you be?" Petunia asked Lily.

"I's fine."

Lily worked on the hand sewing, which was rumpled in a shallow basket balanced on her lap. She drew a fine needle in and out of the delicate cotton. The finished work was bunched at her feet.

Petunia set the bundled food on the weaver's stool next to Clarissa, untied the bandana, and spread it out.

"Dis here's for you, Clarissa. How you be feelin', gal?"

"My leg be throbbin' me bad. But I's glad dat I don't have to be lookin' in Missus' face for a while. And dat be mighty good."

Clarissa's hands mindlessly glided the shuttle back and forth beneath the yarns that ran from the feeder towards her. She shifted her weight from hip to hip and then looked up with a wry face.

"How you be, Petunia?" Clarissa asked, barely able to hear her own words.

"Some of me be feelin' good. Some of me don't. But I sho' be worryin' 'bout bein' in dat big house alone wid dat woman. She be kinfolk to the devil."

In an unusually slow motion, Clarissa pulled the beater to the core of her being and hung on to the slider before she released it to pinch the hoecake. With the quick bread at her lips, she grimaced before nibbling its crispy edge. She gestured with her bottom lip at the bench in the corner.

"Put dat dere under dis here leg."

Using her hands and legs Petunia inched the bench, screeching and scratching, across the floorboards. She lifted Clarissa's limb. The smell of feverish flesh, blood, and Effie's balm stormed Petunia's nostrils. Coughing and choking, Petunia nearly dropped her friend's leg. Clarissa crushed the hoecake, cried out in agony, and knocked the apple to the floor. Petunia picked up the fruit and dusted it off.

"Here, honeychile. Take ya time."

Petunia rubbed Clarissa's back, "Don't you worry 'bout dat leg of yours. It be strong come winter."

Hearing the rustling of fabric and notions, Petunia turned toward the sounds. "What's dat you be workin' on, Lily?"

Lily rested her hands on the top of her sewing. She stretched and arched her back to relieve the fatigue that had trampled her spunk.

"I's gittin' Missus' party clothes ready."

Lily reached over to the blue satin fabric bunched on the floor next to her and fluffed up its ruffles.

"Missus be wantin' dis here took in at the waist."

Lily held up the underwear that she worked on. She lifted up one of the legs to show off the trimming around the hem of it. "Dis here done come all the way from Paree, so Missus be sayin'. Don't rightly be knowin' where dat is. Dey say it be far away. Across dem waters. Not sho' which waters. I knows it don't be the ones we be singin' 'bout."

"She gonna be mighty spiffy in dem. What's dat you be tackin' to dem?" Petunia moved nearer for a better look. Lily's hand prevented a view of what she was sewing into the missus' drawers.

"Somethin' to help Missus when she be sittin'," Lily said with a sly smile.

"Best you take care, gal. I done heard her tell Massa, more den once, she gonna git herself another dressmaker. And you won't have to be comin' back to dat big house no more."

"Dat be just fine wid me."

When Petunia looked at the sewing again, there was something more. "What's dem pretty colors 'neath dem drawers?"

"Dey be socks. I be knittin' wid dem yarn pieces I gits when Missus ain't payin' me no mind."

"Don't no two of dem be lookin' the same," Petunia laughed.

"Don't need to be. Just need to keep dese here feet warm."

Clarissa's body drooped as she moved the beater away from her chest again. This time, she didn't bring it back. Instead, she sat quietly with her hands folded in her lap. Lily and Petunia hushed when they noticed her stillness. Clarissa's eyes were lowered like a preacher collecting strength, getting ready to let loose a special message.

When her head came up, she whimpered, "Whenever I hurts, and I be hurtin' plenty right now. I be thinkin' deeply 'bout my granma. I knows dat ain't many of us be knowin' our ma and pa." Peering at Lily and Petunia, Clarissa asked, "You be knowin' yours?"

The air in the loom house thickened and was difficult to breathe. Lily and Petunia gazed at the floor, keeping their heads lowered like they were taught to do in the presence of white folks. Lily spoke first. Her words punctured the quiet.

"Don't be knowin' much about my pa. I only know what my ma done told me about when she was a gal."

"What's dat she say?" Clarissa asked.

Lily sat firm with her eyes closed. She held her head at an angle. Feeling alone, she spoke into the plum purple light on the backsides of her eyelids.

"She tells me dat, at the end of the plantin' season, when she a young gal, tits just startin' to show. She and dem other gals, all 'bout her same age, was locked in a barn by dere massa. The next day, he shoved dem boys in wid dem. 'We's all naked and cold,' my ma say. Den she tells me, 'dem boys seem to be knowin' what dey s'pose to be doin' . . . minglin' demselves wid us gals. Dat followin' spring, you be born to me,' dat what my ma say."

Lily paused and opened her eyes, but was unable to look at Clarissa or Petunia. Still holding on to her needle, she blotted the uninvited beads of perspiration on her forehead and spoke again with the same uneasiness, but with a stronger tone.

"My ma was traded for two young slave gals. I was put in da care of an old darkie. His name be Old Joe. He was good to me. Dat's when Massa Ben come along and buys me. I's 'bout eight, maybe more, maybe less. Not sure. I be here since den." Lily's voice began to trail. "Don't know no more den dat."

Clarissa turned to Petunia. "What you be knowin' 'bout your family?" she asked.

"Don't know much neither. I's given to Massa Ben by his pappy's sister. I never knowed dat ainty's name. I was her pet. Slept at her feet. Keep dem warm. Dey be mighty cold some of dem nights. It was just 'fore she die from the cholera dat come through here a long time ago. It took a lot of us Negroes, too. I's still a little thing den. Don't rightly know how old. But I knows Massa loved dat ainty of his. He be cryin' a lot when she die. He respect her so . . .," Petunia said while patting the side of her head. "He keep dis here scarf for me. She wanted me to have it and have me. When I's old enough, he gives dat scarf to me. No matter how I misbehave or how mean Missus be to me, he go on keepin' me, 'cause I be a gift to him from dat ainty. And the missus, she be mighty mean to me. Told Massa she didn't want me in her house. Every chance she git, she beat me. One day I runs off. So she say she fix my runnin'. She switch my legs 'til dey's bleedin'. When dey heal, I have dese here scars. Dey don't let me stand properly. I kin tell you, a bunch of coloreds done come. A bunch done gone. But me . . . I's still here. I tells you somethin' more. Listen to me."

Petunia slipped between deeper thoughts as she fluffed her apron. She slowly took in the loom-room dust through her nose and just as slowly let it out. She scratched through the headscarf above her ear as she assembled words in her head.

"One day . . . " Petunia sighed. "Miss Margaret had a gatherin'. She give me a pair of beat-up brogans. Dem toes was pointed like dem chicken beaks. 'Put these on,' she say. I don't be knowin' who dey belong to. Den, she make me serve drinks to dem ladies wearin' fancy hoop dresses. When I comes out of the pantry, a ghost be tying my toes together. I falls. Dem drinks rain down on dem uppity ladies' and dey pretty gowns. Missus grab my hair tight. She yank me to the smokehouse. Dem ladies rushed out of the house behind us. Dey stand on the veranda watchin'. Massa, he come on wid us, but he just stand dere. Don't say nothin'. I's cold and shakin'. She whup me wid dat rope dat's used for hangin' dem meats. When ha arm give way, she lock dat door.

Dem ghosts in dere be tryin' to take my soul to hell. I hears her yellin' at Massa to give me over to dem slave traders dat be comin' through soon. Massa tells her his ainty done give me to him. 'I'm not about to sell her,' he tell Missus. Don't rightly know how long I's in dere. I mark the wall each time dat crow call. Big Bo say I make twenty-one of dem. Reckon my time comin' on soon, seein' how Missus be gittin' meaner and meaner. Done give me scars on my legs. Now, I gots dis here bad eye dat always be weepin'. Remember when you and George Henry first come here? Dat's when she knock me in dis here eye. Say I burnt up her biscuits. Dem biscuits weren't burnt. I never opened my mouth to sass her like she say I done. Dat woman always got the devil's fingers in her eyes." Petunia's shoulders heaved. Her voice filled with anguish. "I don't want to be up at dat house by myself. I's scared of bein' in dat kitchen alone."

Lily gave Petunia a sympathetic glance and told her, "You won't be havin' no trouble up dere 'cause she done hurt Clarissa. Remember what you done told me when she hurt ya eye? Lock herself in dat bedroom of hers? Don't come out 'til Massa ain't upset wid her no more. When she sold Sara, she locked herself in the bedroom 'til he wasn't mad. She be glad to be locked in dere, too. He don't like it when his darkies be hurt and cain't work. I hears him tell her how much she done cost him damagin' his hands."

Petunia toyed with her headscarf more. "Miss Effie done give me a potion to put in her coffee. 'Calm her down a day, or maybe two,' she say. I wants her calm 'til she too old to raise dat hand of hers against me. When dis here potion wear off, everythin' be gittin' back to like it was. Me duckin' and hidin'," Petunia chuckled. The others joined her laughter.

"I still got dem brogans. Gonna keep dem hidden for George Henry. Dey some big. But he be growin' into dem and dey gonna be mighty nice for him."

"He gonna be needin' dem one day. You be sure to keep dem hid," Clarissa said.

"What about you, Clarissa?" Lily asked.

"Didn't know my ma. She be sold away from me when I's still in her arms. My granma be the one dat raise me."

Petunia jumped up. "Best I be takin' leave. Missus don't like for us to be visitin' and talkin'. Dis many of us be 'gainst dem white folks' rules. Missus be gittin' twisted up into one of dem ornery moods of hers. Den, dese seeds won't be doin' what dey needs ta be doin'."

Petunia left, Lily went back to her sewing and Clarissa started the loom moving once more. Few tears fell. Life had squeezed their eyes dry. Most slaves' stories were similar: child taken from mother; masters taking pleasures from women who didn't morally belong to them; young girls victimized at the first sign of puberty and couldn't fight back; men ripped from their families; field hands overworked, most mangled; house slaves degraded; whippings and starvation made too familiar; hands near frozen in the winter months; backs fried in the summer months; a life that they couldn't call their own; and barely allowed to hold onto a thought, even one about God.

9

A Cup of Coffee

Petunia fidgeted with her ear as she followed the dabs of blood dotting the way to a puddle of sickness and pungent stench in the kitchen corner. She tripped over the bloody poker and then staggered away nearly falling. She removed her cloak from her shivering body and hung it on a rusted nail just inside the door. Feeling hollowed out, Petunia buried her face in the folds of the cloak. Her fingers grasped it until they ached.

After some agonizing moments, Petunia adjusted her head wrap, picked up the fireplace tool, and leaned it in the corner with the puke. She counted her steps to the bucket, plunged the hem of her skirt into it, and then angrily wrung out the excess water. Turning on her heels, she gathered an armload of wood and stacked it in the fireplace with yesterday's embers. The heat from the flames dried her tear-wet cheeks as she hung a coffeepot on the hook and set a pot of water on the hot coals. She felt dazed without Clarissa to tell her what to do.

Petunia stood in the center of the kitchen, amassing the courage needed to enter the big house. When she moved hesitantly to the side door, she reached for the handle and paused to send up a prayer to the Lord. After the door closed behind her, she eased down the hall and into the dining room with her palms clasped at her waist.

The house was quiet. An uncomfortable emptiness hovered around Petunia's head. Margaret sat in Massa Ben's chair at the head of the table reading the Bible. As she turned the holy pages under God's watch, Petunia moved a bit closer. She controlled the distance between the two of them not wanting to disturb the aura that Margaret created for herself.

"Sorry I's late, Missus. I be gittin' your breakfast now. Anythin' particular you be wantin'?"

Margaret looked up as if she were seeing a biblical vision. Petunia, startled, hopped back and held her tongue.

"No . . . nothing particular. Take your time. I'm reading. I'm the only one having breakfast this morning. Mr. Mullins and Ann Marie will be having theirs with Dr. Isaac. His filly gave birth during the night. They've left to join him. Ann Marie was excited about feeding the foal."

Some of Margaret's words were clearly spoken, others were tearful and barely audible.

"I be sittin' the table for one, Missus?"

"That'll be fine."

While moving, to back away from Margaret, she kept her good eye on her missus' face. Petunia wasn't sure what to make of her behavior, but she was certain that a storm brewed inside her head and waited to explode like it usually did.

Back in the kitchen, Petunia moved cautiously. She felt Margaret spying on her from the cracks in the walls. Petunia fought the urge to touch her ear. Instead, she rubbed her eye and busied her hands preparing breakfast. She poured a dark, rich, stronger-than-usual coffee into the silver pot and dumped the remainder in the corner to dilute the sickening odor. She spooned two eggs into rapidly boiling water and clipped bread slices onto a toasting rod and spun it over the fire, browning the surfaces. Petunias squeezed orange juice into a goblet but didn't fill it to the brim. She didn't have steady legs and her hands were jittery. She plucked the eggs from the water bath, stood them in eggcups, and filled the silver creamer half full. She placed it and the sugar bowl on a tray along with the coffee, eggs, and toast.

A bone china teacup and saucer sitting next to the tray captivated Petunia. She had seen them many times before, but this morning the flowers on the teacup tickled her senses. Scattered blooms and buds encircled the inside of the bowl. When she held up the cup to admire the outside of it, there were tiny, delicate roses clustered about. Others looped the surface of the saucer.

Petunia had never noticed the flowers before, at least not in such detail. She placed the cup and saucer on the tray and glanced around the kitchen once more. Feeling confident, she opened the knot in her head wrap. Her tense fingers gathered the seeds. Her left hand steadied the right hand over the coffeepot as she rolled the kernels between her fingers crushing them to a fine powder. A gray, cloudy film floated on the steaming coffee before it was absorbed and pulled to the bottom of the pot. Petunia flipped the lid closed and positioned the coffee on the tray.

She inhaled a lungful of cooking air and let it out with a prayer. "Lawd, don't be angry wid me. I be needin' you," she mumbled.

Petunia entered the house and ambled down the hall holding the tray away from her body to prevent her pigeon gait from upsetting the breakfast and coffee service. She dawdled before stepping into the sun's rays filtering through the sheer curtains at the dining room window. She moved slowly, lessening the distance between the table and the tray, until she was able to place it careful and not disrupt Margaret's contemplation. Petunia picked up the cup and saucer. She held the potion above the cup prepared to pour it.

"Shall I serve you now, Missus, while the coffee is hot?" she asked, not recognizing her own voice.

"No, thank you, Petunia. I won't be having coffee this morning."

A twitching in the back of Petunia's neck traveled down both arms to the china cup that clattered in its saucer and to the coffeepot that spat on the back of her hand.

"Ouch!" she squealed and set the coffee service down.

"Are you troubled, Petunia?" Margaret asked in a concerned tone unfamiliar to Petunia.

"I . . . uh . . . be fine, Missus."

Petunia stepped back until she bumped the tall case clock. A chime sounded. She wasn't certain if it came from the clock or her head.

"Are you sure? You seem uneasy."

"I be sure, Missus."

The dizziness in Petunia's head forced her eyes shut. She wanted desperately to disappear in the darkness behind their lids. When she raised them, Margaret had tapped the eggs and knocked off the caps. She was spooning out the yellow-white marbled content, enjoying it with toast and jam. When done, she sipped the orange juice and then pushed back her chair without any indication that she intended to leave the table. Margaret leisurely gathered up the hefty leather-bound Bible and the scattered papers into her arms. Before she rose, she studied Petunia as if she were a real person. Goosebumps coated Petunia's cool flesh from head to toe. Margaret's exaggerated politeness was the kind reserved for highbrow white folks. Her tone was too unlike the harsh one that Petunia knew well.

"Please bring my coffee to the sitting room."

Petunia tightened her grip on the tray. The serving pieces rattled a scary tune as she followed Margaret at a respectable distance. When they entered the parlor, Margaret smoothed her skirt beneath her hips before sitting on the burgundy brocade chaise longue and placing the Bible and papers next to her.

"Put that here before you drop it."

When Petunia flexed her knees to position the tray on the table, her toe stubbed a wrinkle in the rug causing the service pieces to shift. She gulped and carefully adjusted her load. Margaret leaned back on the chaise. She restlessly patted her feet and shifted her weight for comfort. She opened the Bible and thumbed page-to-page not stopping to appreciate a thing.

"I'll have my coffee now."

"I be gittin' it, Missus."

Petunia lifted the pot and tilted it, releasing a thread of dark steaming amber, drowning the flowers in the bottom of the cup.

"Cream and sugar, Missus?"

Petunia minded the inflections of her words along with every move that her hands, feet, and mouth made. They seemed to be disconnected from the rest of her.

"Just a little."

Margaret pulled herself into the corner of the chaise longue and kicked the papers to the floor. She sighed and drew her feet up next to her hips. Then, she accepted the cup and saucer. She puckered her lips and blew across the sweet steaming brew before she sipped it. Petunia neatly stacked the papers and took four steps back, holding her breath as Margaret slurped the coffee and flipped the pages of the Holy Book, too quickly to be reading or noting the biblical art.

"Arrange that comforter over my legs, pleeease." Her words slurred. "Take this, pleeease," slurring more.

Feeling faint, Petunia released the breath that she had forgotten she held in and reached for the coffee cup. She caught the Bible about to slip from Margaret's lap. After finishing the second cup of coffee, Margaret stretched out on the chaise with her head propped against the armrest. Her eyes grew as sluggish as her words. She was gradually pulled into an easy sleep. While her shallow breathing mimicked that of a bird's whistle, the hinges in her jaw loosened, her lips parted, her arms slackened when her shoulders wilted, and her bosom rose and fell with a tick-tock rhythm.

Petunia drew the cover up to Margaret's neck, ensuring that she was properly draped before diverting her eyes from the slumbering body to the ceiling, to offer a prayer of thanks to the Lord and the saints, too.

Hoedown and Death

10

Shucking and Laundry

Petunia's hands shelled sweet peas and diced turtle meat for the midday stew as her eyes followed Clarissa, who moped around the kitchen withdrawn into a private world. She agonized about not being able to be with her boy whenever she yearned for his touch, craved for the sound of his voice, and hankered for the smell of his flesh. She fretted, too, about Miss Effie's slowing down and not being able to spring out of bed. Clarissa didn't like that she couldn't care for her like she wanted to. And, as deep down as a water well, she harbored a passion to be free.

"How you be, gal?" Petunia asked. No answer.

"Help me wid dis here pot." Clarissa gestured with her bottom lip. "Hang it dere on dat hook."

Petunia did. Then, she eased back to her workstation without another word being said, allowing Clarissa the distance she commanded with each of her grunts and groans.

Clarissa braced herself against the workbench cluttered with root vegetables, beans, and an assortment of herbs. She stood on her sturdy leg and massaged the hurt one soothed it when she could. Her face was taut as she chopped and chattered idly under her breath. The words didn't take a single direction. They didn't make sense either.

But Clarissa seemed to understand what it was that she struggled to say.

Finally, she tossed the vegetables and herbs into the iron pot and stirred with a jerky arm. Afterward, she slammed the spoon on the table. She leaned sluggishly with her head slumped between her slackened shoulders. Petunia wanted desperately to reach out and hug her, letting her know that peace was near, even though it wasn't. Instead, she continued to monitor Clarissa with a guarded eye, prepared to catch her if she tilted too far. When Petunia's heart couldn't take any more, she begged Clarissa to sit.

"Rest some. Let dat stew simmer. Got time."

"Cain't be sittin'. It be painin' me to bend dis here leg. Hurt won't ease up. Don't be needin' its company no mo. I's tired of it!"

Petunia lugged two fire logs, one at a time and stood them side-by-side on their ends. She knew Clarissa's pain. Her own legs that were marred behind the knees, ached every day, and wouldn't let her stand like a proud woman should.

"Come on. You sits yourself here. Don't have to bend dat leg so," Petunia said, minding Clarissa's face. "I's sorry for you. Missus done hurt you bad. I know dat hurtin'. I done been beaten like dat, too. After Missus hurt you, Massa give her a good piece of his mind. I know, 'cause I sees dem two on my way to the kitchen. It be dat a day after she done took dat hot poker to you. Missus follow him out the yard door beggin' his forgiveness. I hear him yellin' 'bout how she done hurt you bad. First Sara, den you. She be cryin' and hollerin' how she didn't mean to and couldn't 'splain how it happen. I thought he gonna kill her for sho', but he keep walkin' 'til he gits to his horse. Everybody be knowin' you be his favorite. When she be hurtin' you, she be hurtin' him. Everybody know how he be feelin' 'bout you . . . your cookin', too." Petunia put an arm across Clarissa's shoulder. "Dat leg of yours gonna be gittin' better."

Clarissa brushed sweat from her forehead and glanced at Petunia. "The Lawd . . . he's gonna be easin' my hurtin'. I been prayin'. I know he won't let me down. When I be needin' dis here leg . . . he be makin' sure dat I kin dance dat high-steppin' juba," she told her.

"I knows what you be sayin', Clarissa, but dem words be troublin' me."

"Don't be worryin' 'bout my words. Just keep your mind on dis here meal. Dem hands be sittin' down soon, and Massa Ben'll be comin' in from dem fields for dis here terrapin soup."

Clarissa slapped both hands down on her knees and took in a needed breath of air.

"We talk mo' down at the shed when shuckin' time come. Dat's when dem trees be mighty pretty. Some red, some gold, some both," Petunia said.

Clarissa looked straight into both of Petunia's eyes. "When I sees dem trees bleedin' dem red and gold colors, I be seein' my blood flowin' down dat lane, carryin' me to a hellish place, remindin' me of dat day I's hurt and crawlin' like a animal over dem leaves dat you be speakin' of. I ain't never told you 'bout one of dem nights after the missus hurt me. I be walkin' back to the cabin. Done finish my weavin'. It be real late and peaceful. The quarters got no sounds. All the cabin doors be shut. Couldn't tell of no night sounds neither. Dem pretty leaves was still on the ground. They was all thick and golden with a mix of red. Den it happen. Massa, sloppy wid his whiskey drinkin', snap me up from behind. He twist me around. He be showin' parts of him dat I don't wanna be seein'. Den he hook the back of my legs, pullin' me up to him. I scream wid such a pain. He fall back stumblin', den he stagger off like the drunkard he was. Run fast as he can, trippin' and fallin' over dem nasty bare feet of his. Ain't put a hand on me since den. But lately, his eyes . . . dey be tellin' he got it on his mind."

Petunia was at a loss for words. She rubbed her arm to block the icy breeze that blew through the hot kitchen.

"Best we be gittin' back to dem pots," she said.

Clarissa placed a reassuring hand on Petunia's knee. "I's gonna be fine," she told her.

When Clarissa gestured to stand, she bobbled, nearly knocking her friend off her seat. Petunia grabbed Clarissa's skirt, steadying her.

"Dey been pullin' dem ears down better den two weeks now. You be ready to dance dat juba and do some pattin' under dat harvest moon dat be lookin' down on us when we be makin' fools of ourselves: tappin', kickin', flingin', and flirtin', and sending dem heels up higher den dey needs to be goin'," Petunia laughed.

"I be ready," Clarissa smiled, but only slightly as she hobbled toward the fireplace. "Best we be dippin' up dis here stew now."

Clarissa and Petunia worked in silence, knowing what the other needed to do. The meal had to be on time and to Ben Mullins' liking. They didn't want to upset him and cause them and the others to lose out on the pending festivities.

It was corn-husking eve, just before sundown. Clarissa stood in the doorframe of Miss Effie's cabin. She watched Petunia and the others come down the lane from the big house and the fields. Everyone headed toward the quarters; happier than she could ever remember them being.

"Clarissa. What got you smilin' so, gal?" Petunia asked.

Clarissa nodded her head north, toward the stream that flowed behind the cabins.

"I's here listenin' to dem women washin' clothes. Battlin' sticks poundin' a mighty pretty sound." She grinned. "Listen out yonder. Hear dat?"

"Don't be hearin' nothin'," Petunia said.

"Ain't no yearnin' songs bein' sung. Ain't no snappin' of dat hungry whip dat eats da flesh off dem backs. Ain't no moanin' comin' up out of dem fields nither. Cain't hear no hurtin's. Dat be makin' me smile."

Early the next day, the bedlam around the cabins swelled with gaiety: babies fussed, frogs croaked, children squabbled and rummaged for little pretty rags, young women chattered and laughed, old women hummed while the young men gathered the dancing canes. Everybody, young and old, sang the getting-ready songs with an extra hallelujah. Around noon, they congregated at the base of the alley near the turnpike for the parade up the alley to the yard transformed from a work-yard to a playground.

It was nearly half past one o'clock when Petunia flung her arms and led her perky congregation from the turnpike, up the carriage lane that tracked between the sun-bursting poplar trees and through the slave quarters, headed to the shed. They skipped and sang in voices so angelic that they seemed to deepen the azure of the sky and tease the egg-yolk sun that caused silhouettes to rail along behind them. Petunia's unsteady stride flip-flirted the tails of her paisley scarf looped around her waist and knotted at the back. Mischievous laughter slipped from the lips of the boys who frolicked behind her, captivated by the dipping of her gracious hips.

As Petunia approached Clarissa's cabin, she waved a howdy-hand.

"Hello dere, gal. It be another day, and you still standin' in dat door. Lookin' mighty spiffy in dat skirt wid your hair let down.

Gonna steal a heart for sho' at dat shuckin'." Petunia giggled and dance-walked on, throwing up a vibrant arm.

"Missus done send down word dat she got shirts needin' a quick pressin'. Won't take long. I be seein' you soon," Clarissa hollered after Petunia and chuckled at the boys ogling at Petunia's accentuated rear.

Turtle Jim led his own parade of toddlers gleefully dancing along, following his shadow to the shed. Old Abe came along behind them.

"Ma, I be gittin' now. Dat biscuit and bacon sho' was good."

George Henry ducked beneath Clarissa's arm as she saluted the marchers passing by.

"Take care, boy. I sees you soon."

George Henry rushed to catch up with Sally. He grabbed her hand; the two raced on to the shed. The running and jumping teased up Sally's dress hem, exposing the edges of the red petticoat that matched that of her ma's.

Clarissa hadn't brought her arm down before a butterfly hovered above her hand, brushing her fingertips. She was blinded by the bright orange and black colors of its wings. When she thought to reach for the butterfly, it fluttered away, following behind George Henry, encircling his head. Clarissa slumped to the stoop-step. Her heart raced as she examined her fingertips, straining to see a trace of butterfly dust. She tried to quiet her heart. The butterfly returned; it touched her nose.

"Dat you, Little Man? Dis here a sign you comin' back to me? What you tryin' to say, boy?" Clarissa cupped her palms around the delicate creature. When she opened them, they were as empty as her soul.

On the balcony of the big house, Margaret and Ann Marie watched Ben Mullins crisscross the lush acres below.

"Corn-husking time!" he bellowed and flung his hat above his head. He galloped in huge circles as if he were rounding up his darkies in the field.

Big Bo, Sam, and some of the other hands had made numerous trips to the shed in the oxcart, hauling load after load of the dried corn ears, hundreds of them. They stacked the ears in long piles where the darkies huddled together, singing in one voice, same as they did in the fields, but with a special kind of jubilance:

> *Git on board, little chillen,*
> *Git on board, little chillen,*
> *Dere's room for many mo'. . .*

Ann Marie bent her body over the banister and peeked between the fall foliage at George Henry and Sally, who beckoned for her to join them.

"Please, Mommy, let me go down to the shed."

"That, Ann Marie, is not the proper place for you to be. Remember you've had your twelfth birthday. You're a young lady now."

"But I can see George Henry and Sally. They're waving to me. They want me to come down. Now!" Ann Marie shouted over the railing. Margaret caught her around the waist.

"Take care. You nearly tumbled over that rail. Come with me!"

"Mommy, I hear the music." Ann Marie shook free from her mother. "Listen!" she demanded and waved once more before she reluctantly followed her mother.

Margaret glanced over her shoulder to ensure Ann Marie was still behind her before she raised her skirt to step into the house. Moving with a pompous air, Margaret failed to notice where she was placing her foot and tipped the spittoon that sat near the door. It dumped its ropy content onto her dainty brocade slipper. Margaret flailed her arms and yelled with the gusto of a vulgar man. Ann Marie ducked low. She didn't take another step. Margaret yanked at her skirt, flipping up the rear of the hoop. "Oops!" she cried and slapped it back down, blocking the breeze that smacked at her lower cheeks and forced the front of the hoop up. She pressed it back down and then shook her foot. That sent phlegm flying. A bit smacked her flushed cheek. Margaret thrust back her head with an air of contempt and flicked away the offending gob. Filled with outrage, she hop-hobbled across the sitting room and flopped in a chair.

Down at the shed, Negroes gathered around the oxcart. Mullins stood on its rear, handing each man a dram of whiskey, each lady a jar of molasses. The elderly men and women got a plug of tobacco with their treats. Each child snatched the piece of hard candy offered to them and ran off to enjoy it.

Mullins stepped down off the cart and swung up into his saddle, where he played king of the court. "Start the music, Sam," he shouted at the top of his voice.

Dressed in his best greased kidskin boots and his fiddle tucked under his chin, Sam stomped on a hollowed-out log, announcing the official start for the corn-husking gala.

"George Henry, you and Bo go tell Dr. Isaac to send down his hands."

Ben hurled his hat once more and took off on horseback. He rode with showmanship, galloping as if he were on a young colt chasing after a wild mare, out to the fields and back.

George Henry, with Stu at his side, Bo next to him, a group of hands behind them, and bloodhounds following, they crossed the field headed toward Dr. Isaac's farm. They zigzagged along the meandering path, jumped the freshwater streams, and leaped over the stone walls, keeping up with the other hounds that decided to tag along.

Clarissa's words, "Dem speedy grasshopper legs be a gift from God," sang in George Henry's head as he trotted along. A short time later, he and Stu proudly led Bo, the hands, and Dr. Isaac's darkies back through the fields, stepping lively and singing:

> *Somebody's knockin' at yo' do'*
>
> *O, sinner,*
>
> *Why don't you answer . . .*

Mullins' darkies responded joyously, belting out a tune to the group crossing the fields to join them:

> *Hallelujah,*
>
> *O, hallelujah,*
>
> *O, Who dat a comin' ovah yondah . . .*

The singing stopped when Mullins' hands, at the shed, noted a brawny lad in the midst of the crowd. He was tall, slim, with copper skin, high cheekbones, a narrow nose, a well-formed chin, and a tapered waist. When the breeze lifted his shirt, his washboard ribs and the muscles that rippled up and down them were exposed. His golden eyes were those that only a cat should have. He was too good-looking and too full of boldness to be a slave, some said. He came down the hill with the rest, but he stepped extra high in the tall grass. The sixty or so additional hands made nearly a hundred for husking. Ben shook his head. He was surprised that Dr. Isaac had let his newest hand leave the quarters so soon.

The bloodhounds raced back to the barn with their tongues dangling. Stu followed George Henry on to the hoedown shed. Dr. Isaac's slaves came together with Mullins' same as spokes on a wheel running straight to the hub. They joined in the fun and games and played and worked together as if they were the closest of friends and relatives, even though it was the first meeting for most of them. Dr. Isaac always bought and sold his darkies before they could bond with other people. The strange looking fellow was his latest purchase.

George Henry, now ten years old, busied himself with the big boys. Few could beat him at most games. He tossed the hopscotch stone and jumped the squares. He picked up the marker with the precision of a hawk diving for its prey and never touched a line. George Henry kicked the rag ball farther than any of the other boys and precisely where he wanted it to go. When they squatted to shoot marbles, made from mud and clay, George Henry hit his targets. He always had more marbles in his heap than he did at the start of the game. When he stood in the cane field, playing hide-and-seek, his tall lean body could not be seen. His slim-fingered hands were fast, too, and always reliable when he played ball-and-string. He seldom missed the cup at the end of a stick that wasn't much larger than his thumb. Jumping rope was tricky for him. George Henry's feet often got caught in the ropes, tripping him and tying him down. It was all fun, but he missed his ma and Bo. Bo used to chase him around the yard, but since he had turned fifteen years old, he busied himself with his pa and the other men.

"Come on over here, join the fun," Big Bo said to the new brawny lad who, on that day, became known as Copper Tom.

Sam took a break from his fiddling and came down off the cart to watch some of the wrestling. He, too, invited Copper Tom to join in the fun.

"Go 'head, boy . . . try ya luck," Sam told him.

"Ain't no good at dat."

Copper Tom stayed back, reluctant to be part of the activity. He wanted to compete and felt he could win, always did before, on the other plantations, but he didn't want folks watching him, not just yet. No one insisted that he join the wrestling.

The hoedown was a fun time. Everyone did as they pleased: danced to the music of the drums, ate corn when it wasn't corn-eating time, and horsed around the yard or in the field while others flirted with their love interests. There was no making-to-do on celebration days. Join in if you want, stand back if you don't. Those were the unspoken rules that all the hands respected. Copper Tom moved on, joining the old men nearby.

Turtle Jim, Old Abe, and the other older fellows drew him into their huddle under a tall maple tree that burst with fire-red foliage. Their toothless grins and weak arthritic handshakes didn't bother Tom. He missed his family and friends from the old plantation and welcomed the kindness of these men. Being close to them lulled the uneasiness in his gut. Tom rested against the tree, next to Turtle Jim, who was bent over beneath a floppy-brimmed straw hat, chewing on a long blade of dry grass.

"How you be doin', boy?" Turtle Jim asked.

"Doin' fine."

"What dey call you, boy?"

"Tom. I hear some calling me Copper. It might be Copper Tom now."

"Which you like?"

"Don't matter. Massa gonna change it if it ain't to his likin'." Tom stopped talking as if his tongue had been stolen. "Who dat gal over dere at dem cookin' pots? Dat pretty one."

"Dat be Lily. She runs the loom and do sewin' fa da Missus."

"She be asked for?"

"Not dat I be knowin' of."

"She gonna be mine. I sees to dat. Somethin' 'bout her seem right for me . . . cain't say what it be. But the Lawd be knowin'."

"You take care, boy. Dem kinda matters not easy."

Lily dumped her vegetables into the pot. She could feel the stare and raised her head. She gave Tom a smile and continued working. She didn't have time to take particular note of him or anyone else.

This year, Bo's only interest was arm-wrestling, testing the strength of his well-configured muscles against those of the other young men. He clenched hand after hand, pushing each down 'til sweat dripped from his brows. When his pa stepped up to the big log, he knew that he wouldn't win. Big Bo put his elbow down and held up his receiving hand. Bo gripped it. He felt a special connection to his pa when he did. He looked into Big Bo's face, marveling at the strength reflected in it.

"Git ready, boy."

"Am, Pa."

The log pricked at Bo's bare chest when he braced himself against it. He tightened his grip on his pa's broad, calloused hand that he remembered holding onto when he was a small boy, scared of the dark.

They acknowledged each other in only a way that a father and son can do. Holding on to his pa's hand, the sweat of their palms mingled and trickled down their wrists. Bo knew he was going to lose, but being close to his dad made him feel strong and secure, even giddy at times. Big Bo pulled his boy close. Their damp shoulders smacked.

"On the count of three, you push. Push hard, boy . . . hard as you can."

Bo tucked his feet beneath his hips and dug his toes into the dampened earth.

"One . . . two . . . three."

Big Bo victoriously slammed the back of Bo's hand down on the log. He squeezed it and gave Bo a hardy slap on his back.

"You done good, boy."

"I try, Pa."

Big Bo effortlessly pulled Bo to his feet and put an arm around his shoulder. They sauntered off to find a cooling drink.

Bo eyeballed Tom positioned against the tree next to Turtle Jim. Since Tom was tall, Bo wondered if he could have wrestled his pa's arm. Tom wondered the same.

As Tom hung back, he listened to the old men jabber about aging and going on to the Promised Land. With one hand on top of the other, they unsteadied their fragile bodies on walking sticks. They grinned at the pretty gals who winked, shook sassy hips, puckered their lips, and blew naughty kisses to tease them.

"Um . . . hum. Mighty pretty," the elderly fellas said, each wishing aloud to be a young man again, but only for a moment.

"Workin' in dem fields ain't easy," they'd say with a chuckle and a slap on a knobby knee.

After the young ladies passed, the gray-heads spit tobacco and wobbled over to a nearby bucket to see whose gob landed closest to it.

Turtle Jim left Old Abe and the group to mind the iron spikes hammered into the ground. He wanted to know which horseshoe rang it first. When he returned to the group, the old men were whittling small animals and flutes from softwood and cane. They didn't permit Turtle Jim to handle a knife. His eyesight was poor. He'd already cut off part of his thumb off trying to slice and eat an apple. He joined the joke-telling about when they were young chasing gals, older trying to keep up with them, and now trying to get them to stand still long enough for a better look.

Ben Mullins had sent down a few chickens and a whole hog for the hoedown. The years that the harvest wasn't plentiful, so he sent buckets and barrels of pig parts: ears, feet, heads, maws, tails, and tripe. It didn't matter what he sent this year. Clarissa hadn't shown up to cook it. Petunia had to take charge of the cooking. She didn't want the meal to be too late for fear that Mullins might call back the meat, even though it'd be too much for his family to eat and no way to keep it from spoiling.

The women who had kitchen gardens brought their harvest to the pot: beans, okra, onions, peas, spuds, tomatoes, yams, and squash. Hot corn pone was made after milling some of the dried corn. It would sop up the pot liquor.

Once the dinner bell rang, the feast was served to all. The hands ate until content. Right after the main meal, molasses cakes and fruit pies brought on a host of smiles. Well fed and jolly, the slaves swarmed around the ears of corn. When Sam's rhythms exploded, so did the shucking: ripping down the husk, pulling off the silk, and racing to see whose slaves finished first.

The young gals and the women bent, braided, folded, tied, twisted, and wove the husks. They made dolls, horse collars, baskets, bed mats, mops, and more. The old Negresses smoked corncob pipes and crafted new ones. Sally tagged along with Lily to the ring of ladies. The ground was damp and hard, but you couldn't tell by the smiles on the faces and the mud-splotched soles that stood straight on thick-calloused heels and swayed to the fiddling. The freshly starched, multicolored, homespun fabrics of their skirts spread over the properly outstretched legs. The ladies sat like their slave mothers taught them to do as young gals. Petunia couldn't straighten her legs, so she rolled and tucked her scarf behind her knees.

"Sally, come . . . sit here. I shows you how to make a pretty little toy," Petunia said.

"Be mighty glad to be learnin', Miss Petunia."

Sally plopped down next to Petunia, who pulled her close and guided Sally's girlish fingers. They manipulated the husk into a skirted form with arms, legs, and a small rounded head. When Petunia uncoiled her fingers from around Sally's, Sally hopped up, clutching her new doll. She called for George Henry to show him her creation, but he frolicked with the big boys and couldn't be distracted.

When the sun bounced on the horizon, a victorious hoopla erupted. Dr. Isaac's slaves finished the husking first. The crowd pushed forward, encircling them. The winners applauded as the gang sang and slapped hambone. Mullins gave each winning man and woman two apples and a piece of peppermint candy that they proudly carried above their heads, ensuring that everyone knew who the winners were.

The tangerine sunset was absorbed by the hilltops. The music was replaced with excited jabbering. Petunia looked but still didn't see Clarissa. She pulled her paisley shawl across her back, blocking the chill from the night air and the thoughts of what might have happened to Clarissa.

Turtle Jim, Old Abe, and their buddies were braced against the shed, turning up their horns of whiskey, when Sam lit the lightwood knot torches. They were shipped to Ben Mullins from a friend in New Orleans. The torches flared bubbly yellow and blue-tipped flames. When Sam was done, he got back on the wagon and once more stomped the hollow log. This time, it announced the start of the jivin'. Sam rapidly drew his bow across his fiddling strings and added a strong vibrato. The sound was electrifying; it captured everybody in its musical web.

Copper Tom was a dancer and couldn't resist joining the men who warmed their muscles with a buck and wing: shaking one leg at a time and thudding each foot. They spiraled in a lazy S-line and flirted with the gals applauding them. Copper Tom took particular note of Lily. He watched her most of the day from a distance. Dancing on the sideline with the other gals, Lily let loose a female call as her shoulder dipped toward Tom, letting him know that his attention was welcomed.

"Dat boy got too much grit for a Negro," Turtle Jim said to his old buddies. "Must have been groomed by one of dem Christian families dat might've owned him."

Turtle Jim rubbed his chin and pondered a bit longer.

"He like a buck wantin' to git a gal. Maybe waitin' for his first sip of moonshine. Gittin' his first pair of britches, or maybe itchin' to get to where he don't rightly know. Dem the things dat kin git a young buck grinnin' and hurt at the same time."

"Jim, ya think dat boy gonna see a good number of tomorrows?" Old Abe asked.

"Don't rightly know."

Old Abe cupped a hand to his ear.

"What dat ya say, Jim?"

"I say," Turtle Jim raised his voice. "Dat boy got trouble behind dat smile of his. Somethin' big gnawin' at his innards. Not certain it be Lily neither. If it is, dat could mean real trouble. Lovin' kin spark a happiness dat kin slip into the devil's pen. An unsettled heart wid no way to feed dem desires grapples at ya. Yank a young buck's life quicker den you kin snap a dead twig."

Every slave knew it, but no one would speak it, except Turtle Jim.

The suitors moved on. Bent low at the waist, the men doffed their hats. When their heads bobbed up, they did a dignified walk. Pretty gals answered their calls, and Lily answered Tom's. Her head went back, her bosom rose, lips parted, eyes widened, and her lashes fluttered. She donned a robust smile not seen since she lost her baby boy. Everybody watching knew Lily was smitten for Tom. He captivated her heart. It seemed as if both of them were tipsy from a hefty dose of a love potion.

When the men started juba patting, the gals twirled and snatched their skirts, showing off a kaleidoscope of colors. Lily had the grandest underskirt of all, full of red flair. The ladies danced until it was time to turn the yard back over to the men. They receded and formed a large circle around Copper Tom and the men who waved their canes and arched their backs, deeply as they could. The gents sported high kicks. Then, they fell in step with the ring-shout dance that had no shouting. One by one they slid into a shuffling move. Their heels tapped and feet stamped. One after another, they moved counterclockwise inside the ring of women. The jivers wiggled and swayed while keeping their shoulders stiff. When they were done, the strutters lined up with buckets of water balanced on their heads. They paraded in a straight line, showing off their skills. Even though

Copper Tom was tall, he had no trouble securing his bucket. The young boys who mimicked the men soon found themselves drenched and shivering. George Henry remembered the water bucket practice and decided he'd wait for warmer weather. When Sam's music began to crescendo, the pails were put down.

The men locked arms with the ladies for the cakewalk. The winning couple would each get a hoecake wrapped in a cabbage leaf. Copper Tom extended his arm to Lily. She hooked it in good fashion and fanned her skirt, snapping it with a flip of the wrist. The two exaggerated their high steps and were the envy of most as they promenaded, and then took the hoecake prize.

Before the music cooled down, the men dismissed their partners for their next dance. Lily reluctantly let go of Tom's hand so he could join the other men and she the gals. The fellows bowed their bodies backward with their legs up, bent at the knees. The gals praised the guys with an encore of applause. Some of the men showed off with jaunty somersaults and hog calls when they landed on their feet. Everybody who could, danced the long dog stretch. That was the last dance of the evening. It was an exaggeration of shuffling and clawing. Copper Tom and Lily moved away from the crowd. They were hugged up with a serious tête-à-tête, savoring their last moments, knowing the worst.

Petunia limped into the center of the crowd. The celebrants moved back and danced a buck and wing around her. She squatted close to the ground, stretched her scarf across her back, and flapped the ends of it like wings of a chicken with its neck wrung for frying. Without raising her feet, she did her own juba, flaunting a speedy heel-toe. Then she dipped, swayed, and jiggled her hips. She was a spinning top twirling its colors into a bright marbled ball.

When the fiddling notes faded, Petunia's scarf fell limp. The group divided. Tom and Lily stared at each other. They did what they knew they had to. He joined Dr. Isaac's slaves, who staggered back across the field to their cabins. She and Mullins' other slaves sauntered back down the alley to their cabins, drunken on pleasures, leaving behind an eerie quietness.

Turtle Jim's young charges slept on the shoulders of older slaves. He and Old Abe paraded home alone. They were the last to lay their heads down for a much needed sleep.

11

Troubled Moments

The hoedown was over. George Henry watched Sam snuff out the last torch. Then, he snatched up the victuals and raced Stu to Effie's cabin. With his hand braced on the door, George Henry shooed Stu away.

"Go on back, boy."

The hound tucked his tail and ambled on toward the barn. With heavy paws, he dragged his feet along the ground and twisted his neck to peep at George Henry once more.

George Henry stepped inside the cabin, with his hand still on the door handle, he gasped; basket after basket of overflowing laundry and a disarray of rough, dried clothing, more heaps than he'd ever seen, hid most of the floor.

"I brung you some victuals, Ma. And you, Miss Effie. Wasn't no cakes, pies, or sweets left," George Henry said, not able to shift his stare away from the laundry.

"Dat be just fine, boy. You come on in here," Miss Effie said.

George Henry closed the door and minded his feet as he moved cautiously around the scattered bundles. He placed the food on the hearth.

"Ma," his voice trembled.

"Hush, boy. Done had enough of Missus' orneriness. Don't want ta talk."

Clarissa stepped into George Henry's space and knocked him over the three-legged stool. He crawled to Miss Effie's bed and slumped against it. He drew his kneecaps to his chest and wrapped his arms around his legs. He kept a wary stare on Clarissa as he listened to his heart thundering in his eardrums. Miss Effie stroked his shoulder.

"Gonna be fine, boy. Your ma be upset. She be calmin' down soon."

Clarissa mindlessly snatched up another piece of laundry and spread it across the pressing board. She fussed aloud, wishing with each slam of the iron that she could shred the garments into bits and pieces, and be done with them forever. She looked fixedly at George Henry.

"Got whupped for stealin' dat biscuit and bacon for you. Cain't git caught feedin' you from the big house no more. Be gittin' a heavier lashin' cross my back. I don't be wantin' dat."

"I's sorry, Ma."

"Not your fault, boy. Dat woman be a foul one and her man, too. Dey both be created by the god of evil and the one of meanness. She keep givin' me dis here laundry dat I ain't got enough time to finish. She know I ain't no laundress." George Henry covered his ears, blocking Clarissa's yelling. "She be causin' me to stand on my feet workin' day and night after she done made my leg so I cain't near walk. I's tired. Cain't take no mo'!"

Clarissa's skirt gathers snapped as she angrily jerked her hips. She turned the hot iron bottom-side-up and glared down on it.

"Dis here be remindin' me of dem shackles I wore dat auction day in Louisville. I feels like I'm still chained to dem. I's tired of bein' . . ."

"Chile, I done told you, let dem raw feelin's go."

"I's sorry, Miss Effie. Don't mean to be upsettin' you none. You rest now."

Clarissa's lips quivered. Her tears fell on Mullins' britches and sizzled when the iron glided over them. After she was done pressing, she folded and stacked shirts, britches, and overalls, filling the empty baskets that she would tote to the big house later.

George Henry pulled strings of meat from a chunk of pork and rolled them between his fingers, pulverizing the strings. Then he added a pinch of boiled vegetable to the mushy lump.

"Dis here for you, Miss Effie."

George Henry held the food to Effie's mouth like a mother would to her baby's lips.

"You's a good boy, George Henry."

"I try, Miss Effie. You sip dis here," he said, holding a tin of sweet tea to her lips.

"Ma, you wants some of dese here victuals?"

"I eats dat later, chile."

Still monitoring his ma's behavior, George Henry crawled close to the fire and drew his knees up to his chin.

Clarissa had stopped ironing. Holding her head with a strange certainty, she studied George Henry with a gaze that puzzled him.

"You remind me of your brother. You be sittin' like him wid dem muddy knees under your nose. Gonna be tall like him, too. Done growed out of dat shirt I brung you here in. You be standin' near a head over Sally and taller den most born round your time. You be near tall as Bo. Got dem grasshopper legs, too."

George Henry smiled at Clarissa's bragging words, trying to capture the proud ones and not let them escape his mind.

Clarissa snatched up another piece of laundry from the basket, then another. She pressed some right away; others were crammed back into the basket of unpressed clothes or thrown back on the floor to be hot-ironed later. When the last bit was finished, she told George Henry eye-to-eye, "Things gonna change . . . you wait and see."

"Clarissa. What you got on your mind, chile?"

"Miss Effie, dere a part of me dat nobody kin take hold of. Dat part wants to be free. Time's done come for me."

"You sho'? I hear tell one of Dr. Isaac's boys done been caught runnin'. Dogs brung him back. Best you take care, gal. Things ain't easy out dere."

"Ain't easy here neither. I always done what you tells me: don't sass, work hard, walk softly, stay on Missus' good side, and speak nice to Massa. Didn't none of dem things make my days better. You knowed I done tolerated enough from dem folks. It be my time. Dogs or no dogs, I gotta try. I's dyin' here, Miss Effie."

"Come close. Listen to me, chile," Effie whispered. "If you be havin' your mind set, keep dem ears of yours listenin' for Big Bo's hammers. Word will come to be ready. When he bangs on dem horseshoes, he be tellin' you somethin'. If you don't hear dat hammer, gal, don't you run. He knows what he be doin'."

"How I gonna tell one bangin' from another?"

"You hear two long bangs, den five quick ones, two long ones, a big loud one, den lots of quick ones. Dem the runnin' bangs. Don't you linger when you hear dem. Keep movin'. Let your feet be quick."

George Henry, still holding his legs, asked, "What you be talkin' 'bout, Miss Effie?"

"Don't worry none 'bout what I be sayin' to your ma."

A chill snaked around George Henry's arms. When he grabbed a piece of kindling, Clarissa spun him around.

"Hush. You be seein' and knowin' soon enough. Don't be lettin' your mouth be tellin' nothin'."

George Henry twisted from her grasp and tossed the kindling on the low fire. The flames cast an orange glow that warmed the cabin. Clarissa seemed unaware of the new energy. George Henry settled back down. He took in a heap of warm air and rubbed his arms, smoothing out the goosebumps, trying to temper the hurt he felt.

"Ma, why you be upset wid me? I didn't . . . " George Henry whimpered.

Clarissa peered deeply into the dark of George Henry's eyes, cutting his words off. At first, she didn't say a word, and then she sputtered, "Ain't upset wid you, chile."

Clarissa picked up the three-legged stool and pulled it next to her bedding. She sat on it and slipped her long, skinny fingers into the shucking and straw. She pulled out rags and sorted them by size and color. Bleakness washed over her face when she drew out a swatch of dark blue fabric.

"Ma! Dat be from your auction skirt?"

"Is, boy."

"Tell me 'bout dat day and where we be from."

"Dis ain't no tellin' time."

Clarissa's trembling fingers smoothed the relic. Her expression was the same one that haunted George Henry when she refused to tell him once before about the auction block and their trip from Virginia to Kentucky. He had heard snippets of the tale when Clarissa talked privately to Effie, but could never hear enough to decipher the meaning of what was being said.

"You sleep, boy. I's got work to do."

Clarissa unfolded Gran's old quilt and patched it by the firelight. The aged stitches were faint; some were missing. The message was barely understandable on parts of the quilt. She filled in the vacant spaces with the scraps at her feet. Granma Alice's words called to her with each stitch: "Don't run 'til you know the time is right. Watch dat big star. Don't let the dipper out of your sight. Wait 'til near time for the river to freeze. Keep on dat trail. Look for the signs dat the quilt done told you. Don't stop 'til you cross dem waters to Jordan. Den, go on to Canada, if you can. Dem help you 'long the way."

Clarissa rocked and sewed until day bullied night away.

12

Flounce and Lace

Ben and Margaret, just out of bed and still in their loungewear, sat in a straight-backed, whitewashed, wooden rocker suited for two on the veranda just outside their bedroom. They faced the front lawn and admired the expansive grounds that surrounded their house as they sipped hot coffee, sweetened with cream and sugar, and reveled in the pleasant fall air. It was a welcome respite from the heat and humidity of the summer days.

Margaret cherished the trees that ran along each side of the lane that led to the big house. She couldn't look away from them. The trees were full of the golden-yellow, tulip-like blooms.

"Ben, do you remember the sweet, floral fragrance of the poplar trees? It was so delightful."

"Don't remember much about that, but I can tell you, this 1855 crop was the best it's been in years. Those darkies sure had themselves a good hoedown: husking and shucking, dancing and drinking. They ate better than the king's court. That kicking and parading was something to see. You should have come on down to the shed . . . see for yourself. We got us a good bunch of darkies, Margaret."

Ben slipped his thumbs under the collar of his smoking jacket. His arrogance expanded his chest beyond the lapels.

"We've done well this year. Except for those damn gals. Lily loses her pickaninny and Clarissa hasn't produced a thing since I bought her. Don't seem to be promising a thing any time soon. When I think she might be with child, it never comes to and don't seem that it ever will. I've lost money on that gal . . . and your hurting the other hands didn't help none. But Isaac certainly had a sad and expensive year."

"Why do you say so?" Margaret asked, fanning her face with a napkin, pleased that Ben had decided to divert the conversation to Isaac's slaves instead of his.

"He lost another hand. That makes about five this year alone. He has to buy a new boy and it's not auction time. So, that makes it costly. Don't know which one ran this time. But I know it was a young buck. When you lose one of them, you lose production."

"Why does Isaac have such a problem holding on to his help?"

"Not sure. Could be he buys and sells before his slaves get a chance to be in a family way. That's what keeps most darkies settled."

Margaret set her cup and saucer down.

"Enough of that. It's our time to celebrate. We shall have a grand soirée crossing both lawns. You can ride to Louisville . . . engage a speaker and a few musicians. And, I'd love to have suitable table waiters dressed nicely in finely starched uniforms."

Margaret tilted her head, knowing the rays of the sunrise would blush her cheeks with a rosy-orange tint. She fluttered her eyelashes to suggest a kiss. Smiling and nearly laughing, Ben pecked her on the lips.

"It's best we make do with what we have, my dear. We're lucky. Few can cook better than Clarissa or Petunia, at least in these parts. They'll do a superb job with the help of the hands we already have. The two of them will produce a fine spread. Sam's fiddling will be all the music we need. I can tell your guests a thing or two if you feel that you must have an orator. That way I can keep my profit in my pocket."

"Well! With or without the extras, you see to it that the right people are invited."

"I'm sure you will take care of that, dear."

"It's going to be an impressive affair. You'll see, Ben. The evenings are still warm. I can wear my new gown that Lily sewed for me. It will dazzle you and the guests. Perhaps stir up some jealousy among the ladies."

Margaret inhaled again and drew her shoulders back. She rested against Ben's arm and heaved, pushing her breast above the fragile lace on her nightwear. Aroused by her charm, Ben touched Margret softly at the curve of her neck where his fingers nested perfectly. His thumb toyed with the hairs at her nape. His massaging hand glided across her collarbone and then slipped into her gown, fondling her breast.

"You're warm and wanting, Mrs. Mullins."

Ben's other hand slid to the center of her back, easing her into his embrace. His lips fell over hers, begging for the rest of her body.

"Mr. Mullins! I suggest you stop that and listen to what I have to say."

"I heard what you said, Margaret, but you need to consider an earlier gathering . . . take advantage of the sun. Since it's fall, you'll be able to expose your shoulders a bit longer and won't have to worry about your delicate skin taking on color or my mistaking you for a darkie."

Ben roared with naughtiness as he continued to offer himself to Margaret. She laid both hands on his chest and straightened her arms, moving him away.

"Watch your vulgar ways, Mr. Mullins. You need to be aware of that jug and not generate more gossip for the neighbors. You've given them enough to wag their tongues about: riding drunk last week, falling out of the saddle, nearly breaking your fool neck."

"I shall take care, dear."

"Be sure that you do."

The festive day arrived. Clarissa was in the kitchen well before dawn. She bustled about, sweating and hobbling on her bad leg. She checked the lambs hooked up inside the chimney for smoking. The chickens twirled at the end of ropes, dangling above a low fire. Big Bo tended to the beef, skewered and rotating over a hot spit. The pig was smoldering in a ground pit. With the help of his boy and Sam, Big Bo boned the cooked meat and hauled it in the back of the oxcart to the kitchen. Clarissa and Petunia prepared the meat for serving. The smells of smoked meats, spices, sweets, vegetables, and yeast breads announced the grand happening for nearly a mile around.

George Henry and Sally scavenged for wildflowers. They bunched them in bouquets of lavender, pink, red, yellow, and white. They stuffed them into cans left at the tree by Sam. The two rushed across the lawns, dashing between tables draped with red and white gingham cloths, garnishing each with a can of flowers. When done, they stood back, crossed their arms like grown folks, and appraised their work.

"Let's go tell Ma, Sally."

The two raced across the lawns yelling, "Come see! Come see!"

Clarissa and Petunia poked their heads through the kitchen window.

"You two sure done good," Clarissa said.

"My! My! Dem tables be mighty pretty," Petunia said.

At two o'clock, the nearly 300 guests began arriving in coaches that pulled up to the wrought iron arch overlaid with the last blooms of the season. Sam stood erect, dressed in his best: white cotton gloves; a well-starched, white shirt with a high-standing collar; waistcoat; knickers with knee-high socks; and a black felt top hat.

As the carriages pulled up, Sam opened each door. He offered a hand to the gentlemen. In turn, they assisted their lady who rested a gloved hand on the topside of the arm extended to them. The couples glided under the arch and promenaded between the rose gardens where the gentlemen took leave from them.

The ladies strutted off in pairs, bobbing their silk bonnets; adorned with feathers, flowers, lace; and ribbons, secured with puffy bows snugly tied beneath their chins. They pranced from group to group, chatting excitedly about family, fashions, and friends, as they waved fine, white, linen handkerchiefs trimmed with delicate lace.

The men gathered in small groups. With thumbs tucked into waistcoat pockets, they rocked back on their heels. They grinned, laughed, and chewed tobacco. Some puffed on cigars, others smoked clay pipes that they bit down on while debating local politics.

Up at the big house, Ann Marie sat quietly with her hands resting on her lap, minding her manners. Lily's knee was pressed firmly against Margaret's back as she tugged the corset strings.

"Tighter! Tighter!"

"Got no more pull in dese here strings, Missus."

Margaret's face flushed when Lily tied the strings. Feeling faint, Margaret diverted her attention to the round cage crinoline collapsed on the floor. She stepped into the ring; Lily lifted it to her waist, buttoned it at the rear, and then released the royal blue skirt over Margaret's head. Layers of ruffles slithered down over the hoopskirt. Margaret wiggled her arms through the mushroom-capped sleeves of the tightly fitted bodice that left her neck and shoulders exposed. Lily looped each tiny pearl buttons that tracked up the back of it.

"My dress! What have you done to it? It's much too tight."

"I . . . I sew it the way you say, Missus."

When Margaret raised her hands, Lily stooped to avoid being struck. She adjusted the hem of the skirt that didn't need adjusting.

"I can hardly take in a decent breath. Let me sit a minute."

"Oh! No, Missus. You might muss up your dress. I kin loosen dem corset strings," Lily said, peering up at her missus.

"Mommy, I'm sure it wasn't Lily's fault. It must have been the breakfast cakes . . . "

Margaret raised her hand again. This time, it was to caution her daughter.

"You can go to your room until time to greet the guests. And where are those white ribbons that I bought for your hair?"

"I misplaced them and had to use the pink ones. They match my dress nicely," Ann Marie said and bolted from the room before she could be questioned more.

While her hand was still up, Margaret noticed her curvy figure in the wardrobe mirror and turned herself. Without taking her eyes off the image, she admired what she saw.

"Missus, you sho' be lookin' mighty pretty in dat dress. I'll put dese bosom flowers and gloves on the dressin' table wid your other things. Should I let dat dress out, Missus?"

"Leave it. I just won't eat. Take my vial of smelling salts with you as you leave. Lily! . . . Was that a wolf I heard?"

"Was, Missus."

"I surly hope he keeps himself up in those hills. I don't need any unnecessary excitement today."

Margaret shuddered at the thought of the wolf, and quickly abandoned the worry. She didn't want to consider the chaos that one of them might cause if it got hold of a calf, broke into the smokehouse or worse, snatched the meats from the buffet table.

Lily arranged the lace gloves and the lemon-yellow and white flowers on the table next to the multicolored, jewel-tone, glass beaded purse and silk fan. She picked up the scent bottle. Lily's finger studied its shape. It was a small, ruby red, beveled cylinder that lay perfectly across her palm. Before dropping it into her apron pocket, she appreciated its coolness, the brass closures at each end of it, and its smoothness.

"If dere's nothin' more dat I kin do for you, Missus, I go help Clarissa in the kitchen."

"Before you go, tell Ann Marie to come down to the foyer."

"Yes, Missus."

Margaret lifted the small bouquet of flowers, tied neatly with a ribbon, to her nose. She took pleasure in the fragrance before she tucked them between the soft moons of her bust. She glanced in the mirror before she hung the purse, no larger than a man's hand, on her wrist. Pleased with what she saw, she gathered the lace gloves in her hand and walked over to the window. Margaret gandered at the guests below as she adjusted her gloves; her fingers appreciated the seams of the slim fourchettes as they slipped through the finger casings.

Humming to herself, she lifted her skirt, tiptoed over to the wardrobe mirror, and swayed as if she were waltzing around a grand ballroom. Feeling dizzy, she curtsied adoringly to the figure in the mirror. Rising up, she stood face-to-face with her image. She fluffed the ruffles, brushed off the creases, and smoothed the pleats that had shifted. Satisfied with what she saw in the glass, she picked up her fan and descended the steps that led down to the foyer. Two large wingback chairs, one on each side of the new huntboard welcomed her, but she chose to stand not wanting to muss her dress.

In the kitchen, Clarissa sliced and stacked meat on large oval platters; baked deep dishes of corn pudding; boiled, buttered, and creamed vegetables; and filled basket after basket with freshly baked biscuits, cornbread, soda bread, and yeast rolls. The hands stood just outside the kitchen door, well dressed in their fine serving garbs: new white aprons, fresh blouses, and tow shirts worn with well-pressed skirts and trousers. They awaited for commands from Clarissa, who meticulously considered each dish, assuring that it was presentation-ready before sending it out.

"Come and git it," she cried.

Lily, along with the other hands, retrieved the casseroles and platters at the kitchen door. Petunia grabbed the handles of the breadbaskets. With their backs erect and their shoulders steady, the well-dressed slaves balanced the dishes and baskets on their heads. Clarissa shielded her eyes from the sun as she proudly watched her team parade, in step to the big table. Young darkies waited in a cane-straight line swaying peacock-feathered shoofly fans. They moved them in unison, assuring that no pests alighted on the food.

George Henry told Sally, "Ain't never seen so much food. Be more den was at the corn shuckin'."

"Come here." Clarissa cupped their chins. "Stay 'way from dem tables. Dere food ain't ours. Go on down to the cabin 'fore trouble finds you."

George Henry pulled Sally along. "Come on."

"Naw. Miss Clarissa say stay 'way."

"Come on. We looks quick. Den, we go on."

George Henry and Sally crawled underneath the tables until they found a suitable spying spot. Sprawled out on their bellies, they inspected the gentlemen, who twirled their ladies up to the center of the circle and back again. Hoop skirts swished and swayed to the music of Sam's fiddle.

Back at the big house, Margaret held Ann Marie's hand as they prepared to present themselves to the guests.

"Just a minute, Mommy. I need to get my parasol."

"Hurry, Ann Marie! The guests are waiting."

Margaret watched the ladies and gentlemen out on the lawn, cackling with one another. She chuckled at the sight of the children frolicking about. Engaged in fun and games, the boys chased the girls across the lawn.

Ann Marie returned and followed Margaret out of the house. They stopped briefly at the top of the grand stairs leading to the front door. Ann Marie opened her parasol and hurried down the steps. She scampered off to join her friends, whose soft-colored party dresses flounced with buttons, bows, laces, and ribbons that highlighted the folds and gathers.

"Come back here!" Margaret called to Ann Marie.

"Ahhh!" the ladies gasped from behind opened fans as they appreciated the exquisiteness of Margaret's ensemble and Ann Marie's beauty.

"Look! George Henry. There goes Miss Ann Marie and Miss Margaret be mighty upset wid her, too."

"But she won't be gittin' no whuppin' like we would if we be goin' off like dat."

"Ooh! Wee! Miss Ann Marie dress be mighty pretty. Look at dem shiny ribbons in her hair. Wish I had just one of dem."

"Shush," George Henry said.

Margaret descended the stairs with majesty. As she ventured from one small group to another, she offered small talk about the weather, the new huntboard, and troublesome slaves. Then she sashayed, person to person, extending a limp hand to the gentlemen to be acknowledged and a cheek to the ladies for an air-blown kiss. By the time she arrived at the head table, most eyes were on her. With all the drama that she could muster, she elegantly raised her skirt to lower herself into a small chair.

"Ouch!"

She sprang up, frantically fanning her face. Her cheeks flushed a bright crimson. Her legs trembled beneath her weight. When Margaret's arms shot up, her purse spun like a boomerang above her head, and then clobbered her on the nose. She sneezed repeatedly, loudly passed gas, and tumbled over the guest seated next to her. She straightened her back, sniffled herself, and yelled hysterically for Lily.

"I'm comin', Missus."

Lily waved from the other side of the lawn. She rushed between the guests to reach Margaret before she yelled for her again. Margaret grabbed her, holding on so tightly she numbed Lily's arm.

"Are you wantin' to dance, Missus?"

"No I'm not! Get the smelling salts! I feel faint."

Lily retrieved the vial from her pocket. In her haste, she pulled the glass stopper from the perfume end of the bottle, splattering its contents on the two of them.

"Oh, Missus, I's sorry. I's so sorry," Lily cried.

She dabbed Margaret's dress with her apron. The smell of the sweet magnolias nauseated Lily, causing her stomach to churn.

"Stop that fuss. Open the smelling salts. Be quick, gal!"

Margaret hurriedly wrapped her hands around Lily's and inhaled deeply. Her head was thrust back by the pungent odor and sting from the salts.

"Come! Come, gal! I'm fainting . . ." Margaret sniffed the salts a second and a third time. "There's something in these drawers other than me."

The other hands watched from across the lawn as Margaret pulled Lily along. Big Bo and Sam tucked their heads into the folds of their arms to stifle their hoots. The gals used the tails of their aprons to muffle theirs. Margaret shot each of them a piercing glance as she continued along with Lily. As soon as they entered the bedroom, Margaret bent over. She tilted her hoop, exposing her rear.

"Do you see anything?" she demanded.

"Don't see nothin', Missus."

Lily carefully plucked off the burrs, tucked them into her sleeve, and then finger-dusted the bottom of the bedroom chair.

"Try sittin' again, Missus?"

"Hum. That's a bit strange. I don't feel a thing."

"It must be dat chair dat you be sittin' on. I goes and gits it, Missus."

Lily dashed out of the room before her sides ruptured from glee.

"Take it out to the rear yard. Burn it!" Margaret hollered from the top of the stairs.

"Yes'um."

Out on the lawn, Ben Mullins enjoyed the jug, turning it up for a hefty slurp each time it passed him. When his gait faltered, he kissed a darkie smack on her lips, causing the proper ladies to frantically fan themselves and pass smelling salts beneath their noses. George Henry and Sally rolled onto their backs, kicking up their heels with laughter. If that wasn't enough, Ben plummeted into the lap of a guest dressed in buttercup yellow. She leaped up, dumped him on the ground, and shook out her skirt. With her teeth clenched, she stepped over him and stomped off. Before he regained his composure, he missed his footing again and plunged facedown on the slippery ground. When Mullins raised his head, his forehead, cheeks, and chin were smeared with mud. He crawled toward George Henry and Sally. Their heads were butted together. They were unaware of his presence until they smelled his whiskey breath and heard his garbled speech.

"Yooou-you. Coooo-come wit-wit-with me. Yooou-you, too."

When George Henry and Sally stood, Mullins nabbed them. He clipped the two, one underneath each of his arms, kicking and screaming. The party ladies and gentlemen ate, chatted, danced, and laughed. They ignored the commotion as Mullins, with his war paint drying, wobbled down the carriage lane to the smokehouse. Slaves, old and young, feared that place. Too many had been incarcerated there: whipped, raped, starved, or strung up for days.

"We be good. Won't spy no more. Please, Massa, let us be. We go on down to dem quarters. You see. Please! Please, Massa!" George Henry squealed, and Sally bawled.

Mullins stumbled on. He didn't slow his steps until he kicked open the smokehouse door and dropped the two on the floor.

George Henry and Sally cowered beneath the monsters that swung in the shadows above their heads. The bacon, beef, and hams that dangled from the rafters made them wet their pants. Mullins tied a length of rope under George Henry's arms and knotted it at his chest, and then tied a piece around Sally and strung the two up between the rumps.

"You pickaninnies gonna swing 'til you're smoked and cured."

The door crashed shut, leaving George Henry and Sally in pitch-black darkness. Sally sobbed and hiccuped until her throat was raw.

"Don't cry, Sally. We gonna get free," George Henry whispered and then listened to the outside sounds. He could hear music and laughter coming down from the twin lawns.

Clarissa's steps were laborious. Sweat dripped from her brow. Her clothes were matted to her body. Her leg had swelled and smarted something awful as she hobbled about, to arrange meats and vegetables on the serving trays, while Petunia, Lily, and the other hands ran them to the big table. Finally, the cakes, pies, molasses, taffy, and chilled sweet cream were served with after-dinner coffee. It was an indication that Sam would soon fiddle the last song.

The orange hue of the sunset, at the edged of the horizon, lingered behind a light blue-gray scrim. The guests lined up for the coaches that would drive them away, leaving a lazy streamer of dust behind. The gentlemen, with wives on their arms and a clear indication that they had shared the contents of the jug more than once, needed Sam's assistance to get back into their carriages. By the time the last guest left, the sky glistened with a full harvest moon that appeared to be so low that it could be touched. Deep black shadows were forced across the grounds by its brilliant white light.

After the hands cleared away the tables, chairs, and trash, there was little evidence of a soirée except for the crushed grass. Clarissa and Petunia put away the last of the place settings and returned to the quarters. Miss Effie and Bo were fast asleep, but not George Henry.

"Where my boy at?"

"Ain't he wid you?" Effie asked groggily.

"Naw! He ain't wid me."

Before Clarissa could say more, Lily burst through the cabin door, unable to catch her breath. Wringing her hands, she staggered in circles, calling between sobs, "Where my gal? She ain't in our cabin. I thought she be here." Lily's eyes scanned the cabin. "Lawd! Lawd! What done happen to my gal? And George Henry? Where he be?"

"Bo, run! Pound on dem doors. Don't miss none. Ask 'bout dem chillen," Clarissa said.

Bo knocked on every door and spoke to everybody. He returned, bent over and winded.

"Dey seen dem! Massa done took George Henry and Sally down to da smokehouse."

Lily fell to her knees, reached toward the heavens, and then pulled her praying hand down to her midsection. Bent over, she tearfully rocked and wailed, "Oh, my Lawd! Dat man done killed and smoked dem babies. He gonna slice dem. Den he gonna feed dem to the hogs. The devil done come for me 'cause I done been cruel to the Missus. I knowed I shouldn't put dem burrs in her drawers or stitch dat dress up like I done."

Heaving and sniffling, Lily reached for Effie's hand. "I's done lost too many babies. Cain't be losin' my only gal, Sally. It be hurtin' too much. Oh, Miss Effie, I done made dem Gods plenty angry wid me. What I gonna do?"

"Hush now. You wait. Things gonna be fine. You see."

13

Smokehouse Fears

George Henry wiggled until he slipped free from the rope and plummeted to the floor with a thud and a bounce that made his teeth clack.

"Don't leave me, George Henry!"

"Shush. Gotta find somethin' to stand on."

"Cain't see you. Where you at?"

"I's here. You better hush. Dey gonna come and git us if you don't. Den we be gittin' a lickin' for sure."

George Henry's hand snaked along the floor, feeling for the baskets. He touched the rough weave of one, turned it over, and stood on it. As soon as his weight added pressure to the bottom of it, his foot went through to the floor.

"Ah!"

"You hurt?"

"Naw. Somethin' just run across me."

Up on his hands and knees, George Henry floundered about in the dark. He touched something and jerked his hand back. After realizing it was lifeless, he reached out again. It was a wooden crate.

"What you doin'?"

"Findin' somethin' to stand on. Hush!"

George Henry dumped out the hams and stood on his find. He was boosted up, but not far enough to get a good hold onto Sally's legs. He jumped down and smack into a side of beef, sending it swinging and spinning on its hanging rope. When the side swung back, it whacked him from behind, knocking him to the floor.

"Oh, Lawd! Don't let dat be the devil dat be gettin' after me. Ma already gonna skin me when I gits back to dat cabin. She be plenty mad wid me."

George Henry sat in the dark, trying to think clearly about what had just happened and what to do next. Bats fluttered above his head. One swooped down and brushed the side of his face. Then it happened. A warm glob plopped down on his upper lip.

"Eee!" He smacked at it with the backside of his hand.

"George Henry! You hurt?"

"Naw. Dat bat done drop poop on me."

George Henry adjusted the crate he had been standing on and stubbed his toe on another one. Consumed with fear, he lurched; his lips kissed another side of beef.

"Oooh!"

"George Henry?"

"Hush up. Don't talk. I done told you 'fore. And stop dat cryin'."

"You bein' mean to me."

"Ain't! You, hush."

George Henry emptied the second crate, stacked it on top of the other, and stood on the two. He flung his arms, caught hold of Sally's dangling legs, and hoisted her up.

"Untie dat rope."

Sally's fingers groped at the knot. When it loosened, their weight dropped with a forceful thud.

"I's sorry, George Henry." Sally hugged him around his neck, gripping him as tightly as she could. "Dis here darkness scare me," she cried.

"Let go! I cain't breathe."

George Henry pried Sally's arms from around his neck. She latched onto his shirt while he patted the wall, searching for the way out. When he found the door, he opened it a finger's width, sneaked a peek, and shut it. It didn't catch; a sliver of light crossed the floor.

"Hycus!" he said.

George Henry covered Sally's mouth before she could respond. He dragged her away from the sunrays, into a dark corner, and pinned her against the wall. Warm tears trickled over the back of his hand.

The cat-o'-nine-tails drummed against the doorframe.

Bang!

Sally flinched.

Bang!

She flinched again.

"Who's dere?"

Hycus whacked once more, and then he smacked the tails against his leg, disturbing the odor of the trousers he seldom took off. The stench of horse sweat mingled with the smells in the smokehouse made George Henry tighten his throat muscles, blocking the purge from his gut. After a long while, Hycus pulled the door shut. He shuffled back and forth, toeing the gravel just on the other side of it. Satisfied that no animals were inside, Hycus moved on. His footsteps faded, but his stink lingered. When George Henry sensed it was safe, he lowered his hand from Sally's mouth. He slumped against the wall ready to cry, but he couldn't. He had to be brave to get Sally back to the quarters unharmed.

"Dat man come near to gittin' us," she whispered.

George Henry touched her lips like his ma did when it wasn't safe for him to speak. Sally cowered behind him. She held on to his damp shirt and pulled herself closer to his sweaty body. They stayed put, bundled together until there was no sight, sound, or smell of Hycus.

George Henry told Sally in a low-whispering voice, "Ma be worryin'. She gonna git me wid dat big switch. Miss Lily be mighty upset, too, 'cause I be gittin' you in dis here trouble. Miss Effie, she be rollin' in her bed. Mad as a cat dat got his tail stomped on."

Sally pulled tighter on George Henry's shirt 'til her forehead was butted into the mid-section of his moist back.

"Ma, Ma. I want my ma," she cried.

"Shush. It's time to be gittin'. Stay close to me. Dat sun be mighty bright. Dey be seein' us if we ain't careful."

George Henry held on to Sally and peeked out again.

"Let's go," he said.

Keeping low to the ground, they squat-walked alongside the bushes until a rustling from the other side paralyzed George Henry. He gulped hard and curled into a ball. Sally fell over on her side behind him. The footsteps didn't stop. They only grew more intense. George Henry shuddered, waiting for the bullwhip to thrash his backside. Instead, a sniffling and licking tickled his heels. George Henry threw his arms around Stu's neck.

"It's you, boy! Git on back to the barn," he whispered, and then scratched Stu behind his ears. The hound rolled over for more patting.

"Not now. Git, boy!"

George Henry took Sally's hand again. Stu scrambled to his feet. The three skedaddled along the shrubs. George Henry and Sally crossed the alley. Stu stood guard and watched after them.

Before George Henry could fully take in his ma's presence, she, Lily, and Effie screamed with pure delight. Sobbing and shaking, Sally fell into her ma's lap. Lily held onto her as tightly as possible.

"Thank you, Lawd Jesus. You done give me back my gal. Didn't know smoked babies smell so good," Lily cried. The others laughed out loud.

"Ma, you smell mighty pretty, like a bunch of flowers," Sally said.

"Dat be Missus' perfume dat she didn't intend for me to be wearin'." Lily laughed.

Clarissa hung her arms over George Henry's shoulders and squeezed him. Her clothing and skin smelled of smoked meat, vegetables, sweet breads, and confections. Clarissa grinned as she dragged her fingertips from his hairline through to his nape, pulling his head back.

"Why your nose so?" she asked, feeling full of love for her boy.

"I falls down in the smokehouse. When I gits up, a side of beef kick me in the face. Den, bat droppin's plop on me."

Clarissa laughed as she pulled a rag from her bosom and dabbed his nose.

"I don't think dis here from no bat," she said, showing George Henry the bloodstained rag.

"Miss Clarissa, George Henry . . . he save me from dat evil man . . . dem hounds, too," Sally said proud enough for both of them.

"Your boy's done growed up," Effie said.

"Dat's why I tells you, it be my time."

"Clarissa, you sho' 'bout dat?" Lily asked.

"I's sho'."

Ben Mullins passed out and was carried up to his bed. He never remembered what he had done that night at the lawn party and no one ever spoke of the incidents at the big house or the one at the smokehouse. Life went on as usual, until Effie came down with the fever. Things around the quarters changed then and were never the same.

14

Effie's Journey

Slave songs floated across the fields and through trees stripped naked by the brisk fall winds. Big Bo's hammer pounded unsteady pings and pangs that didn't fit the beat of the songs being sung in the fields. The slaves sang excitedly about freedom, stars, signs, rivers, trains, and a man named Moses going on to Egypt land. "Let my people go," the voices begged.

Perplexed, George Henry hurried to the cabin. He rushed through the door into a dim afterglow of the fire. His ma had not bathed Miss Effie. Her sweaty body, the garlic tied around her neck, and the rotten potato stitched in her nightgown pocket reeked.

"How you be, Miss Effie?" George Henry asked.

"Rheumatism won't leave me be. Got no peace today, boy."

George Henry lit the kerosene lamp. He raised the wick for more light and dragged the three-legged stool next to Miss Effie. Taking his time, he adjusted her covers. Her thin, pale skin was cool and damp to his touch. Lately, she had gotten up only to take care of her personal needs. Some days she couldn't do that.

"You eat, Miss Effie?"

"Not much. Been painin' so I cain't swallow. Dis here potato and garlic fixin's ain't doin' me no good."

"I git you some ashcakes and sassafras tea. You be feelin' better, Miss Effie. You want me to fix dat hole in your cover wid dem stitches you done taught me?"

"Not yet, boy. Got somethin' I need to be givin' you. Bring dat doctorin' bag. Look in dere. Git dat hanky dat I taught you dem stitches on."

George Henry's finger shifted through the whatnots until they grasped the red plaid rag. He laughed at the large, clumsy stitches that he made when he was a little boy. Some where white, some were black, and others were blue. When the hanky opened, two flint stones rested on his palm like a pair of plucked out owl eyes.

"Miss Effie, dese here be mighty pretty."

"Keep dem in your pocket. Dey be yours now. You gonna be lightin' dem fires from now on. You knows how I done showed you."

George Henry's fingers flipped the stones, knocking and sliding them around in his hand, making him feel grown up.

"Miss Effie, dese here remind me when we squat in front of dis here hearth dem nights. My hands could hardly hold on to dem. I butt 'em against some twigs and leaves. You keep hollerin' at me, 'Strike 'em! Strike 'em again! Strike 'em hard!' Den a puff of smoke seep out."

"You be big enough now to be usin' dem. Take care when you do, boy. Some of dem fires be quick to catch. Don't need to be tellin' nobody how you gits dem stones. Dey be yours now."

George Henry stuffed the plaid rag and owl-eye stones into his pocket. Overwhelmed with a manly kind of feeling, he grinned and added fresh wood to the fire. When the flames perked up, his shoulders drew back proudly. He reached for the oil lamp and pinched the wick. He dropped a piece of sassafras bark into the pot that hung on the fireplace hook. While he waited for the water to heat up, he rotated the stones between his fingers again and again. The tapping sound they made kept beat with the songs rambling through his head.

When the water bubbled, George Henry fixed the tea and helped Miss Effie sip it.

"Things be different in dem fields today. Hands be singin'. Dere words be tellin' things. And Big Bo . . . his hammer . . . it be poundin' in a strange way. What it mean, Miss Effie?"

Between bites and slurps, Effie sorted her words. "Somebody gittin' ready to run, boy. Don't rightly know who. Songs didn't say. Nobody be talkin'."

Miss Effie rested for a moment. Then she looked at George Henry.

"Best you don't be knowin' and tellin' neither." Effie settled back to catch her breath. "Keep dem knowin's and hearin's in your head, boy."

Effie closed her eyes. A strange stillness settled over her. George Henry touched her arm. Her eyes opened. She let out a dry breath and sank deeper into her pillow.

"Want me to tighten dem bed ropes? Dat bed got a sag in it?"

"No, boy. My limbs be too weary."

Shortly after the night bell, Clarissa and Bo stumbled in exhausted. They fell into their beds and didn't speak or eat. Lying on her back, Clarissa softly sang, "Follow the drinkin' gourd."

Before his head was down, Bo drifted into a serious slumber. Miss Effie groaned the tune of death. George Henry squeezed the stones in his pocket until he, too, slept.

Later in the night, just outside the cabin door, hounds, wagons, and horses created a ruckus.

Thrashing her arms about, Clarissa tumbled off her bed and drew herself into a quivering lump. Effie pulled the covers over her head. Bo crawled to the corner and hid beneath his blanket. George Henry couldn't move; his entire body shuddered.

"Don't seem like those darkies came down through these quarters. Let's move on," they heard Dr. Isaac say outside the door.

Finally, the wagons and sounds faded into the hush of the night air.

"Ma, dey done gone. We's safe now. Thought dem horses and dat cart was comin' through dat door when dem wheels screeched against dem stoop steps."

Effie panted a mix of words. George Henry put his ear to her parched lips.

"What you say, Miss Effie?" Her lips moved as she struggled to speak, but not a word came out. Her chest filled with air and collapsed. When it rose again, a warm breath carried her message.

"Dr. Isaac . . . his boys . . . " She gulped. "Dey goin' after dem." She gulped again. "Dey be his runaways."

George Henry repeated Effie's words for his ma and Bo. Clarissa was still too frightened to hear what he had said.

The remainder of that night was eerie and drawn out. Effie gargled and rattled through most of it. Clarissa whimpered off and on. Bo continuously flipped and flopped on his bed. George Henry lay still. He was troubled by the search for the runaways and what Effie had told him about not knowing what he might know.

When the rooster called the following morning, George Henry added a log to the fire and stoked it. An explosive yellow-orange flame melted the chill lurking in the cabin.

In a whisper, to not disturb the quiet, George Henry said, "Mornin', Miss Effie." There was no answer. "Miss Effie, you hear me?" he whispered a bit louder . . . still no answer.

George Henry thought Effie's face was too tranquil and brushed her cheek with the backside of his fingers . . . still nothing. He poked her shoulder and snatched his hand back. His face tightened.

"Ma!" George Henry's voice choked.

Clarissa came from behind him. She placed her hand on his shoulder and squeezed it.

"I's here, boy."

"Miss Effie's got no breath."

George Henry gently tucked the loose covers around Effie.

"The Lawd done took my Miss Effie. She be my life. What I gonna do widout her?" Clarissa cried.

Hearings the cries, Bo scooted off his pallet. He clung to Clarissa. She trembled in his grip. He peeked around her at Miss Effie.

"She done gone on?" he asked.

"Be so, boy. You stop dat slobberin' now. No need for you to be sad. She done cross over to the good world. She be keepin' an eye on us. Go quick! Let Massa know. Den, go tell Big Bo to bring down the casket and dig her buryin' spot. We gonna put Miss Effie under dat big oak tree out back. He be knowin' where. Tell Sam we be needin' the coolin' board. Hurry, boy."

Without thinking, Bo did as Clarissa said. His long legs didn't seem to belong to him as he moved up the lane toward the big house and then on to the barn. As Bo approached the cabin, Clarissa's cries could be heard out in the alley. He opened and closed the door, but didn't move or make another sound. George Henry was folded over his ma's back, trying to temper her grief.

A loud knock on the door disturbed the mourning. Bo stepped aside. The door sprang open. Ben Mullins stepped in and removed his hat. A ghostly breeze pushed past him, ruffling the flames, nearly extinguishing them. Without speaking, he bumped George Henry aside and knelt so close to Clarissa that his knee tugged at her skirt. Mullins swept Effie's cover back. When he did, he knocked Clarissa over with an elbow to the left side of her head. She waited for the next blow, but it didn't come. Instead, Mullins grabbed the arm that she shielded her head with. He shoved his fingers through her hair and gripped a fistful. Twisting his hand, he tugged Clarissa up to her knees.

"Gal, you need to know what it is I'm doing."

"Yes, Massa," Clarissa's voice bristled.

George Henry anchored his foot to challenge Mullins, but his ma stopped him with a cautioning eye.

Mullins released Clarissa to rest his hand on Effie. The anger drained from his face, leaving it slack and pale. He moved Clarissa away from the bed and crawled toward Effie's head. He placed a lemon-sized mirror beneath her nostrils and then slid it back into his pocket, "She's gone," he said. Mullins sounded like a child who had lost his mother. Shaking his head in disbelief, he discreetly flicked away the tears gathered in the corners of his eyes.

"Take care of Mammy. She was faithful to me. Looked after me properly. She never failed me. I'll surely miss her. Petunia will manage the kitchen today and tomorrow. Bo, you're big enough to live with your pa. I'll let him know you're coming."

Mullins didn't leave right away. He stood politely by Effie's bed, thinking of his boyhood and his love for her. George Henry was certain that he saw his eyes fill with the same kind of wetness as before. Mullins' body moved as if his boots were weighted with heavy bricks. With his hand on the door handle and his shoulders wilted, he put his hat on and left slower than he came.

That night, after Miss Effie's body was placed on the cooling board, Clarissa fed George Henry and Bo. The boys had gathered close to the fire and spoke in hushed voices to not disturb Effie's journey to the next world. When Clarissa was ready to tend to the body, she shooed them off to bed and warmed a bucket of water. She got a fresh cut of lye soap and collected her best drying rags as well as the lavender oil that Miss Effie loved. With an all-over sunken feeling, Clarissa carefully disrobed the body, washed it down, oiled it, and dressed it with a fresh gown. When she forked out Effie's wet hair, the tines caught hold of the kinks. Clarissa grimaced as if she had caused her pain.

With all the gentleness she could muster, Clarissa repositioned the coverlet over Effie, folding the edge back with the accuracy of a straightedge. When she did, the sweet smell of lavender rushed from beneath it, hinting that life might still be there. Clarissa gazed down on Effie's angelic smile.

"You sho' pretty, Miss Effie," Clarissa said and kissed the cold and hardened cheek.

Bo raised his head. "Miss Clarissa, don't want to be leavin' you and George Henry."

"Your pa's a good man. Got a lot to teach you. You a big boy now. 'Bout to be a man. Big Bo be mighty proud to be havin' you wid him."

"You been my ma. George Henry been my brother. I be missin' you. George Henry, too."

"You be up at the barn and the blacksmith shop. We be visitin' when we can. You be gittin' them long britches you always been wantin'. You sleep now, boy. Don't let dem worries be disturbin' your mind."

When George Henry and Bo were stretched out with sleep. Clarissa unrolled Gran's old quilt.

"Ouch!" she cried when the needle pricked her finger.

The next day, Mullins watched from the balcony as his slaves slow-walked down the alley, toward the quarters. When they reached Effie's cabin, they went down the hill to the oak tree, swaying and humming in a low tone. At the gravesite, they prayed and joyfully sang out Effie's favorite ballads. Clarissa served everyone a taste of lemonade before they returned to their work.

The cabin felt empty and lonely that evening. Clarissa held onto Gran's sleeping quilt. She didn't stitch on it or sing to the moon. She just rocked back and forth 'til time to feed George Henry and Bo. They ate a dish of fresh roasted carrots, bacon, and corncakes that were prepared earlier. Afterward, the boys rested and thought their thoughts. Clarissa rocked and mumbled to herself before calling on Effie.

Miss Effie. You dere? I be callin' on you, and you ain't cold in your grave yet. But I done stuck my finger. Blood done fall on dis here quilt when I's patchin' on it yesterday. Dere be a bunch of dem bloodstains. Don't know which drop be my ma, my granma Alice, or my great-granma Mary. Dem blotches lookin' like a bunch of mud-red flowers. Dis here be another sign. My blood done join dem dat's done gone on to the glory land. Dey be watchin' over me and George Henry.

Clarissa finished her talk with Effie and took note of George Henry. His eyes followed Clarissa as she put Gran's quilt down and clutched on to Miss Effie's coverlet. Feeling the need to be close to her, she pressed it to her bosom. She pined for her like she did for her Granma Alice when she was taken away.

Miss Effie, dere be too much sufferin' and too little joy to balance dem hurts. Life ain't 'posed to be dat way. Dat loaf of bread ain't never gonna rise up enough to feed me and my boy like we needs to be fed. And Petunia . . . she brung dem brogans down from the big house for George Henry. Dey was stuffed wid two fine pairs of heavy socks. We talks more before it be gittin' time.

It was one late fall evening, chilly and dewy when George Henry sat against a tree not far from the grave. His ma rested back on her heels and bowed her head. Her back curved like a sickle. She wailed, and rocked, and prayed aloud about her need for a change in this life and to be free of her troubles. George Henry watched and said his own prayers. He wasn't sure in which direction life would spin without Miss Effie.

On the fifth Sunday after the burial, the cold was numbing. A persistent drizzle and sleeting rain coated the ground with icy slush. Bundled in her woolen wrappings, Clarissa looked out.

"Dis here weather be remin' me of dat time dey brung us from Virgini to Kentuck to be sold. You be too young to be rememberin' dat."

George Henry examined his ma's grief-filled face as he gathered up Miss Effie's old blanket and followed Clarissa down to the grave. When she took her usual place by the earthen bulge, he draped the cover across her back and went on down to the creek. He mindlessly skipped rocks on the water as he thought about Miss Effie's death and how his ma had become a stranger to him. The water rippled out into ringlets that dissolved with the current.

"Wish I could make dis here uneasiness go away like dat."

George Henry shrugged his shoulders and threw the rocks down. He shoved his hands into his pockets and recalled what Miss Effie had told him many times: "Be strong. Be brave. Be good."

With those words on his mind, George Henry staggered back to the gravesite but didn't move close to Clarissa. She was still sitting on her heels, and now, wringing her apron. George Henry studied her from a distance.

Miss Effie, I knows you's dere, and I's here. But, I wants you to know, I cain't take no more of dis here life. Been here ten years and tryin' for the last two of dem to move on, but my leg keep me back . . . wouldn't let me go. It be my time now. I been hearin' dem songs from the field. Dey say the time done come, time to git on board . . . dat train's a comin'. Comin' through Kentuck, just 'fore dat big auction dat be comin' in January. George Henry and me . . . we be gittin' on dat train. Dat singin' been sayin' three of Dr. Isaac's hands done already run. Doc's bloodhounds tracked one of dem down. Name's Jim. We ain't knowin' him. He was a new hand dat come from Virgini. Petunia say she hear Massa say he was a stubborn buck. Give Doc sass and run the first night he had him. Dey say Tom, the one dey call Copper Tom, was wid him. Massa be watchin' us day and night . . . when we's sleepin', too. Ain't gonna let dat discourage me none. I done prayed and prayed. It be my time. I be knowin' it. Ain't nobody gonna turn me around. We gonna git on dat train . . . gonna find dat freedom. Miss Effie, you watch over George Henry and me. We gonna be movin' on . . . and it be soon. Just waitin' for Big Bo's hammer to tell us when. Gotta go. My leg cain't take no more. It be smartin' somethin' awful. I be back. We talks later.

Clarissa didn't say anything more. When she stood, spasms in her leg caused her to grimace and stumble. She glanced down at the grave, and then at the sky. The icy rain had stopped falling, but the nippiness in the air lingered.

"Let's be gittin', boy, 'fore we be catchin' the misery."

Clarissa braced her hand on George Henry's waiting shoulder. He was glad he could support her weight. Before taking a step, Clarissa tilted her head again.

"Lawd, dis here boy be mighty strong. Wid ya help, we be gittin' on dat train."

"What's dat you be sayin', Ma?"

"Hush, George Henry. I be talkin' to the Lawd. Not for you to be hearin'."

As Clarissa and George Henry traced their footprints back to the cabin, her heel bumped a wedge of rock.

"Ma! Ma!" George Henry hollered, running behind her tumbling body.

"Lawd, Jesus! I don't want to be fallin' down no more hills."

He reached for her.

"Leave me be, boy. I'm goin' back up dat hill. Gonna keep on goin'. Ain't gonna fall down no more."

"What you mean, Ma?"

"Never you mind."

Clarissa stared down for a long moment at the skid marks her heels made. Gesturing with her chin toward the tracks, she said, "Dey make me remember my Granma Alice."

"How, Ma?"

Clarissa nodded her head for George Henry to go on up ahead. Lily was coming down the lane from the big house with a good-sized basket balanced on her head. Her bouncy stride hiked her skirt above her ankles, exposing her homemade socks. They didn't match, but they spoiled her feet with bright colors. The corners of a green and white towel had escaped from beneath an oilcloth that covered the basket. Lily brought the basket down from her head to rest it on her hip.

"How you be doin', Clarissa? You, too, George Henry?"

"We fine. Been visitin' wid Miss Effie some," Clarissa said and caught hold of the wraps slipping from her shoulders.

"You all muddy. Your clothes and dem covers . . . dey be torn and soiled."

"I be fine. Feet come out from under me. No need for a fuss."

George Henry walked away from his ma and Miss Lily. He didn't know what to say or do.

"Massa Ben done sent dese victuals down from the big house. Dey be for you and George Henry."

Lily offered the load to Clarissa but she refused to touch it. Lily raised Clarissa's arms. One at a time, she fastened them around the basket as if Clarissa were a child.

"Dis here food be from the Lawd."

Lily knew Clarissa didn't want anything from Massa Ben or Miss Margaret, but she knew, too, that Clarissa and George Henry needed the food. Since Miss Effie had been bedridden and not able to move about the grounds, the usual stash of victuals had shriveled to a few pieces of smoked bacon, some salt, a small piece of sugar cone, and not more than two measuring tins of cornmeal.

Lily put a soft arm around Clarissa, who had drawn her shoulder inward until her chin grazed between her collarbones. Lily squatted, twisted her neck, and peered up into Clarissa's face.

"You wants me to sit wid you and George Henry tonight? Keep you company? I kin wash dem clothes and covers you got on and stitch dem, too."

Clarissa's lips quivered. "Got no need for dat. We be fairin'. Gonna fix George Henry and me some victuals. Doubt it be des here. Den, I lays myself down. My burden be mighty heavy. Gotta long walk I gonna be takin' and it gonna be soon."

Clarissa's tone softened when she told Lily, "I knows you be hurtin' about Tom. He gonna make it. Den he send for you and Sally. We gotta believe dat. It be luck how you two come together and be a good match. Dat don't happen often. Take care, gal. Hope be all we got in dis here world."

"I done hear from Tom. It be more den once. Got word he done made it to dat freedom up in Ohio. He be on his way to Canada. Don't know no more den dat right now. I sho' be wantin' to hear more," Lily said and straightened herself.

When Clarissa's head came up, her face was drained and her eyes were swollen, puffy, and red. Lily looked straight into them. What she saw troubled her, but she knew not to press Clarissa about matters any further. She hugged her tightly. George Henry knew that Miss Lily sensed that it might be the last time she laid eyes on them. Letting go, she said, "You take care, gal. Keep ya'self safe." She hugged Clarissa once more.

"George Henry, you . . ."

George Henry wrapped his arms around Lily. "I's scared, Miss Lily," he moaned.

"You be fine. You 'most a man now and can help ya ma. Sally and me gonna be prayin' for you and ya ma," Lily said, feeling saddened by what she perceived might be.

Clarissa had gone into the cabin and set the basket on the stool. She brooded over the contents as she folded the oilcloth into a tight roll.

"Tuck dis here behind dem fire logs wid dem victuals," she told George Henry when he came through the door.

"Ben Mullins be tryin' to show his respect for Miss Effie. Gonna takes more den dis here food," she mumbled.

"Ma."

"Hush. No mood to be talkin'. Just do as I tells you, boy."

15

Clarissa's Family History

Clarissa leaned against the cabin wall, peering between the window and the ill-fitting shutter and pondering the time Ben Mullins visited the cabin early the day before Miss Effie died.

He stood looking down on her. She was too sunken in her deathbed to sit up. Miss Effie's frail fingers rested on Massa's arm when he had not invited the touch. I thought he would back away from her like he had the day I fell into his arms when I didn't want to. Instead, he gently patted her hand. She pulled it away to draw her fingers across her forehead damp with perspiration. She coughed and wheezed; sick tears floated over her cloudy eyes. She turned her face toward Massa Ben and opened her eyes more fully. Miss Effie reached for him again. He took her hand, welcoming her motherly touch. "Put my body near dat tall tree back of dis here cabin. It be mighty pretty about now." She stopped speaking to collect another laborious breath. "Dem angels needs to be knowin' where to find me when dey come git me." Effie's hand shook when she tightened her grip on Massa's hand to convey the seriousness of her words. "It's not your time, Mammy," he told her with as much care as possible. "Comin' fast enough," she told him. When Massa left the cabin that night, Miss Effie was still on her back, too weak to roll left or roll right. She mumbled to me, "When I'm gone, come talk to me. Come whenever you be feelin' the need." Miss Effie's voice trailed to a hush. I put my ear to her dry cracked lips. The sassafras tea that I had helped her sip earlier scented her breath. "Don't keep dem bad feelins pinned up inside you," she said to me wid moony eyes. "Like I done told you, gal . . . dey eats you raw." Effie gulped, then looked at me. I didn't know it would be the last time that we'd look eye-to-eye. Den she say, "We thinks more clear when we be talkin' 'bout dem things dat troubles us." Her lips parted. No words came from them. Her body collapsed like an empty flour sack. Her rapid sips of air faded into a slow rhythm. Each breath seemed to be the last. "Hush, Miss Effie. Don't be talkin' no more. You be needin' your strength, and I be needin' you here wid me and George Henry." My Miss Effie couldn't wait any longer. Sometime during that night she left with dem angels to go be with her Lawd.

Thinking back on those days weighed heavily on Clarissa. She turned away from the cold air seeping pass the shutter and through the cracked window. Feeling lost, she gathered the bedding and sat in the rocker. Clarissa pushed Effie's cover up against her cheek and inhaled the residue from the lye soap that she had bathed her with and then crimped Gran's old quilt that lay across her knees.

George Henry rested on his pallet. He was reluctant to take his eyes off his ma for fear that she might disappear, forgetting to take him with her. He got up and eased to the rocker, careful not to interrupt her quietness.

"Ma," George Henry said with a slight voice. "Why you keep holdin' on to dat old quilt on your lap?"

"Hope. Lots of it be stitched up in dis here."

Clarissa held on to the word *lots*. She thought a long while before she spoke again.

"George Henry," Clarissa said to him with a fixed gaze. "Guess you be old enough to be knowin' 'bout dis here. You done seen better den twelve harvests and be standin' tall like your brother Toby. Look some like him, too."

Clarissa smoothed the wrinkles in Gran's old quilt as if dusting away the strange feelings. She rocked, stroked, thought, and thought more. Then she leaned into the light of the fire. Ghostly shadows slithered across her face.

"When I was a babe, I didn't know my great-granma Mary. She done gone on to be wid the Lawd. But dey say she wrapped her gal, Alice, in dis here. When Granma Alice give birth to my ma, Molly, she done the same for her. Dey say my ma was tall and fiery. Miss Helena couldn't do much wid her. Dat's the woman dat owned us when we be livin' in Maryland.

"Thought we be from Virgini."

"Are. But dere be a time 'fore den. Just you listen." Clarissa continued, "Grandma Alice loved to fish. Miss Helena, she send her 'bout every day to the river, 'cause she be likin' to eat dem critters, too. Granma put a knot in a string. She hang it in dem waters. When she snatched it out, dere be a fish on it . . . another . . . and another. She would leave two or three in the bush . . . fry the rest for the missus. Missus never knowed we cooked and ate dem fish left in dat bush for us."

"I had brothers and sisters . . . some dead, some sold. Don't know how many of dem I had. Cain't rightly remember all I been told. When we first come here, I wraps you in dis here cover."

George Henry reached up. He drew the tail of the quilt down over his shoulders and rested his head against Clarissa's knee. It was soothing to her to have the weight of his head against her.

"Ma, I know your great-granma Mary done gone on and your ma, too. What done happen to Granma Alice? You ain't never said."

Feeling a heavy weight in her chest, Clarissa slowly reclined in the chair. The rocking back and forth over the swells in the floor didn't ease the heaviness in her chest, like it did some nights. She bit down on her bottom lip and held on to it.

"Granma Alice . . . she take care of me after my ma was took from me." Clarissa squeezed her eyelids shut. Without opening them, she said, "Like she done birth me."

"What done happened to her?"

"You wants to know too much, boy."

Clarissa's stomach twitched. Her eyes swelled with tears. Her back slumped. She sucked on her lips. It was a drawn-out while before she spoke again. When she did, she tilted into the light of the fire.

"One day when I was a young woman, Miss Helena sent me, wid your brother Toby and dem twins, to the orchard. Want us to fetch pears."

"Where I be, Ma?"

"Ain't been birthed just yet. Toby . . . he be nigh ten years, and dem twins . . . dey be nigh two. One named Mary after my great-granma, the other Molly after my ma. Wish I had a third gal. She'd be my little Alice."

"What den, Ma?"

"When we gits back to the cabin, long heel marks was in the mud near the door."

"Like dem you made by Miss Effie's grave dat day you be falling. Dat's why you be upset, Ma."

"Dey was remindin' me of my granma and when she was took from me. I prayed dat day dey don't belong to her. And dat blood I see be comin' from dem chickens always peckin' in the yard. My heart be feelin' like it's done been ripped outta me. I opens the door. My Granma Alice . . . she was gone and blood was in her mussed-up bed. I's scared. I rushes out of the cabin. Toby come up behind with a twin in each hand. I's yellin' for my gran. 'Done been sold, chile,' an old woman's voice say to me. Never knowed who dat woman was."

"Ma, what you do? Toby? The twins?'

"Not nothin' we could do. We's powerfully unhappy. I lays dere on Gran's bed, right on dat blood. My babies . . . dey lays dere wid me. I cries like a chile dat's done had its sugar tit snatched. Toby, he just stand dere. Too young to be knowin' what to do for me. When I turns over, I feels a lump and lets my hand search the straw. It be dis here quilt. I hugs it, never lets it be away from me after dat. Done brung me luck when I be needin' it."

"How dis here quilt and us git here?"

"Where?"

"Massa Ben's place."

"Don't rightly know where to start tellin' 'bout dat."

"Where our people be from, Ma?"

"Don't rightly know. Kin only say dat my granma say my great-granma Mary come from Africa to dis here America on dat boat dey always be tellin' about. Done told you she made dis here quilt and gives it to her gal, Molly, who sewed on it some. Grandma Alice got it when my ma, Molly, was took away. Then, I got it when Granma Alice was took away."

"Start dere, Ma."

Clarissa weighed George Henry's curiosity before she drew her hand down his cheek. Stroking it, she said, "You growed enough to be knowin', boy. You always done good not tellin' what's not to be told."

Clarissa fixed her eyes on the burning logs. She reflected a little longer and then eased out of the rocker. She sat next to George Henry and adjusted the two covers over them.

"One day Miss Helena say she done had enough of us darkies. Dat's when she sold me, Toby, and my twin gals to Massa Montgomery and his woman, Miss Bessie. She was his wife of several years. Dey don't got no chillen. It just be the two of dem. She be a fine woman. Never treat us bad, always be playin' dat harp. Dey say her music be dat of dem angels up in dem heavens. One day we be taken in a wagon from Maryland to Virgini. It be a long trip. Didn't have to walk none. Dey stopped for us along the way to take care of our needs. We's cryin' a plenty on our way to where we be goin'."

"Why so, Ma?"

"Happy dat we's bein' sold and bought together. When we got to the Montgomery farm, dey gives Toby, the twins, and me to your pa, Jake. He be the kindest old man dat I ever knowed. When you come along, we all mighty happy. Had plenty to eat. The cabin be warm. Our backs be spared. Not beat like most. Jake be takin' care of dere horses, and I done the cookin' up at the big house. We's livin' good as slaves could. Dat is, 'til dem last days wid Massa Montgomery. He be losin' his money and land. Gamblin' it say. Dat be when he and the missus fall on hard times. Had to sell everything: cattle, house, land, belongings, and even all us slaves–the ones in the house and in the fields.

"One day we gits hauled off to Kentuck. Be some time ago, but I never forgits dat night. It be in late December . . . maybe early January 1846. Not sure which day, but I knowed it be after Christmas. Weather be mean and cold. Folks be talkin' 'bout it. 'Not to be forgotten,' Massa Montgomery say."

"How old I be?"

"Two harvests, maybe some. Never was sure which day you be born on. But I knowed it be warm, and dem trees be mighty pretty. Full of color and all. The sky . . . it be the best dat I ever seen, blue and white wid a bright sun smack in the middle of it. Dey put you in my arms. We brush noses. I kiss dem cheeks of yours, den I puts you to dese here breasts of mine."

Not taking her eyes off the fire, Clarissa groped with memories of her journey from Virginia to Kentucky to be auctioned. She studied George Henry from the corner of her eye.

"Where dey be now?"

"Who?"

"Pa, Toby, dem twins."

"Don't rightly know. But you and me, we's here."

Clarissa took in a warm breath not sure if she wanted to keep telling. She leaned against the rocker and sorted her thoughts. When she did glance at George Henry again, he was inspecting her face.

"Ma, I don't remember Toby and Pa. Done forgot what Mary and Molly be lookin' like."

"You's too young to be rememberin'."

The pain of recalling the hellish ordeal had drained Clarissa. She drew her legs up, folded her arms across them, and lowered her head, resting it on her knees. She was too exhausted to tell more. George Henry sat quietly waiting for more telling.

Bought, Sold, Enslaved

16

Virginia to Kentucky

Clarissa, Jake, twelve-year-old Toby, the four-year-old twins, and two-year-old George Henry cuddled close to the fire. The icy rain scratching on the wooden shingles lured Clarissa into a deep slumber. It was the horses, hounds, and Montgomery's covered wagon, nearly filled to the brim with furniture, jostling outside the cabin door that woke her. She sat straight up. Her hands trembled, same as they did whenever she heard hounds.

"Come outta dere," Bodan shouted. He was Henry Montgomery's overseer, a brutish fella with leathery skin and rotten teeth that protruded from beneath a nose broken in a tavern brawl. In a splintered second, he busted through the door. "Git! Git!" he kept yelling.

Clarissa was on her knees drawing Gran's old quilt and George Henry into her arms. Jake had sprung off his bedding wide-eyed and tumbling over his feet. He plucked up the twins tucking one under each arm. The family didn't know what was happening to them or where they were being taken. Barefooted and smelling of burnt wood, they shuffled toward the wagon in the cold Virginia night air. It was unusually frigid and dark. There was no moon and not a star in the sky.

Bodan's feet were parted, his heels were dug into the slush. He held on to the horses' bridles, steading the skittish pair.

"Git up in dat wagon!" He said.

"Gittin', sir," Jake said. He and the twins were the first to the wagon.

Turning his face away from the shackles slung over Bodan's shoulder, Toby sprang up into the wagon. Clarissa couldn't see Toby's face, but she felt his fear. She was sure that he was remembering the times he was locked in those irons for just being a young buck, liking to run.

"Where's you takin' us, sir?" Clarissa asked.

Bodan cut a nasty eye at her and raised the cat-o'-nine-tails. He snapped the poppers, slicing up ice and earth.

"I be gittin', sir."

Clarissa scaled her way up into the wagon and curled around George Henry. The twins wrapped their arms one around each other. Jake and Toby bunched next to them. Her boy and man's heavy breathing echoed each other. Clarissa stretched Gran's quilt until it covered everyone.

"Don't cause me no trouble back dere. I won't hesitate to use dis here whip on your backsides and shackle you to dis here wagon."

Bodan hung the chains on a nail and flung a bunch of fusty blankets at Clarissa and her family.

"Cover up. It's gonna be a long, hard ride."

The end gate of the wagon was slammed shut and secured with a chain. Clarissa winced when the feedbox was fastened on the rear of the wagon. The clatter made her tighten her grip on George Henry. Bodan clomped to the front of the wagon.

"Go on back. Git, you ugly hounds!"

Bodan climbed over the jockey box mounted on the front of the wagon. He plopped down on the bench that squeaked as if he were about to fall backward into the wagon. He kicked the brake loose and tugged on the reins.

"Giddy-up! Giddy-up!"

He lashed the rumps of the animals with the same gusto he used to flog the darkies. The horses neighed and clopped off down the alley leading to the main turnpike. The sound of dog paws trailed off into the distance, replaced by the sounds at hand: horses on the outside of the wagon, shifting whatnots on the inside, and rocks and gravel kicking the bottom of the wagon. Clarissa was sure that she had entered the back door to hell.

Toby reached for Clarissa. "Ma, I be powerfully cold. Dis here bouncin' me bad as a buckin' horse. I be feelin' sick."

Clarissa shushed him. Toby didn't speak again. She knew he had closed his eyes. She knew, too, that the fright had caused him to bite down on the inside of his mouth and that blood dribbled down his chin. Toby gagged and the putrid smell of his stomach's contents filled the wagon. Clarissa wanted to squeeze Toby's shoulder, but she couldn't find it in the dark.

"Take care, boy," she said.

Toby couldn't see her mouth or hear the words that came from her lips.

The wagon rumbled on, headed down the road to some place the family could not imagine. Sleet continued pelting its bonnet while freezing winds hacked at the family beneath it. The shackles continuously clanged a threat. The pots and pans needed for cooking on the trail, whacked against the sideboards nonstop. Clarissa struggled to shut out the space around her. She wanted to rest her thoughts, but couldn't find peace, not even inside herself, where her heart raced and her breath choked her.

Bodan stopped the team along the way. He got down, stretched himself, took care of what he needed to take care of, and then brought the horses to the feedbox. He didn't asked if the family had any urges. The smell of horses munching oats caused Clarissa's stomach to growl and pain her. When the horses had enough, Bodan brushed them down and praised them before clicking and leading them back to the front of the wagon. He hitched the animals to the tongue, climbed back up on the bench, and continued down the turnpike as though he were alone. After nearly a full day on the trail and daylight starting to fade, Bodan stopped the wagon. This time, he came around to the rear, took off the feedbox, and removed the chain that held up the end gate.

"Come on out of dere. Take care of your business. Don't go far, and don't be long."

Once on the ground, Clarissa put George Henry on her back and drew the quilt over the two of them. She and the twins hobbled off to the bushes. Toby and Jake took to a big tree with a few straggly red leaves clinging to it.

Toby stopped walking and knelt. He locked his fingers together. He prayed that God would watch over them. When he was done, the family hurried back to the roadside. Bodan had placed their food on the ground. It was a filthy tin plate stacked high with cold beans, rancid cornbread, and a tin cup of cloudy water. Clarissa and her family squatted around the food. She pinched up beans and mashed them between her fingers, trying to warm them before feeding George Henry. The twins fed each other while Jake and Toby helped themselves to the beans and cornbread. Clarissa ate the leftovers. They passed the cup and gulped the murky water to wash down the food.

"Ma, how long we been in dat wagon?" Toby asked.

"Near to a day. Maybe some of another, I reckon. Hush. Keep a movin'. Cain't be caught talkin'."

It was another day and some before the wagon stopped again for the family. That's the way it was until they got to a town sitting on the banks of the Ohio River.

Bodan guided the horses off the road and pulled them to a standstill. Men gathered in small groups outside of the wagon. They bellowed about the new stock that had just rolled into Louisville. Feet shuffled clumsily to and fro. Horses neighed and stomped about. Manacles rattled a wrenching noise. Henry Montgomery's voice was heard above the commotion.

"How was the trip from Virginia?" he asked Bodan, still perched on the wagon bench.

"Not much to tell. Got the furnishings and the darkies back dere. I be taking care of dem for you. When dis here auction's over, I'll sleep some. Den, haul the goods on down to New Orleans to the missus."

"My stock's going to have to be kept together. Pens are full. Take them over to Matthew Garrison. He'll lock them up. He's the only one that's got space for more hides. Be sure to mind that whip. I don't want any markings on them. I need to get the best price possible."

"No need to worry. I takes care of dem, sir."

Bodan tipped his hat and jumped down from the wagon seat. He hurried to the rear of it, removed the feed box, and released the end gate. He took the shackles from the nail and snatched the blankets off the shivering family.

"Get out!"

"Comin', sir."

Jake lifted the twins out of the wagon, Toby leaped over his back.

"Hey! Where you goin', fella?"

Clarissa froze, unable to move.

"I's right here, sir."

Clarissa continued bundling George Henry in Gran's quilt. Bodan grabbed a corner of it. When he peered from his pox-marked face at Clarissa, he let go. He didn't want a problem that might bring on a whipping.

Stump, a drunkard whirling around on his peg leg and tipsy from too much moonshine, hobbled up for a better look at the new stock. He poked Clarissa where he shouldn't have been poking. The gesture prompted Toby to move closer to his ma.

"Where we be?" he asked in her ear with an eye on Stump.

Clarissa tapped Toby's hand. This time, it let him know to mind his ways, fearing the trouble that his action might lead to.

The shabby family followed Bodan to the pen. He shoved Stump and the crowd aside. Men gathered along the footpath. They sported notes and bags of gold coins as they gawked, spoke ugly among themselves, and groped at the darkies whenever one passed close enough to be touched.

Garrison, a short, stocky, beastly man with a wiry growth on his face and a chewed-up hat drawn down over his ears, had folded his coat back to ensure his gun, poking above his belt, could be easily seen. He held the gated door open. Clarissa slowed her pace. The smell of ailing slaves inside the pen provoked her stomach. Her feet stopped and her arms clasped down on George Henry a bit tighter.

"Keep moving."

Garrison's bottom lip twitched. He nudged Clarissa in the back of her knees with the butt of his whip. Her legs buckled, but she caught herself before falling to the ground.

Once the family was inside the pen, the door slammed shut. The key turned inside the lock, creating a dreadful noise. Clarissa backed away from the door and sat on the cold, damp, gritty floor. She pulled George Henry into her lap. The twins curled themselves into the fullness of her indigo skirt. Toby sat as close as he could to Jake who squatted behind his family.

Toby drew his red, mud-stained knees, discolored during his prayer to the Lord, up to his chest. He wrapped his arms around them. Jake stretched his long cotton-plucking limbs around his family. He wanted to keep them safe even though he knew that a Negro had no say about his kin.

Clarissa peered over her shoulder at Jake. She committed every part of him that she could see and smell to her memory: hairy chin mole, milky eyes, thick smooth lips, sunken jaw, tobacco-stained teeth, bent shoulders, and even his warm, piney breath. The more she studied him, the more she yearned to embrace him and be cuddled. The whimpering of the twins brought her mind back to the waiting–for what she didn't rightly know.

17

Auction of 1846

Toby moved along on his hands and knees. He squatted in front of Clarissa and peered into her eyes.

"We gonna see another tomorrow. And we be together, Ma," he said, as calmly as he could. When Clarissa put her arms around his trembling body, she knew how scared he was.

"Jake, what's gonna become of us?"

"Don't rightly know, Clari." Only he called her by that name.

"Let's go!" Bodan shouted over the deafening moans choking the air inside the pen.

Clarissa and her family's eyes shifted toward the door. Jake squeezed them for what he knew would be the last time.

"I seen us folks separated like dis 'fore, Clari," he said, trying to blend her into his very being, not wanting to let go.

Clarissa clutched George Henry and the quilt as she wrestled to stand. She shuddered and he fell from her grip to the floor. She plucked him up and kept moving.

"Come on! Come on! Sit down here, wench. Gotta put dese on ya. We'll be walkin' to the courthouse grounds. Don't want to be chasin' no runaways today. It be too cold."

Bodan fettered Clarissa's ankles with an icy cuff. He chained her to Toby and Toby to Jake. Then he connected the three of them to a heavier chain that he held onto.

"Let's go!"

Clarissa carried George Henry and the quilt. The twins, Mary and Molly, toddled along next to her. Their fingers were intertwined. They sobbed and shook so Clarissa felt ripped at the core. Jake moved along as surefooted as he could until he stepped on uneven ground. He tumbled over, taking his family down with him. The irons bit into his ankles. Bodan raised his whip. He gave each of them a spiteful eye. Remembering what Montgomery told him, he lowered the whip. Even so, Clarissa was sure she felt the sting of the rawhide on her back. Bodan herded the lot of them over to the courthouse lawn where he removed the irons. Grimacing, Jake chewed on his bottom lip. Clarissa was heartsick at the sight of his raw ankle.

Toby shifted his eyes from one point to another, not settling on any one thing. When the auctioneer started calling folks, Negroes were dragged up to the block, one and two at a time, sometimes a whole family, until they got to Henry Montgomery's stock.

Bodan gnawed on a piece of straw that he wiggled at Toby.

"Git on up dere," he said to him.

Jake patted Toby on the leg, passing on as much sentiment as his soul could wield.

"Dis here stock's fresh in from Virginia. They a good-looking bunch," the auctioneer said.

Henry Montgomery stood next to his property, but directed his speech to Bodan. Clarissa listened attentively, mentally recording each word.

"What do you think I'll get for them?"

Bodan spit the masticated straw at Clarissa.

"Don't rightly know. Word is the sales are good."

Montgomery raised his hand, interrupting the calls. He viewed his slaves, checking them for visible marks. When he was face-to-face with Clarissa, she blurted between clenched teeth loud as she could, "Massa! Sell us together, please, Massa."

"Got no control over that."

Montgomery gave Clarissa an apologetic shrug and walked away. His words severed the last thread of hope that held her life together.

Montgomery nodded for the auctioneer to continue. When he picked up his gavel a lightning bolt struck a near by tree, illuminating the courthouse lawn. The world seemed paralyzed until a thunderbolt assaulted their eardrums and rocked the grounds. Every soul around ducked, the Negroes and white folks. It was a phenomenon that was out of place for that time of year. But it didn't stop the auction.

"Come on! Come on! You first. Get yourself on up there," Montgomery ordered.

Bodan yanked Toby from Clarissa's grip.

"Ma, I be good. I be seein' you again. I promise, Ma."

Bodan shoved the boy along, not letting him say more. Toby mounted the auction block with all the pride allowed a slave. Startled, George Henry grabbed Clarissa's shirt, pulled it over his head, and sobbed on her bosom. The two rocked as if they were riding a wild wave. Clarissa kept her sight on Toby. Her eyes traveled the length of his body, head to toe and back up, again and again, locking each detail of him into her memory: his smooth milk-coffee skin; his broad shoulders; his slim legs; his dark, tight curly hair; his narrow nose; his big marble eyes; his beautiful white teeth that made a perfect smile; and his muscles just starting to grow manly. She took particular notice of the brick-brown, butterfly shaped birthmark on the back of his neck. The wings fluttered whenever he turned his head, lifted his arms, or moved his shoulders. Clarissa was especially proud of Toby's height.

All of the mothers in the slave quarters in Virginia had a hankering for a boy like him. He was Miss Bessie's favorite. When she thought no ears were was listening, Clarissa heard her say to Montgomery, "Toby's a handsome one. He's a good worker with a good temperament. He'll do well."

"Jump, boy! Jump!" the auctioneer commanded.

Toby leaped plenty high. His overalls hiked up to his knees. The crowd cheered and butted against the auction block for a better look.

"Turn yourself around. Bend over. Touch your toes," the announcer said. His hand patted Toby like he was a premium steer. The auctioneer turned to the bidders. "Look here, I say. This boy's got what you want in a buck. Stand up, boy," he said to Toby, still bent over. "He's got a sound back. Open your mouth. Got all his teeth in that head of his. This here buck is surely a prime one. He's strong as any of them. Gonna grow to be a mighty fine producer. He'll make a good-looking flock of pickaninnies. What do I hear for him?"

"Turn him around," a man in the crowd shouted.

The auctioneer grabbed Toby's shoulders, spun him on his heels and then slapped his back. George Henry raised Clarissa's shirt and stared at Toby who stood cane-straight, peering into the space above the heads of the men that yelled at him. Jake's hand rested on Clarissa's shoulder. He wanted to comfort her in the ways he knew best but couldn't. Instead, he whispered, "Lawd, watch over my family and me as dey sell us away from each other. Keep us safe from dem heavy hands and dem whips dat hurt so bad."

Clarissa caressed the backside of Jake's weary hand, resting on her shoulder. She knew the pain in his heart was greater than that of the knotted and swollen joints in his fingers inflamed from years of picking cotton, breaking hemp, and now agitated by the frigid weather.

"I'll give $700 for that young buck," somebody yelled from the crowd.

"I give $750."

"I give $1000."

The bang of the gavel resonated through Clarissa's body.

"Sold!"

The caller told a young man, not much older or bigger than Toby, to pay his money and move his stock along. Toby looked at Clarissa. A drop of blood nested in the corner of his mouth. That was the last time she saw his eyes. She watched him walk away. The butterfly on the back of his neck vanished and took a part of her with him. Engulfed by damnable men, the boy was gone.

"Come on, boy. You next," the caller said, with his arm stiffened and the handle of the mallet aimed at Jake.

"Get on up dere, boy," Bodan said.

Jake gripped Clarissa's shoulder, not wanting to let her go as he readied his old legs to take their troubled steps.

"You gotta be brave, Clari."

Next thing Clarissa knew, Stump had caught hold of Jake's overall straps and had yanked him up on the block, causing him to stumble. When Jake's feet were steady, he planted his heels stubbornly beneath his weight, same as whenever he strung up a hog to be slaughtered for Henry Montgomery. The crowd butted against the block. They jeered, haggled, and scoffed among themselves.

"Quiet down!" the auctioneer blurted. "This here boy comes with high recommendations. They say he's got good manners, dependable . . . reliable, too. Got the bent-back disease and somewhat worn out, but he's got plenty of work left in those bow legs of his."

Jake clasped his hands across his front, sucked in his gut, raised his shoulders, and then drew down an invisible curtain, locking out the world around him.

"Don't take my man from me. Sell us together," Clarissa pleaded as loudly as she could. Only George Henry seemed to hear her pleads. His spidery fingers smudged the tears from her cheeks and his clasped his arms around her neck. Over George Henry's shoulder, Clarissa's stare sent all the affection that they could to Jake. Jake never flinched, but she knew, that he knew, she had sent the love. His ear twitched, taking her mind back to their private times together.

Bang! Bang!

"Do I hear a bid? This man is old. But I say, he still got work in those legs. I ask you again, dis be the third time, maybe a fourth. Do I hear a bid?"

"Three hundred dollars," a husky voice bellowed.

Bang! Bang!

"Sold! Come get him."

Jake was gone, swallowed up. Clarissa shivered like a scared puppy.

"Get those cute little wenches up here," the man hollered.

"Come on, you two," Bodan growled.

Mary and Molly crawled up on the block. They clutched each other tightly. Their teeth chattered a duet.

"Ma," they cried.

When their voices reached Clarissa, she gaped, studying them. They seemed one body with two sweet faces that glowed from beneath a wooly halo. *I love you,* Clarissa said with the secret sign that she had taught them to use when it wasn't safe to speak. With two fingers at her lips, Clarissa quickly flipped them around, not letting them leave her lips for fear that she might reveal that she was sending a secret message to her girls. The twins' unsteady hands did the same, sending love back to their mother.

"What you give for these gals? Two's always luck," the auctioneer said.

A man, howling like a bloodhound dog, yelled, "Put dem little wenches up on a crate. We need to see those gals."

The bargaining men debated: how much the same-faced gals would fetch, their differences, their likenesses, how cute they were, and how they'd like to get their hands on them. The ruffians crushed against the block. Confused by the loudness of the rambunctious crowd, the twins wept profusely.

Bang! Bang!

"I ask you one more time. How much do I hear for these here gals? Best look-alikes I've ever had up here."

The first cry was "$400." The next was "$800." From far back in the crowd "$1200," was heard.

Bang!

"Sold."

The cheers caused the earth to tremble beneath Clarissa. She sucked in a gulp of air, twisted her hair achingly tight, and pulled at her ear 'til it bled.

"My gals gone," she mumbled over and over as she wildly rocked herself.

"Next," the crier said, and didn't look Clarissa's way even though he had sold her family away from her, except her baby boy.

Stump, chewing snuff and spitting, came face-to-face with Clarissa. Without warning, he snatched the quilt from her arms and pulled her close. She could taste the whiskey smell from his breath and the tobacco that he chewed. Before shoving her up on the block, Stump flung Clarissa around as if she were an oversized rag doll. George Henry had tumbled out of Clarissa's lap. He scuttled about, struggling to get on the block with her. When he did, he grabbed a bunch of her skirt. Whimpering like a puppy, he spun his body into its fullness. Quick as a frog traps a fly, his voice was gone.

"Hold on there. Here's a wench and her pickaninny," the auctioneer called.

Clarissa never took her eyes off the quilt that lay heaped on the lawn, showing hints of its story. Stump trampled on it with his muddy boot. His peg was tangled in the trail going north. The quilt flipped him and then looped around him. The crowd shoved and kicked his drunken body as he fought to free himself from the cover. His sw head crashed against the auction block, knocking him unconscious. A stranger dragged him off, pulling the quilt along until it caught on a stray nail. The rowdy crowd grew hysterical with laughter. Clarissa bolted, trying to leave the auction block to fetch the quilt. Bodan caught hold of her shirt.

"Where're you goin', gal?"

When Clarissa tried to shake free, his hands clutched her upper arm. Fraught with anxiety, her body stiffened, waiting for death by the hand that held her.

"Best you stay put."

Bang! Bang! Bang!

The mallet commanded attention from the crowd.

"Time is precious."

Bang!

"Heed what's going on up here. These two got to be sold 'fore dark comes. Look here! This woman's a small octoroon. She's rare: can cook, do laundry, run a loom, and sew. She's worked for the best of them, high class and higher. Can even pick cotton if need be. That boy wrapped in her skirt . . . he's less than three years, maybe nearer to two. He's a bit on the frail side, but plenty healthy. Feed him, fatten him some, and let him grow. He'll produce a hearty and good-looking herd for you. Now, what do I hear for these two?"

"I gives you $250 for dat little darkie," a crude farmer said.

A stiff-necked businessman, wearing a black suit and fancy hat, stepped in front of him. "Eleven hundred dollars for that wench!" he hollered.

Not to be outdone, Luke Johnson, the town lawyer, belted, "I'll give $1200 for that Negress."

A tall, hat-waving farmer said in a low, drawn-out voice, "Make that $1300."

When the crowd heard the bid, they became nearly lawless, shoving and cheering. The farmer snatched Clarissa off the auction block. That's when she knew that she and George Henry would be separated for life. She was shoved along unable to feel, think, or speak. She couldn't even cry out for her boy.

Bang! Bang!

"I didn't say sold. Let that wench go!"

Clarissa clambered back up on the block and swooped up George Henry. He clamped his arms around her neck and his legs around her waist. She squeezed him as he fought to breathe.

Bang!

"The bidding's not done yet!" the auctioneer warned again.

Ben Mullins stepped out of nowhere, waving notes above his head.

"I'll give you $1450 for that gal and her boy."

Bang!

"Going once. Going twice."

Bang!

"Sold to Ben Mullins."

"Come on up here, Ben, and pay your money."

The mob mumbled in disbelief and backed away, creating a narrow path to the auction block.

"You sure got yourself a sweet bargain this time. That wench and her pickaninny gonna do you good. Come spring, they would've fetched at least $1500."

Ben Mullins flashed a doubtful smile.

To move quickly, Clarissa put George Henry down and leaped off the block. With him clinging to her skirt, she gathered the quilt in her arms and hugged it to her face. A heavy hand shoved her and the boy to the back of the auction block. She leaned against it, too exhausted to cry.

They stood, waiting for Ben Mullins to claim them. He was still on the courthouse lawn, considering the unsold Negroes as if he might buy another.

"Next."

Bang!

"Sold . . . next."

Bang!

"Sold."

Slave after slave, gone. Clarissa didn't know where to, just gone. An old black woman, wrinkled from time, stood next to her, so close their arms brushed. Gray hairs wired out the woman's ear. She smelled of cooking grease and animal sweat.

"Your gals done gone on to St. Louis wid a massa name Smith. He be wearin' a gentleman's coat and hat," she whispered to Clarissa. Her sweet breath warmed Clarissa's cheek.

"Thank you kindly," Clarissa said, but didn't think that the woman heard her. Clarissa didn't raise her head and never saw the woman's full face, but felt her kindness. The old lady was sucked into the crowd, gone, like Jake, Toby, and the twins. Could she have possibly been the same messenger who told Clarissa that her Granma Alice had been sold? Not knowing what else she could do at that moment, Clarissa pleaded with the Lord to give her family back to her.

George Henry squatted close to Clarissa, lifted her skirt, and crawled beneath it. He sat his bony rump down on her foot and fastened his cold, twig-thin arms around her leg. It wasn't long after that they were loaded into the back of an oxcart parked at the edge of the Louisville Turnpike, facing south.

"You belong to me now."

Ben Mullins took his stock back to his farm, about forty miles down the turnpike. He was pleased but uncertain about with his purchase, especially the boy who seem small for his age and frail, too.

18

Frocks, Feathers, and Fuzz

From the upstairs window of Mullins' bedroom, he marveled at how the hunter's moon illuminated the trees and the outbuildings, turning the farm grounds into a bewitching canvas with picturesque shadows as black as onyx. Each shape sported deep angles, elongated lines, and perfect curves. In spite of his calm demeanor, uneasiness festered inside Mullins.

Clarissa and George Henry strolled down the carriage lane, moving away from the big house. They shouldn't have been out and about once the evening bell tolled. Clarissa carried her head wrap in her hand. She tilted her head, allowing the cool air to bathe her face and lift her hair away from her neck. George Henry abruptly fell out of step with her.

"Come along, boy. What be troublin' you?"

George Henry couldn't muster another step.

"Dat place. Ma . . ."

He pointed at the smokehouse, unable to steady his finger. His eagle eyes caught sight of something butted against the structure. A hump was poked out from a mound of mud and leaves.

"Ma . . ."

"Shush, chile. Dat might be a wild animal or wee slave."

"If it be a slave, it be dead."

George Henry rushed toward the find.

"Stop! Don't touch dat!"

George Henry froze. Only his eyelashes fluttered as he tried to see more. Clarissa squatted and extended her arms. She picked up a twig and cautiously poked the scraggly bundle. It didn't move. Using the stick, she teased it away from the foundation of the smokehouse. When she had determined that it wouldn't bite and was only an old knapsack, she gathered it up and knocked off the crud. Clarissa stretched it open to peek inside.

"Ah!" she gasped and staggered back.

When she stopped, she looked around to ensure no eyes were on them. Almost certain that the curtain in Mullins' window shifted, she glanced once more at the window. On one was there.

"Somebody be at dat window. Best we be gittin'."

George Henry trailed behind Clarissa's quickened pace back to the slave quarters. She shoved open the cabin door with one hand. As she entered, she kicked over the laundry basket, dislodging its contents.

"Ma! You troubled?" George Henry asked.

"No."

"Dat baby? It be dead?"

"Hush, boy!"

Clarissa right-sided the basket, added her load, and piled on the unwashed shirts, skirts, and britches. She stood back with her hands on her hips. She stared down at the washing. Her thoughts were hazy and scrambled. Exhausted, she plopped down in the rocker.

"Follow the drinkin' gourd," she sang in an unsteady voice.

"Ma, dat baby?"

"Ain't no baby, boy. Dem Massa's old coats."

Clarissa stopped rocking and sprang from the chair. Down on her belly, she slid her hand beneath the bed, grabbed a small can of

168

red pepper and picked up the bent-handled spoon off the floor. She wedged the tip of it under the can's lid and popped it off. Standing over the victuals hidden behind the heap of firewood, she tilted it, dusting the floor around them with the pepper.

"Whatcha doin', Ma?"

"Hush up, boy. Put yourself on dat sleepin' straw. You don't see nothin'."

Clarissa sealed the can and sat back down in the rocker. She was still as a Virginia opossum playing dead. The beastly sounds of the blue-gummed hounds grew intense as they neared the cabin. Clarissa squeezed the can to keep her hands from shaking; her fingertips were cold and blue.

"Ma!"

"Hold your words, boy."

George Henry burrowed into his sleeping straw, pulled the covers over his head, and spied with one eye.

Bang!

When the door sprang open, Ben Mullins was standing there with his hounds. Clarissa's heart flipped, the same as it did that day in the slave pen when the door slammed shut on her life. Mullins didn't knock like he did when Miss Effie was alive.

"Whatcha doin' in here, gal?" Ben cast an inquisitive glance about the cabin.

"Just put my boy to bed, Massa."

The hounds stretched their necks, pulling Ben toward the fire logs.

"What do these hounds want from that corner?"

"Don't know, Massa," Clarissa said.

She kept her sight glued to the pepper can in her lap. Her consciousness seesawed from the stacked logs to the laundry basket. Her thoughts were about to shift back to the logs when George Henry retched and gagged. His stomach dumped its last meal of grits and greens into his nightshirt that he held to his mouth to hold back the vomit.

"What's wrong with that boy of yours?"

"He be fine, Massa. Just got hold to a chunk of spoiled meat."

The persistent hounds barked and jerked Mullins nearer to the food.

"Massa! Best you hold dem hounds. I just spilled dis here pepper over dere."

The dogs whined from the burn of the pepper in their nostrils. George Henry puked once more. Mullins drew back on the leashes. His shoulders swelled with anger.

"Look what you've done to these hounds. I got a good mind to let them loose on your hide."

"I's sorry, Massa. Dis here pepper can falls out of my hand. Didn't mean no harm to dem hounds."

Mullins lugged the dogs out the door to the yard. They whined and dragged him in circles as they pulled him up the alley.

Clarissa closed the door and fell to her hands and knees. She pressed her forehead against the floor, thanking the Lord. "I knowed you'd keep me and my boy safe. And I knowed you be lookin' after us. I thanks you plenty."

Clarissa unearthed the knapsack from beneath the laundry and emptied it at her feet. Two musty, crumpled-up, double-breasted frock coats spewed out. She shook them with a swift flip of the wrist. A grayish-brown dust cloud rose up around her face. Coughing and sneezing, she admired the tattered, cocoa-brown garments that would fall below her knees and George Henry's, too. With the coats across her lap, Clarissa fingered the threads where buttons should be. With the back of her hand, she brushed away debris clinging to the prickly fibers, and then slipped her hands in and out of the pockets, wiggling her fingers, pleased that the pockets were intact.

"George Henry. Git up. Come here, boy."

Clarissa lifted the soiled nightshirt up over his head.

"Put dis here dry one on. Git dem victuals from behind dem logs. Dump dem in dis here knapsack. Take care, boy. Don't git in dat pepper."

Clarissa placed a smaller pouch in George Henry's hand.

"What dis here, Ma?"

"Salt. Pour dat over dem victuals after you put dem in dis here sack."

"Ouch!" George Henry cried when he pinched up a clump of salt.

The grass cuts on his fingers were still fresh from picking weeds at the big house. He took his time salting the meat, ensuring each piece of was properly coated. He closed the sack, hid it behind the firewood, and rinsed his hand in the water bucket. Then he sat by the hearth to untangle his thoughts: food, sack, salt, shirt, coats, and no dead baby.

After that night, George Henry watched Clarissa more closely. She often stood behind the cabin door, resting her head against it. Maybe she prayed, maybe she thought her troubled thoughts, but always paused before she opened the door. This night, she hesitated longer before she thrust her head back and released the latch. When the door was ajar, the night air rushed in, teasing the flames and stealing the warmth. With her eyes on the stars and in a mysterious voice seeping from her lips, Clarissa sang, "Follow the drinking gourd."

George Henry knew that Negroes weren't allowed to own anything, not even a stone in their pockets. Clarissa's actions could get her lashed and sold down the river in a snap, leaving George Henry with no ma, when he already had no pa, no brother, and no sisters. Not sure what to make of Clarissa's doings, he burrowed into his pallet and waited for her to return to the ma he was more familiar with.

Several moons later, Clarissa's needle kept a steady rhythm, looping one stitch after another, mending Gran's old quilt.

"Ma, why you keep patchin' on dat old cover-up? It be lookin' mighty worn."

"Dis here winter gonna be wicked. We be needin' all the coverin' we kin git. My bones been tellin' me so. Dey be hurtin' somethin' awful," Clarissa said, not able to divert her attention from the stitching, or the mound of laundry that hid the coats. George Henry knew that she was thinking about how to make the frocks warmer.

The following evening, guided by the moonlight, George Henry sneaked to the loom house and sat on the front porch. Swinging his feet, he looked around before he climbed the stairs leading to the weaving room. He got a whisk broom from a basket next to the big loom and dragged it back and forth across the floorboards, trapping all the lint that he could on the straw tips. He piled his collectings by the door. When he was done, he sat on the top step just outside the loom room, plucked the last fuzzy lumps from the bristles and crammed all the lint into his pockets. George Henry was so excited about his adventures that he had not listened for footsteps. With his ears fully alert, he eased down the steps on his rump.

Once back on the porch, George Henry's eyes explored the night for evidence of Hycus and the hounds, which he didn't see or hear. He took off running until a sudden thumping sound stopped his feet next to a fence post. He was pushed to his knees from behind and licked on his cheeks.

"Stu, you scare me to death. Let me be, boy."

George Henry teased splinters from the post and used them to tack the sides of his overall bib to the front of his shirt. When he got to the chicken coop, his head did a quick side-to-side. He swept his hands along the ground where the chicken wire trapped feathers. He closed his fingers around the soft down. Stu licked George Henry's hands as he stuffed fistfuls of feathers into his homemade pouch.

"Come on, Stu."

The two raced on to the cabin. George Henry burst through the door, panting and bumbling around.

"What keep you, chile?"

"I . . . I's workin', Ma."

"Sit down. Catch you some air."

Clarissa never took notice of the bulges in George Henry's overalls. She was cooking and cleaning as she agonized about being free.

"Ma! Ma! I got some . . ."

"Hush, boy. Just git yourself ready to eat dis here food."

George Henry answered the whining and scratching at the door. He sent Stu back to the barn and watched him trot off before sitting back down on the damp, earthen floor to wait for his meal. Clarissa dished up taters and fatback from the iron pot that hung over a bright popping fire. She set the bowl of steaming food on the three-legged stool in front of George Henry.

"Eat 'fore dem victuals be gittin' a chill on dem."

Clarissa dragged the rocker up to the fire. She slid into the chair and stitched down the last scraps on the spot where Stump's peg ripped a hole in Gran's quilt. Clarissa never looked to see if George Henry was eating. Her mind was on the quilt. She had left the rip until near last, not wanting to forget the anger she felt that day at the auction. When she was done with her sewing, she rolled the quilt up and tucked it behind the logs with the victuals. She went back to staring at Master Ben's wash. Tears puffed her red eyes and then clung at the edge of her lids before they tumbled onto her cheeks, trailed across her chin, and dripped on her hands folded in her lap.

"Ma, why you be so?"

"Ponderin', boy."

Clarissa smiled weakly when she took particular notice of George Henry.

"How I gonna make dem raggedy old coats warm? Ain't got nothin' but dust and straw.

"Look, Ma."

George Henry plucked the splinters from his britches and spooned out heaps of feathers that floated down to Clarissa's lap. She raised the sides of her apron, trapping them. Before she could exhale to express joy, George Henry emptied his pockets. Clarissa's chest expanded with pride as lint balls and feathers danced on her lap.

"You done good, boy."

"Ma, don't want you to cry. You save dem tears for dem whuppin's. We gonna be warm dis winter, when dey ain't lookin'."

Without a word, Clarissa stashed the cotton and feathers in a large tin box. She went back to rocking and singing. Her eyes glowed like fireflies on a moonless night.

"Follow the drinkin' gourd," she crooned gleefully.

Late the next evening, George Henry busied his fingers, stuffing the lint and feathers into the linings of the tattered coats. After the last bits were forced through a gap near the collar of one coat and through the armhole rip of another, he tacked both, using the tiny, even stitches that Miss Effie had taught him. George Henry folded the coats as if they were brand-new and returned them to the bottom of the laundry basket beneath the dirty wash.

"I's proud of you, George Henry."

George Henry felt the same pride he had on the smokehouse day when he returned Sally to her ma.

Escape

19

Run for Freedom

One evening toward the end of the 1855 harvest, Clarissa stood in the doorway of Miss Effie's cabin. The sunset polished the leaves left on the oak trees to a bright red and burnished the straggly golden leaves on the poplar trees that lined the sides of the alley from the turnpike, up to the twin lawns. Like everyone else in the quarters, Clarissa listened for the sound of the night bell. When it rang, cabin doors slammed shut one and two at a time. The hands ate, tended to their aches, and rested if allowed to, but not Clarissa.

"Ma, I's cold. Bell's done rung."

"Hush chile, you be warm later. Wait here."

Clarissa draped Effie's coverlet over her back and went down to the oak tree. George Henry grabbed his cover, followed, and stayed far enough behind to avoid detection.

Can you hear me, Miss Effie? Clarissa waited, giving Effie time to know that she was there. *I's sorry I ain't been able to visit wid you lately. Been gettin' ready to go. Hates to leave you here, but my time's done come. The other night, I stand at the door lookin' out, studyin' things real good. When I was done, I close it. I stare down at the floor, thinkin' my thoughts. George Henry knowed my mind done took me to another place. He don't be knowin' where.*

Dem traps be next to me. Ropes be all tangled up. In the secret pockets under my skirt, I had a cut of fatback and some old biscuits dat I done stole from the kitchen in dem. I be waitin' for dat thick, deep darkness. When it come, I flung dem traps over my back. Pushed what might happen to me, if I gits caught, out of my mind. I crawls to the creek. Dem smells and sounds of the water be lettin' me know when I's at dat spot, where I be needin' to be. My fingers dig into dat mud . . . make a nice size hole. Den wiggles dem traps in and sets dem doors. When I's satisfied wid my work, I squats low to the ground, den looks around me. Don't see nothin'. Don't hear nothin' neither. Den I be gittin' up on my feet.

Miss Effie, Hycus come up on me from nowhere. My heart fish-flop. ' 'Bout stop dead, sho'nuf. Good thing it be dark and he don't see dem traps. He say to me, "You know the rules, gal."

Before I stand good, he done lifted me up, rip my shirt off, and smashed me against dat tree. "Hug it! Hug it tight!" he keep hollerin'. Next thing I knowed, he done throwed dem nine-tails over his shoulder and brung 'um down on my back. I falls down. "Lookin' for my boy dat gone to fetch water and ain't come back,' I tells him. He push me again. Dat tree bark be hurtin' my chest and scratchin' my cheeks. 'No one's out in dis kind of darkness, gal," he say to me.

"Ma! Ma!" George Henry hollered.

When Hycus heard his call, he lowered the whip. He didn't want no trouble from Massa. He walk on off into dat night . . . leave me clingin', cryin', bleedin', and frettin' wid fear. Miss Effie, I be so scared, I wanted to bury myself right dere wid you. It was George Henry dat took my hand and led me like a horse back to the cabin. I send for Lily. She help me wid my hurts.

Dat next afternoon, George Henry keep watchin' me. "Ma, you wants some of dis here water?" he say. Den, next thing I knowed, he holdin' out a gourd to me. I closes my eyes and slump down next to the door. My whole body be weepin'. Sweat done run down me . . .

front and back. I ponder how I gonna tend dem traps. George Henry . . . he still standin' dere. I tells him, "I drinks dat water when I gits back."

Miss Effie, I be too nervous and scared. I couldn't swallow.

"Make a hefty fire," I say to my boy.

"Ma, you goin' back out dere?"

"Gotta, boy. If I don't, won't be no meat," I tells him.

When the darkness come, I rolls myself out dat door wid my ears listenin'. What'in no bird sounds, no leaves rustlin', even the creek water be restin'. Kin only hear dem insects and critters dat be scratchin' and screechin' to git free. I kills 'em, den ties dem up in dat old green shirt and scurry on back to the cabin.

George Henry be waitin'. He done made the fire. I charred, skinned, boiled, and fried dem critters, den hides dem. "Don't speak of dis to nobody," I tells George Henry. Miss Effie, my boy look me in both my eyes. "I won't, Ma. I sews up my lips 'fore I let dem tell a word." Miss Effie, he done growed up. I done got the word, like you say I would. I be ready. My leg done healed real good.

A few days later, Massa done gone on a trip. I believes it be for some Christmas things cause it be gittin' close to dat season. Dey didn't have much of a Thanksgiving to speak of. Miss Margaret be feelin' poorly. When the last light of the day be startin' to fade, I goes on back down to dat creek. I catches fish and frogs. I picks some dried grapes left on the vine from dem summer days. Den, I plucks up dem walnuts dat's done fall. Den I sneaks back to the cabin wid my stash tied in my apron. I fries dem fish and frogs and hid dem pickin's.

When I be done, I sits close to the cabin door. I listen for dem boots. It was the whistle of the cold wind comin' through dem cracks in dat cabin door, dat disturbed my driftin'.

Gotta go! Sorry I done kept you so long, Miss Effie.

By the time Clarissa trudged back up the hill from her visit with Effie, the sky had darkened to a blue-black dark as coal. A heavy bang rang in her ears unlike any she'd ever heard before. It must be a late workday for Big Bo and he's being heavy handed with the hammer, she thought. Clarissa lifted her skirt to widen her stride when she heard two resounding bangs, louder than the first. Five quick solid strikes followed them. She became anxious and unable to determine which direction to go, left, right, or keep moving straight ahead. She closed her eyes, commanded her hog-heavy feet to step, and then, struggled to get them on the stoop.

Inside the cabin, she braced herself against the door. Her skin crawled beneath a sudden sweat. The hammer sounded again and again. She got down on her hands and knees and nervously rooted out the knapsack, and then emptied the basket that contained the frocks and brogans, and now a pair of Massa's old boots stuffed with socks. Petunia left the boots next to the stoop not long ago. She said they were too worn to be any good for Massa and said Massa Ben thought that Miss Margaret had disposed of them anyhow. Petunia didn't think that he would question the missus about their whereabouts.

Clarissa slipped into one of the coats, pulled on the pair of socks and then the boots.

Bang! Bang!

Clarissa's eyes shifted as if someone had knocked at the door.

"Movin' fast as I kin, Miss Effie. I be hearing' dat hammer."

Clarissa tied a shawl around her head and neck. She stuffed Miss Effie's scarf into her pocket and then remembered the thick warm nightgown that was kept folded under Miss Effie's bed pillow.

Bang! Bang!

Clarissa fell over.

"Help me, Miss Effie," she cried.

Back on her knees and trembling, Clarissa crawled to the rope bed. She laid her hands flat with her fingers stretched out and her head bowed. She rested on Effie's pallet. At that moment, she craved Effie's touch like she had Jake's on lonely nights. Clarissa felt the softness of Effie's gown and drew it toward her heart. She wedged it into the knapsack, right on top of the victuals, and then snatched up the chunks of meat that she nibbled on earlier. She slipped them into the pocket of the frock coat. Clarissa hesitated before taking a much needed breath of air.

Bang! Bang! Bang! Bang! Bang!

"I's comin' fast as I kin."

Clarissa squeezed the knapsack, recalling its contents: apples, bacon, birds, chicken, corn, cornmeal, fish, frog, grapes, grasshoppers, hominy, mushroom, nuts, possum, snails, snake, squirrel, turtle, and Miss Effie's gown.

Lawd, dis here seems plenty to eat, but it's gotta get us fed 'til we gits to dat freedom. We be needin' you to bless it and us, too.

Bang!

"Dat be a big one, Miss Effie. I be gittin' your wooden box."

Clarissa fished underneath the bed. Once she had the box in her grip, she drew it out and dumped its load into the sack. The amber bottle bumped its way to the bottom. Next, she snatched up Effie's medicine bag and unloaded it on top of the other goods. Without seeing, she knew it was ash for cuts and scrapes, balm for cuts and bruises, cockroaches and dry rattlesnake for fever, hard candy and whiskey for coughs and colds, hair balls for earaches, hog hoof for infant colic, frogs and toads for snake bites, tobacco for bleeding, a string with sixteen knots to prevent malaria, and sugar for bleeding and infections. Clarissa pushed the sack aside. She folded over the sides of Gran's quilt, rolled it into a tight bundle, tied both ends with a cord long enough to secure it across her back. Then she looped the rope around her waist.

Bang! Bang!

Clarissa whispered into George Henry's ear. "Wake up, boy. Git yourself in dis here coat, dese socks, and dem shoes."

George Henry smelled the smoky meat that Clarissa chewed before he heard her words. Pawing at the coat, he scratched for a sleeve opening. He wiggled one arm and then the other into them. Next, he shoved his feet into the socks and stepped into the brogans.

"Ma, who dese shoes and socks be belongin' to? Where we goin'?"

"Hush, boy. We talks later. Hold on to dis here knapsack. You take care. Our life be in it. Gnaw on dis here."

The meat had the same smoky smell as his ma's mouth. Clarissa held tight to the cuff of George Henry's coat, ready to dash out the door.

"Gotta be brave, Clari."

Clarissa stepped back on George Henry.

"Ma?"

"Dat be your pa. He be talkin' ta me."

Clarissa pulled the door open further. She looked for Hycus but didn't see him. The latch clicked when they went out the door.

Bang!

Clarissa and George Henry rushed to the rear of the cabins. They step-stumbled down the hill to the first ridgeline near Effie's oak tree.

"Wait here. Hold on to dis. Don't you move, boy!"

Clarissa slept with Effie's coverlet ever since Effie went on to the Lord's world. If she left it behind, she knew that she just might as well crawl into Miss Effie's grave and venture onto the next world.

Bang! Bang! Bang! Bang! Bang!

"I forgot your cover. I be gittin' it and be on my way."

Clarissa didn't need the moonlight to find her way. She had been up and down that hill fetching bath water, drinking water, wash water, as well as the Lord's water on Sundays. She knew the hill like she knew the butterfly wings on the back of Toby's neck.

Unable to see, Clarissa's foot landed on a bundle that sent her headlong into the cabin. On her knees, she snatched it up.

Bang! Bang! Bang-bang-bang-bang-bang! . . .

This time, the two hard bangs were followed by five steady bangs and a trail of ringing ones. They were too many and too quick to count.

Feeling the weight of the hammer on her back, Clarissa shoved the sack under one arm and crept to Miss Effie's bed. With a trembling hand, she gathered the coverlet scrunched up in the far corner. She swooped it into her arms and dashed out the door without pulling it shut behind her. Her heart kept rhythm with the hammer that told her, her feet should be running. She bustled back down the hill and was knocked silly by a stray branch that caused her to lose her load.

"Dat you, Ma?"

"Is."

Clarissa retrieved the haversack and Miss Effie's coverlet. She groped in the dark until she detected the toe of George Henry's brogans.

"Let's go, boy."

"Ma, cain't see. Where we goin'?"

"Hush! Don't want nobody to hear. Dem hound dogs be near."

"I be scared, Ma."

"No need to be. Just keep movin'. I tells you when to stop."

The sound of Big Bo's hammer kept Clarissa along. She and George Henry hiked down the hill toward the northbound turnpike and crossed it to follow the creek that followed the road. They circled the bend in the creek, which passed Powell's Run, flowing toward High Grove. The hammering faded into the stillness of the night and was replaced by a sudden crunch. Clarissa's entire body quivered as the noise magnified, sending her and her bundles to the ground.

"Ma, it be Stu."

George Henry threw his arms around the dog's neck. Stu licked the salty dampness from George Henry's cheeks and whined to be patted.

"Cain't play, boy. You gotta go on back. Git! You git, now!"

The hound tucked his tail between his legs and ambled back into the darkness. George Henry listened after Stu's departure. Then he slipped his arm through Clarissa's.

"Come on, Ma. Let's be gittin'. Cain't stop 'fore we be startin'."

George Henry threw Miss Effie's quilt across Clarissa's shoulder. They hiked until daylight. They crouched behind a tree that grew close to a hill, rested, and then slept. He and his ma woke when it was night and continued north for hours, lapping the far reach of the creek where they were greeted by a tinge of orange, blushing from behind the treetops. When they shoved their goatskin pouches into the icy water to fill them, the clopping of hooves and howling of dogs sounded in the not-so-far distance.

"Lawd, have mercy!" Clarissa cried. She snatched up her pouch. "Git your goat skin and dat haversack. I gits dem victuals and my tote. Hurry, boy!"

The wagon wheels vibrated the earth beneath Clarissa. Her feet became fixed in the mud; she was sinking. George Henry grabbed her cold, wet hand and pulled her back into the woods. A sleeting rain began to fall, burning their faces and blurring their vision. They scaled one rugged hill, tumbled over another, and then plowed through shrubs and bushes. Without warning, Clarissa fell into a dark hole. She groaned with pain when George Henry tumbled in on top of her. Warm blood trickled down her forearm from a gash on her wrist.

"I's sorry, Ma. Didn't see you." George Henry said tearfully.

"We been snatched by the devil. He done pulled me into hell, boy!"

"Naw, Ma. Dis here be a cave."

George Henry tugged Clarissa into the darkness far enough to be shielded from the weather and not be seen in the strong daylight, coming up fast. The cave was small, but large enough to hold six to eight people and stretched a good distance to the rear. The cave's ceiling was too low for them to get under.

"Ma, we kin stay here. Dem horses and hounds done gone over yonder. I gits us some firewood. We be warm soon. Put your head on dis here haversack."

"The victuals!" Clarissa shouted. "Go find dem, boy! Dey be where I done fall."

Clarissa put her head down on the haversack; the smells of Lily and Petunia surfaced. "You's here! You be lookin' after me and George Henry," Clarissa said, and then fell into semiconsciousness.

George Henry clambered out of the cave. Sleet pelted his face, numbing his cheeks as he fumbled along the trail now camouflaged with fresh snow. Not far from the cave's opening lay the snow-coated knapsack. A raccoon hunkered down next to it, peering peevishly at George Henry.

Hunched over, George Henry cautiously approached the animal. The raccoon's fur, tipped with glistening ice crystals, stood straight up. George Henry lowered his body to his left knee. Not looking away from the creature, his right hand blindly searched for a clobbering tool. When his fingers detected a rough gnarly stick, he wrapped them around it. Taking his time, he tightened his grip, raised the stick above his head, and held it steadfast. He dipped his left shoulder and cautiously reached for the sack with his free hand. The varmint hissed, gnashed, and bared his teeth.

George Henry snatched his hand back. Still gripping the stick, he slowly brought it back down and tried to hook it to the strap of the knapsack to tease the victuals nearer to his foot. The raccoon clamped his teeth down on the sack and wobbled backward, dragging it along while keeping an *I-dare-you-to* eye on George Henry.

George Henry pitched the stick and lunged ahead. He grabbed the tote with the hungry raccoon hanging on to it. He swung the knapsack above his head. A snap of his wrist sent the critter flying into a tree. The raccoon landed on his back, stupefied. When its wits returned, he staggered off in a drunken fashion, hauling his furry tail behind him. George Henry didn't wait to see him disappear into the woods. He rushed back to the cave. His stomach pained at the thought of nearly losing the victuals.

Clarissa sat straight up. "What take you so long, boy? I thought you been caught."

"Sorry, Ma. Didn't mean to be worryin' you none."

George Henry sat next to Clarissa with the knapsack on his lap. Curled over it, he breathed deeply.

"Ma, your arm. It be troublin' you?"

"Some."

Clarissa had ripped a piece of fabric from the petticoats she wore to keep warm. She had used a strip of it to tie a piece of tobacco to her wrist to stop the bleeding.

"Dem victuals?"

"A raccoon, Ma. He snatched dem."

"Did he . . . ?"

"Naw, Ma. I got dem here."

"You done good, boy."

Clarissa blew another sigh that whistled throughout the cave. Feeling chilled, she pulled out Effie's gown. The whatnots from the medicine bag and fixings from the wooden box shifted, creating a slight ruckus. Clarissa's hand scrambled to find the oilcloth. She dragged it out and caught hold of a few pieces of meat that she offered to George Henry. He chewed and was too hungry to care what it was and drank from the goatskin to wash it down. Clarissa, glad that she hadn't sent back the basket of food and the oilcloth back with Lily that night, spread the cloth between her bottom and the wetness of the cave floor.

"Put dis here over you, boy."

George Henry spun his body into Miss Effie's coverlet and took in the smells that he knew well: lavender water, rose oil, and lye soap. They comforted him, but made him miss Effie's love. Clarissa drew her body into a soft curve beneath Gran's old quilt and wrapped her head with the gown. Outside the cave, hail brushed the trees and fallen leaves. The sounds created a restful haven inside.

"Ma, we be needin' a fire.

George Henry wedged the sack of victuals in close to Clarissa and went back into the woods. His eyes scanned the forest floor for his furry friend as he gathered an armload of wood. He sorted the limbs and twigs by size, and stacked them just inside the cave's opening. The heftier ones were used to concoct a fence across the entrance of the cave.

"Dis keep us safe, Ma. If one of dem wild critters come near, we be knowin' it."

George Henry arranged the smallest twigs in a spoke-wheel pattern and filled the center with bark chips and fallen leaves. He felt in his pocket for the flints. He slid them palm to palm before he clicked them together. When he did, they flipped out of his hands. He blew a warm breath on his fingers before picking them up. "Strike 'em. Strike 'em hard," Miss Effie's voice echoed in his head. He tried again. There were sparks, but the kindling refused to ignite.

"Ma, don't know what to do. Dampness won't let dis here fire catch on."

Clarissa ripped off another piece of her petticoat, further up and dry.

"Use dis here, boy."

George Henry placed the swatch among the twigs and sat back on his haunches. He rubbed his hands together. Cupping his fingers, he blew on them and tried again. This time, knocking the flints together took his mind back to Big Bo's hammering. The rag puffed out a light smoke.

"Won't be long. We be warm soon, Ma."

George Henry blew on the small flames. The fire caught hold. When he stacked on more wood, the sudden light disturbed the bats on the ceiling. They frantically circled overhead before settling back down again.

"Boy, I ain't seen what be in dis here haversack. Just been sleepin' on it." Clarissa's fumbling fingers fiddled until the haversack opened. The sight of the paisley scarf caused her to sigh so deeply that she nearly lost all her senses.

"Lawd Jesus, dis here be Petunia's. What she gonna do widout it? I knowed I shoulda looked inside dis here bag 'fore I takes it." Clarissa moaned again when she turned the sack upside down and her hand unexpectedly brushed against a lumpy of softness as the content plummeted onto her lap.

"Oh, my! My! Dese be dem socks Lily been knittin' for more months den I got fingers and toes to count. Dey be for her and Sally. What dey gonna do now? How dey feet gonna be warm?"

"Miss Lily and Miss Petunia . . . dey cares about you, Ma. Wants you to be warm."

Clarissa was overwhelmed with the love she felt from the friends she left behind. George Henry peeled off the wet, threadbare socks that stuck to Clarissa's bloody feet and slipped a dry pair on them. He laughed to himself at the funny mingled colors.

"Wherever you be, I be lovin' you plenty," Clarissa said to the spirits of her friends.

She rolled the haversack into a log to lay her head on. She didn't realiz at first that something more was inside. She didn't need to pull it out, but she did. The whiffs of sassafras tea, tobacco, sweat, and healing ointments told her that it was Turtle Jim's old straw hat. Clarissa whimpered as she wrapped her head and neck with Petunia's scarf and plopped the crown of the hat down over her face, creating a private space. She conjured up visions of those she had left behind. Without disturbing the hat, Clarissa felt for Miss Effie's scarf stuffed in her coat pocket. She twisted it around her cold, tingling fingers.

As night continued, the cave darkened and filled with the smell of smoky musk and bat droppings. George Henry stretched his limbs and rubbed sleep from his eyes. Breathing deeply provoked a cough. He tossed more kindling on the fading fire and stoked it until there was a full blast of firelight. The bats fluttered once more. Clarissa sat up and handed George Henry a piece of dry fish, and then took some for herself. A slight breeze tickled her lashes. She tightened Petunia's scarf under her chin and stared at her feet. She felt Lily cozying around her toes. With little else to do, Clarissa told George Henry to say his prayers and ask God to watch over them. She closed her eyes and did the same.

"Ma, you be pining. Whatcha got on your mind?"

"Petunia be in dat kitchen alone. She be skittish, too. Ain't got me to tell her what to do. Dis here scarf what give her comfort. And Lily, her feet be cold while mine be warm. She be missin' her Tom . . . feelin' a powerful emptiness. I shoulda looked in dis here bag, but Big Bo hammer kept pushin' me so I couldn't think none."

After George Henry and Clarissa had been in the cave two days, she swayed back and forth, mindlessly chewing, trying not to swallow the bit of meat in her mouth. George Henry watched for the darkness of night to come. At the first sign of it, he called to her.

"Done been in here long enough, Ma. Weather be some better. Best we be gittin'."

"Gotta wait 'til the sky be dark, boy."

"I be knowin' dat, Ma. Just be itching' to be gittin' on . . . wantin' us to be ready when the time come."

A star glittered in the black velvet sky. George Henry took down the fencing. Clarissa gathered their belongings. They tracked north for ten more days, counting wasn't easy. They hid in the brush, bundled in the covers, ate, stayed put during daylight hours, and ran only at night. Their toes pushed groundswell after groundswell behind them.

Clarissa sobbed out loud. "Cain't go no mo'. I be cold, hungry, and tired. My legs be givin' way."

"Come on, Ma. Cain't stop here. Daylight startin' to show. Dat train you done told 'bout . . . it be comin'. We be gittin' on it."

George Henry wasn't sure about the trains, trails, stars, or anything else the field hands sang about. But he knew that Clarissa believed and pulled her up on her feet.

"We gonna git on dat train, Ma! Let's be gittin'."

The frigid ground stung the balls of Clarissa's feet that puffed through the soles of her boots.

"Cain't go on no more!" Clarissa sank to her knees. "You hear dat, boy?"

"Ma, dat be gunshots!" George Henry said, raising her back to her feet.

"Best we hurry. Dat next shot might be for us."

Following the North Star, they clambered, crept, and stumbled among the naked trees. George Henry nudged his ma up and down the gorges. She dragged one blistering and bleeding foot after the other while crying and mumbling her prayers.

Not much could be seen since the snow had started falling. George Henry slowed his pace and stepped behind Clarissa. He was ready to catch her if she tilted too far. He listened intently for wagon wheels and barking hounds. A bright flash of color flickered among the snowflakes. George Henry's head twitched and his feet fumbled. He nearly knocked Clarissa down.

"Take care, boy."

"Ma! I sees where we kin hide."

George Henry squatted for a better look.

"Over dere."

Crawling, he led Clarissa toward a thicket and forced himself through a slight opening. She followed until they were both beneath a downed tree with a root base tall enough for them to stand beneath. Clarissa smoothed out the oilcloth and sat on it. She removed Turtle Jim's hat from her head, knocked off the snow, and laid it close by. Smiling, she remembered how proudly he wore it when he chewed on grass and leaned against a yard tree.

"Be missin' your brother and dem others," Clarissa told George Henry. "Dis here mud conjures dem up. Toby's knees always be smellin' like it."

George Henry examined the new hiding space before he responded to Clarissa's words.

"Ma, don't be thinkin' 'bout dem sad times right now. Wait 'til we's free."

She leaned back. "Thoughts won't let me be, boy."

Clarissa unscrewed the lid on the salve, teased out a pea-sized lump, and rubbed it on her sore feet. She snatched her hand back when it touched the thick mass of scars on the side of her leg, causing them to tingle. She was glad the scars were not behind her knees like Petunia's were, or she wouldn't have been able to run away. Barely able to speak, Clarissa handed the jar to George Henry.

"Put some of dis here on your feet."

Shaking so from her thoughts, Clarissa dropped the jar into her boy's lap. She drew her legs up, held onto herself, and prayed her soothing words.

190

"Ma, I knows you be hurtin' 'cause you be missin' folks, but you cain't be makin' no fuss. Dem hounds might be comin' after us."

"Soundin' like your pa, boy. I be wishin' he was here wid us."

Clarissa strained to see George Henry's face in the scanty daylight.

"You go on. Git yourself some of dat possum. It be smoked like you like it."

Clarissa rested her head on her knees. George Henry knew that she was asking God to keep them safe.

20

Molly's Quilt

George Henry searched for a piece of salt-encrusted food in the bottom of the knapsack. When his hand touched what felt like dry meat, he grabbed it and some wrinkled fruit. The sweet-salty flavor pleased his tongue, but his belly wasn't satisfied. His gut yearned for additional pieces of food that couldn't be spared. George Henry knew not to eat more and picked the meat and fruit from between his teeth. He minced it until there was nothing more to it and then swallowed the puree.

"Ma, where dat freedom be? We done come a mighty far piece."

"On the other side dat river. Towards the big star, dey say. We be near it. Dem gunshots we be hearin' the other day, I thought dey be from dem hunters. 'Cept the shootin' didn't stop. Dem folks around here be bringin' in the new year, 1856. Dat could mean we near dat river town, Louisville. If dat be so, dat be where I's sold away from Jake, Toby, and my gals. Couldn't see enough in dis here snow to be noticin' nothin' dat I might 'member from dat day on da auction block."

George Henry fixed his eyes on Clarissa as she retrieved the bundle from behind her back. Her hands and fingers didn't stop fidgeting until the knot loosened and the roll fell open. She flipped the quilt. It landed on their laps. Sunbeams filtering through the shrubs polished the appliqués, giving each a fresh look.

The boy mulled over what he had never seen before. First, he took note of the trail running from south to north, dividing east from west. Then he eyed the indigo patches that rippled across the quilt, east side to west side, splitting the north from the south. There was also a log cabin and more.

"Ma, ain't never seen all dis 'fore. You always keep Gran's quilt folded or dis side laying against you."

"Time wasn't never right for showin', boy."

Clarissa buried her face in her hands when Gran's words entered her head.

Don't run 'til you know the time be right. Watch for dat big star. Don't let dat dipper out of ya sight. Wait 'til it be near time for dat river to freeze. Keep on the trail. Look for dem signs. Don't stop 'til you cross dem waters onto Jordan. From dere, you go on to Canada, if you can. You be safe den, gal.

The boy wondered what Miss Effie would think about the stitched-on snippets making a cabin, fire, sky, rivers, trails, trees, small wings, and other things that George Henry couldn't identify. His fingers traced along the indigo river.

"Ma, ain't dis some of your auction skirt?"

"Is, boy."

George Henry rested his mouth and studied what he was seeing: a bit of his old shirt tied around the tree, pieces of Bo's hemp britches fashioning a tree's trunk, and snippets of a green shirt creating treetops. Not sure what the fluttering white birds; falling golden leaves; flaming candle; and wooden cross high in the sky, not far from a white glowing star are made from.

Clarissa straightened her back, tilted her head, and sucked in cold air through her nose. Then, she slumped forward with her neck stretched.

"You hear somethin', Ma?"

"Not sure, boy."

Clarissa studied George Henry before she said, in an uneasy voice, "Dis here coverlet be showin' us the way."

Her eyes flitted back and forth from the quilt to the bush in front of them. She spoke, but seemingly not to George Henry. She fiddles with the cover, but her eyes were fixed on the thicket as her words floated about.

"See dat log cabin and dem windows? What dem logs be tellin' you, boy?"

"Cain't rightly say, Ma."

"Dey pointin' north, tellin' you which way to be gittin'. Only one window got a light. Dat 'cause dem fires be goin' out. Folks be leavin'. Others be gittin' ready to run."

Clarissa's fingers crossed to the tall tree with a bright orange cloth stitched down on it. She nudged the knot of the rag and slipped into a trance that stole her from the present.

"What dat you be jigglin', Ma?"

George Henry's words drew Clarissa's focus back to the quilt.

Half murmuring, she said, "Dis here be a sign. When we sees it, it be tellin' us we's venturin' north, gittin' close to dat Gloryland."

When George Henry dragged his scrutinizing hand across the quilt. His jarred fingernail snagged a patching thread, stopping his hand next to Clarissa's.

"I seen it, Ma."

"Seen what?"

"Dat sign. The rag you be talkin' 'bout."

"What you mean, George Henry?"

Clarissa didn't take her sight off the clue neatly stitched down and around the tree.

"Come on. I shows you."

Pushing aside the quilt, George Henry and Clarissa wormed from beneath the tree roots and squatted in front of the overgrowth. The snow had covered their footsteps. George Henry pointed to the tree not far from them.

"Dere, Ma. Over dere."

"Where?"

"See dat twisted tree?"

George Henry extended his arm.

Clarissa brushed snow from her eyelashes. Her view followed the length of George Henry's arm until she had sight of the bright, red and green plaid rag. Surprised, she pulled him close.

"Dat rag. Dat be it, boy! Means we be on the trail headin' north. Come on. Best we be gittin' back or we won't be knowin' dat freedom."

Once settled, Clarissa drew the quilt over their legs. Her fingers meandered up the zigzag path, past the campfire. They idled at the edge of the dark blue waters, but weren't ready to cross over.

"Dis here . . . it be the river dey be singin' about in dem fields. We gots to be gittin' across it, boy."

"Dat be the Ohio, Ma?"

"It be so, dey say. Like dem songs the slaves be singin' when dey workin' in dem fields and comin' down dat lane to the quarters, tellin' us about dis here river, what we be needin' to know about and be needin' to see, and to be doin' when the time come for runnin'."

"Ma, the day we be runnin', I hear dem slaves singin' in the fields and Big Bo's hammerin' was easy to hear. Make me speculate why he be hammerin' late into the night, after the slaves done stop singin'."

George Henry was struggling to make sense of things when a twig snapped and the sound of footsteps made him gasp. Clarissa pounced on her boy, folded her body over his, and forced him down.

"Ma! Got no air! I be chokin'."

"Dey out dere!"

"Ma!"

The shuffling noise and crunching of snow moved nearer, invading the quiet. Clarissa eased off of George Henry's back. She threw the covers up over them. They strained their ears to identify what they couldn't see. George Henry squirmed to free one eye. He peered into the stares of eight deer. Spooked, they flipped their blinding white tails and were soon lost among the snow-flocked trees.

"Ma, dey be whitetail deer. Sho' wish I could run . . . hide like dem, too."

Clarissa flounced the covers, shaking off the debris. She swayed back and forth as she embraced Gran's old quilt. Her eyes were still and blank.

"Ma." No answer. "Ma, don't leave me. Ma!" George Henry wailed, thinking she was going on to be with Miss Effie.

"I be scared, boy. Thought Master Ben and dem hounds . . ."

Clarissa hushed. She shrugged her shoulders and blinked her eyes nervously.

"We be safe now, Ma."

Clarissa didn't respond. She went back to holding tight to Gran's old quilt. George Henry bundled her in Miss Effie's coverlet. He covered Clarissa's hands with his and teased the quilt from her grip. He stretched it across their laps with the trail side up. He remembered what he heard Miss Effie say many times. *"Talkin' makes things better."*

"Look here, Ma."

George Henry captured Clarissa's stare and guided it down to the quilt, where the brown patches were stitched on.

"Dat trail be goin' north. What dem dark marks near the river mean?"

George Henry released Clarissa's gaze from his hold.

"Dat be blood, boy. It be from dem needles of the mammies dat done sewed on it. Some I knowed. Some I don't. It be too painful to recollect 'bout."

Clarissa arched her fingers on the trail. They crept with a long dog stretch toward the rough cross and the glowing candle at the top of the quilt.

"What dey mean, Ma?"

"Dere might be Christians dere dat can hid us . . . help us git on to Canada if we be needin' dem to. Dis here, it be the small drinkin' gourd. Dat be the North Star we be followin'.'"

Clarissa's index finger traced the darkened edges of the star worn with time and its dreams. Then she hopscotched them from patch to patch, touching each one with a deeper thought.

"Ma! Dem dabs." George Henry glimpsed closer. "Dey be made from Miss Effie's old white nightshirt?"

"Ain't, boy. Don't rightly know whose gown or tow shirt dey be made from."

"What dey mean?"

"Dem tears. Granma Alice say dey tack dem down wid threads dipped in blood from kinfolks dat done gone on. Don't rightly know who dey all was. Could be my ma or my great-granma. Don't exactly 'member who dem tears belong to. Dere be so many. Look here, George Henry. See dat woman and her baby?"

Clarissa's hands levitated over the quilt.

"Don't see dem, Ma."

"Dey dere . . . be put on wid dem big chain stitches, lookin' same as dem chains dey be puttin' on us Negroes. Dat woman's face be showin' the pain of slave women dat be losin' dere chillen and families. No different den when I done lost mine. Dat baby, it got no eyes cause it cain't see no future."

George Henry moved his head backward and forward and up and down.

"I see dem, Ma! What about dem birds dat be flyin' all over the quilt?"

"Dey weren't always dere. I stitch dem on. Dey be flyin' north. The way we gotta go." A fresh sadness seeped across Clarissa's face. "Dey be takin' my people on to better a place. Maybe it be heaven or maybe right here on dis here earth. Dat bird dere, it be my man Jake bein' carried away wid his legs and back hurtin' him from all dat cotton he done picked and hemp he done broke, 'bout all his lifetime." Clarissa pointed to a bird in the center of the quilt. "Dis one, it be carryin' my twin gals." Clarissa's eyes flickered from the birds to the eyes of the woman chain-stitched on the quilt.

"To where, Ma?"

"Don't rightly know. Dey be so young. But dis here one, it be my big boy, Toby. He might done run on to Jordan."

A slight smile puffed up Clarissa's cheeks for a sliver of a second.

"Dis one here, it be Granma Alice. And dat one's Great-granma Molly."

"What 'bout dat one?"

"It be Miss Effie. She be sittin' next to the Lawd watchin' over us, makin' sure we gits to freedom. I got two more birds. I be puttin' dem on when we gits to dat Gloryland on the other side of dem waters. Dey be you and me, boy."

"What about your ma, my Granma Mary?"

"She dere."

Clarissa's finger dabbed the wings of a bird that fluttered beneath the cross.

"Dis be her."

"Ma, what freedom gonna be like?"

"It be time for me to rest, time for you to play, time for all to pray."

"Will I like it?"

"Sho nuf, honeychile. What I done told you, it be what my Granma Alice done told me and Great-granma Mary done told her. If I gits caught, grab dis here quilt. Run wid dem grasshopper legs 'til you be safe. Don't speak what I tells you to nobody. Only tells your family. Dere family tells deres and deres tells deres. Dat's how it's gotta be."

George Henry sat in the hush of the moment. He didn't know what to think or feel and didn't want to lose his ma like he had his pa, his brother, and his twin sisters.

Clarissa softly sang, "Follow the drinkin' gourd."

George Henry had to strain to hear her voice, not sure if he was hearing or dreaming. He gladly drew his eyelids shut against the day.

21

Scary Chase

Night came and a canopy of dark clouds smothered the moon. Clarissa couldn't see her hands and feet or the meat that she held. She tossed the chunks inside her shirt and reached for George Henry. Gently shaking his leg, she urged in a low raspy timbre, "Wake up, chile. A storm be brewin'. Gotta be gittin' 'fore we cain't."

"No! No! Don't wanna go. Too cold. Too dark. Dat freedom be too far!"

Clarissa's hand climbed George Henry's back. When she felt his tight, curly nape, she cat-arched over his back and laid her head behind his ear, with soft whispers she told him, "Freedom near. Cain't stop now."

George Henry turned his head. He peered into the face that darkness didn't allow him to see.

"I tries, Ma."

George Henry tucked the haversack that he slept with his head on into his waistband. Afterward, he tightened the rope that held it in place and his britches up. Clarissa secured the covers on her back and fastened Turtle Jim's hat under her chin with a tight knot. She stood, took in filling breath and closed her eyes before she slowly let it out. She parted the brush. Disbelief smacked at her when she stepped into deep, thick snow that coated what seemed to be the entire world.

"Come on, boy."

The sudden sound of bloodhounds forced Clarissa to pivot in nervous circles, not moving from the spot where her feet were embedded in the snow.

"Lawd! Where dem dogs at?"

Disoriented and not able to budge, Clarissa fidgeted with her skirt and slapped the knapsack against her leg, whipping up the tattered petticoats. George Henry grabbed her hand.

"Let's git! Ma. Dem hounds gonna eat us and my gut be howlin'."

Hand-in-hand, George Henry and Clarissa headed north fast as their tired, sore feet and achy legs would transport them. Remembering the beef jerky, Clarissa reached into her shirt and snared the meat. Her feet never stopped.

In a bouncy voice, she said, "Chew on dis here, boy."

George Henry snatched the offering and popped it into his mouth.

"Don't swallow 'til you have to."

He chewed the smoky nugget that didn't temper his cramping gut or the feeling of hunger that had haunted him too long. He swiftly shifted his thoughts from his stomach to his ma. George Henry held fast to Clarissa as they bounded through the dense forest, not sure where they were headed, but the turnpike could still be seen.

Brambles and thistles tore their clothing and clawed their feet and legs. They waded through half-frozen streams, fell over their feet, jumped over downed trees and limbs, skittered up and scurried down hills. Some of them were steep and some were slight. George Henry's focus was diverted by the uproar on the upper road. When he turned toward the sound, he thought he looked down a double-barrel shotgun that was aimed and ready to fire at them. The sound of thudding horse hooves rumbled through the naked trees, snatching a wagon side-to-side. The hind part blurred as the wagon veered off the main turnpike, trailed by a pack of bloodhounds.

"Ma, Massa Ben and Mister Hycus, and dem dogs, too. Dey done gone on. I thought dem horses gonna clamor up my back." George Henry's voice quavered from between his cracked and bleeding lips.

Clarissa, barely able to breathe, snapped up George Henry's coattail.

"Stop!" she told him. She tearfully cried, "Cain't go no mo'!" and then toppled over, taking George Henry with her into a snowdrift.

"Ma, you hurt?" George Henry asked from his sitting posture.

"I's fine, boy. But I be so wore out."

George Henry didn't move for several stretched-out seconds. He took note of his weary legs before commanding them to stand him on his feet. Once up, he slipped his hands under Clarissa's arms, took in a deep breath and tugged her to her feet. He held her near to prevent her from falling. Clarissa adjusted her hold on the sack and lifted her skirts. Wet and ice coated, it was a punishing weight and bogged her down. When they were both steady, George Henry took the knapsack from Clarissa and tucked it under his arm. He gripped a heap of her skirt and petticoats, to lighten her load.

"Come on, Ma. You can lean on me. Dere be a big rock over yonder with a good swell. Keep dis here snow off us. Cain't no eyes peer down on us neither . . . not from dat road."

Clarissa lugged the weight of her body along. Her feet slipped and slid in the undergrowth that was iced and choking the path. She fell out of George Henry's grip just feet from the boulder.

"Don't want to be fallin' down, Lawd," she mumbled.

George Henry shoved his palms below Clarissa's shoulder. He tugged her once more, dragging her heels through the snow until they were cupped by the hollow of the huge stone. When he glanced back, he was pleased that the heavy snowfall had already camouflaged their tracks. Once underneath the rock, George Henry propped his mother against the wall of the stone and put the knapsack down next to her. She teased the oilcloth from her shirt band and sat on it. She wept and shivered as she unraveled her filthy skirt and shredded petticoats. George Henry layered the covers over her thin body that wasn't much more than bones.

"I's tired, boy."

Clarissa's voice was spindly, and the heaviness in her chest didn't allow her to take in enough air to recover her strength. Her pleading eyes skimmed over George Henry's face.

"Cain't make no fire, Ma. Dey might see dat smoke."

Clarissa eyelids lowered. George Henry knew she was praying like she did when times weren't easy.

"Ma, I seen dem horses. Dey turn down dat other fork in the road. We be safe for now."

George Henry patted Clarissa's frail hand like Miss Effie did his, chasing off loneliness. He wished deeply that she were with them at this eerie moment.

What would she say? What would she tell me to do? Miss Effie always had the answers dat we be needin', when we be needin' dem. And we be needin' now. She help the sick, took care of us little darkies, fed us when dere was no victuals, and calm Massa Ben when he be ornery and mean to the field hands. She could even make Hycus put down dat whip when no else could.

Clarissa looked sorrowfully at her bleeding feet. She massaged them with balm and pleaded with them to stay strong. She ripped several strips from her shabby petticoat, bandaged her feet, and then stuffed the boots to block the holes in the soles. When she pulled on a fresh pair of socks, she was slow and deliberate, relishing the softness that encased her feet. George Henry took the last of the salve and did the same to his feet. It was a good thing that his brogans were larger than his feet. The wrappings made them snug and a smidgen warmer.

George Henry removed Turtle Jim's hat from Clarissa's head, adjusted what was left of the shawls and scarves around her face and neck, and then scooted under the covers next to her. There was no body heat between them that he could detect. George Henry heaped piles of leaves, mud, and twigs on them, hoping to trap what little body heat they might generate. When he shifted his weight, his hand detected something soft, squirming, and warm. Gritting his teeth, he quickly snatched his hand back.

"Somethin's under here wid us, Ma."

"You sure, George Henry?"

"Uh-huh. It be fuzzy. Warm, too."

"Take care. Might bite."

George Henry explored what was next to him.

"Ma! Dey be young rabbits," he said and stroked the critters, welcoming their warmth.

"Good thing I's so weary or I'd skin dem and make a hat wid ear covers from dem hides. Den eat what be left of dem."

"Ha-ha!" they crowed.

The chuckling knocked Clarissa over. When she pulled herself back to sitting, she brushed away the laughter tears and retrieved a small chunk of victual and a biscuit. She popped the bread into her mouth and blew on her hands to warm the meat between her palms.

"Dis here meat for you. The crumbs left from dat biscuit be for dem babies."

Clarissa braced herself against the cold wet stone and closed her eyes, blocking out the darkness and fear that sickened her.

George Henry's lips clutched the turtle meat before he drew it into his mouth. After he finished his victuals, he brushed the breadcrumbs together in the center of his palm. He licked his finger, pushed it down on the bits, and pointed it at his new friends. They nibbled at the morsels. Their wiggly whiskers tickled his fingertip. One spry kit hopped into his palm, claiming his share. Just then, the earth vibrated beneath George Henry.

"Ma! Dey done come back!" he whispered.

Clarissa was slumped over and nearly comatose. She didn't hear her boy's call and didn't move. George Henry threw himself over her and slapped his free hand across her gaping mouth. Clarissa's ribcage quaked beneath his weight. Her heart thumped against his chest.

Ben Mullins drove the horses at a full gallop. They kicked up gravel, snow, and ice that crashed against the wagon. He yanked on the reins, stopping the team directly above the hideout. The horses' hooves pummeled the ground, creating an odorous slush. The icy mess slithered along the formation of the rocks and down the backside of the boulder where George Henry and Clarissa hid.

George Henry's hand tensed when Clarissa's tears rolled over it like Sally's did that day in the smokehouse, bringing on a rush of uneasy feelings. He pined for Miss Effie and now he missed Sally, Lily, Petunia, Bo, Big Bo, Sam, and the rest of the servants and field hands left behind.

Mullins snatched off his hat and smacked it against his leg in disgust. Snow plastered the side of his face. He flicked it away and forced his hat back down on his head.

"Do you see them?" he asked Hycus.

"I was sure I saw something move when we turned off the main road back there."

"Must have been a deer, sir."

Mullins stepped over the wagon bench and stood behind it for a better look. Steam wafted from his nose and mouth. Hycus, who raised up in his stirrups, scrutinized the river. Mullins noted an unusual quietness in his overseer's manner but dismissed it because they had been on the road for nearly three weeks. They were both fatigued, mentally and physically.

Mullins cleared his throat to raise his voice above the rush of the river. He shouted, "We got off to an early start 'cause they left that cabin door open. We have searched along the creek from the quarters north to the river more than once. Haven't seen sight of them yet. They must have taken up with some of those runaways that seem to vanish underground. I don't understand how a woman and boy could outpace a pack of dogs and a team of horses."

Ben stepped back over the bench. He slouched down in his misery, pining for what he seem to have lost. With his booted foot braced on the footrest, he leaned forward, supporting his upper arm against his knee.

"The day following the festivity, I went down to the smokehouse. Meat crates were overturned. Hams were scattered. I heard wolves howling from the hills, the day of the affair. Seemed evident that they had ransacked the smokehouse. I'm thinking differently now."

Hycus continued eyeballing the river. He kept his stare away from Ben when he muttered, "I heard somethin', too, dat night just before daybreak. I checked the smokehouse, nothin' was dere."

Hycus squeezed the horn of his saddle, shifted his hips, and tightened his legs against the fenders. He was disgusted that he had not gone inside the smokehouse that night. He reared up once more, and goosenecked for a better view of the river.

When Mullins dragged his finger under his drippy nose, he sneezed out a wad of snot on the back of his hand and upper lip. He plucked a hanky from his coat pocket, shook it out, and cleaned away the mess.

"If they got a ham, they got distance. Four of Dr. Isaac's darkies that ran took several of his laying hens with them. Dogs brought one of the runaways back. He was pretty well chewed up and had a mess of feathers clinging to his hide. It wasn't that tall one they call Copper Tom, but he's out there somewhere. With that white people's upbringing of his and being able to read and write better than most and knowing how to blend in with them, he might have made it all the way to Canada. Don't know why Isaac bought him. Those smart, white-looking Negroes never do you any good and cause a heap of trouble besides. There was no word about the others. Guess they might have made it north, too. A little food can get a darkie over the river and damn near to Canada."

"Yes, sir, it can."

Without thinking, Ben snatched off his hat again and angrily knocked it against his knee before quickly putting it back on his head. The snow clumps that dropped from it melted around the toe of his boot, puddling on the boards. By the time Ben finished reflecting, Hycus had sat back down in his saddle, but was still eyeing the river.

"Don't see a thing out dere, Boss," Hycus said, avoiding Mullins' stare. "Look at dem hounds . . . tongues hangin' out of dere heads. Dey stretched out like sides of beef waitin' to be strung up. Dey're done for, sir. Cain't detect no darkies no more. What smells the rain ain't washed out, the snow done froze."

"Stay in your saddle. I'll get them."

When Mullins loaded the last of the dogs into the wagon and threw horse blankets over them, Stu jumped out and staggered off.

"Come back here, you crazy hound."

Mullins chased after Stu. He snatched up the hound by the scruff of his neck and threw him back into the wagon with the other dogs.

"If I didn't know better, I'd think that hound was tipsy on moonshine . . . whining and crying, crawling on his belly, wagging his tail. He nearly went over that ledge. I've lost two good darkies. I don't need to be losing a hound, too. He's been one of my best breeders."

Confounded, Mullins choked the reins and shook his head. "Never thought Clarissa and that boy would get away from me. Look there," Mullins gestured north. "Those rapids are kicking up a nasty fuss out there. See that crack in the ice midway out? It's pretty evident no one could cross that river without being taken under. I'm turning this team around. Blizzard's getting worse, slapping me like I'm the runaway darkie. Let's go!" Ben Mullins suppressed his sigh as he yanked on the reins and shouted, "Giddy up!"

He flailed the leather straps against the horses' steaming rumps and turned the team around with a strong pull of the straps. The wagon veered, sending another heap of slush slithering down the boulder.

Clarissa buckled when George Henry rolled off of her. He flicked the ice off the back of his neck, about to fall inside his shirt.

"Ma, dey gone. Done turn back. Did you hear what dey say? We be at the river. It be frozen. We kin cross it and den git on dat train."

"Lawd help us," Clarissa said, shuddering and praying as she struggled to prop up her weight.

George Henry stiffened his arm. He thrust open his hand and saw the warm, bloody mess in it.

"Ma! I done killed some of dem rabbits. Didn't feel it in my hand. Didn't notice the one dat be by my knee neither. I's sorry." George Henry turned up his face, "Lawd, I don't mean to be killin' dese here critters."

"You hush dat yammerin', boy. We gits caught if you don't. God's done forgive you. You didn't mean no harm. He be knowin' dat."

"I be wantin' to git to dat freedom, Ma."

"God wouldn't let no rabbits keep you from dat."

Using a rock, George Henry hollowed out a foot-sized piece of icy earth, laid the animals in the hole, and covered them. He washed the blood and mud from his hands with fresh snow, dried them on his britches, and stuck them under his armpits for warming.

"Ma, give me Miss Effie's gown."

Too drained to question George Henry's request, Clarissa handed him the knapsack. He lifted out Miss Effie's woolen gown and meticulously unfolded it to verify no food chunks or any of Miss Effie's potions were caught in the folds of it. Clarissa had seldom used it and kept it dry. George Henry tied the other rabbits in one of the sleeves and butted it against Clarissa's feet. He swaddled her legs with the remainder of the gown and bundled her with the bedding.

"Boy, dat feel mighty good. Ain't been dis warm since we's in dat cave."

"We be warmer if Stu could'a stayed."

"You loves dat dog. He be lovin' you, too. He gonna be missin' you, boy."

Daybreak arrived, showing off a dusty tinge of bluish lavender with a misty orange underskirt. George Henry was already awake. Clarissa was huddled beneath the coverings with her feet against the squirming bunnies. When the sun was fully up, George Henry squat-walked to the front of the boulder and separated the growth.

"Ma! Come see. It be the river."

"I's here, boy. I sees it. Come on! I shows you somethin'," Clarissa said.

Back under the rock, she put her feet on the bunnies, covered her legs, and flipped Gran's quilt trail side up.

"Remember how dis here quilt be showin' us a cross, a star, stairsteps, and a candle on the north side of dem waters?" She tapped each appliqué.

"Uh-huh. Dat's where we gotta be gittin' to," George Henry said.

"Dat's right, boy. But you know, we gotta wait 'til darkness come or we be gittin' caught. We gonna cross dem waters when it be dark."

When the day faded, the moon glistened with a serious brightness, making it unsafe to cross the frozen water. Wariness gripped Clarissa. She folded her arms across her chest, glared at the moon, and then drew herself into a tight fetal position.

"You be listenin' for dem hounds and wagon wheels, Ma?"

When she didn't answer, George Henry kept the rest of his thoughts inside his head. He spent the remainder of the night scrutinizing the moon.

The next day broke with thick clouds scudding across the blue sky, covering and uncovering the sun. George Henry gazed at the part of the sky where the "following star" should be. Clarissa sang, "Follow the drinkin' gourd." Her voiced fluctuated as if she didn't believe her singing words.

"Ma, how long 'fore we be gittin' to dat freedom?"

"Soon, boy. Victuals 'bout gone."

"Tell me more 'bout dat train."

"You wait. You be seein' soon enough."

22

Crossing the Waters

On the north side of the Ohio River, along the Indiana shoreline, there were slaves, some freed, some nearly freed, and others who ran from their masters and circumstances. Before George Henry and Clarissa were runaways from Ben Mullins' farm, more than a dozen darkies hide on the north side of the Ohio River were they camped among evergreen trees so thick they could barely see the light of the moon. They waited there for the "freedom train" and chatted about the harsh snowfall and how glad they were that it had stopped falling.

A woman with bare ashen legs clopped about in her over-worn shoes collecting kindling that she added to the dying fire. She and the other women spread their coverings and clothing around the campfires to dry them and warm their bodies. In small pots they boiled nuts, dried fruits, and vegetables carried from their old plantations and farms, or what they gathered along the trail. The men skewered and roasted a wild boar and birds on sticks fashioned from shaved branches. When the time came to eat, everyone cozied close to the fires and enjoyed their share of the victuals.

On the south side of the river, George Henry munched on a fistful of smoked meat and dried fruits. He savored the salty-sweet flavor that he never tired of. He and Clarissa didn't usually both eat at the same time, but she decided it was a special occasion and should be treated as such. George Henry felt a sense of comfort in his gut that hadn't been there since the night they left the cabin.

"Ma, dis here the best meal we done had on dis here trail."

"It be nigh to the last. You enjoy it, boy."

"Sho' hope we makes it."

George Henry went back to figuring on the constellations. Clarissa packed the last of the victuals in the knapsack and folded it over into a tight bundle, tied it with a bit of rag from her petticoat, and wedged it into her skirt band. When she stood, it fell through to her feet. She put it under her bosom with the haversack and tightened the knot that held her shirt on. Clarissa and George Henry waited, and they waited more.

On the third night, Clarissa noticed clouds crossing over and under the new moon. The North Star scarcely had a twinkle in it. Not taking her eyes off the sky, she saw a heavier cloud blot the lights of the stars. She peeled Miss Effie's quilt off George Henry.

"Ma, whatcha doin'! I's cold."

"Time to be gittin', boy."

Clarissa rolled the covers and secured the ends of it with rope. Petunia's scarf was drawn over her head and knotted under her chin. Clarissa was still wearing the last pair of socks that Lily had knitted. She was warmed by the love she felt. When she looped Effie's thready shawl around her waist to hold up her skirt, she had flashbacks of when she first arrived at Miss Effie's cabin so frail she could loop her skirt around her body twice. Clarissa shook her head to ward off those ugly memories and enable her mind to think about the glories of freedom.

"Git up, chile. Time done come for us. Gotta cross dem waters."

Clarissa flung the rolled-up covers across her shoulder, tied the dangling rope ends around her waist, and reached for George Henry once more.

"Let's go, boy!"

Pulled by the rushing sound of water, they moved awkwardly through the snow, not stopping until they were at the fringes of the river. The sight of the ice, black as ink, sent a dismal chill through George Henry.

"Feet won't go, Ma. And dat river . . . it be lookin' mighty rough. Like Massa say."

A slab of ice, big as the side of a barn, washed close to the shore. Clarissa abruptly pulled George Henry onto it. They scuffled about until they had a steady footing.

"Ma! Dis ice be cold . . . burnin' my feet. Cain't go no more."

"Hold on, boy. Don't let go! Step easy, now."

George Henry and Clarissa trudged across the floe. The river water shimmied against the bottom of the ice, causing them to lose balance with some steps and fall with others. Struggling to move north, they picked themselves up time and time again. They could have been mistaken for two sea-drunken buddies holding onto each other.

"Clari. Clari," a voice to her called from the hills.

"I's comin', Jake."

Clarissa moved ahead of George Henry, keeping her eyes fixed on the trees from which Jake's voice called to her. Seeing the break in the ice, George Henry yelled, "Stop, Ma! Stop! Ain't no more ice!" Clarissa couldn't hear him above the roar of the river.

George Henry rushed to catch Clarissa like he did at Miss Effie's gravesite, but the ice swayed. He fumbled and Clarissa plummeted, disappearing in the midnight waters. Her head bobbed up to the surface and back down.

"Go on, boy."

She went under before resurfacing again.

"God, take care of me," she gurgled when a wave washed over her face.

"Hold on, Ma!"

Joe, one of the young Negro boys from the north shore campsite, was collecting rocks when he heard the commotion. He saw George Henry rushing to Clarissa, whose head bobbled in the water. The boy charged back up the hill, zigzagging through the hiding trees.

"Ma! Pa! Done seen slaves comin' on the ice. One done fall in the river."

Using his grasshopper legs, George Henry leaped across the break in the ice. He fished for his ma, but she slipped away. Just at that moment, the moon rolled out from behind a thick dark cloud. The star on the quilt glowed from below the waves that rippled over Clarissa's head.

George Henry reached in and grabbed the star. He jostled his ma onto the floe. A jagged wave elevated the slab of ice and sent them, gliding on their bellies, toward Indiana. Just as the ice touched land, another wave pushed beneath it. The turbulence sent them skimming back toward Kentucky. Without warning, the floe dipped fiercely. The rapids catapulted them up and slammed them onto the Indiana shore. Winded and soaked, George Henry crawled to Clarissa. She had landed facedown and appeared lifeless. He rolled the dead weight of his mother's body frontside up. In the moonlight, he saw an expressionless face. He gently shook Clarissa's shoulder like he had done to waken Miss Effie from her death.

"Ma! Ma!"

Clarissa didn't respond to George Henry's touch. He knew she was dead. Her skin was translucent and had never been so cold, colder than Miss Effie's when the angels took her to Gloryland. George Henry caressed Clarissa's head. Believing that she had gone on to be with Miss Effie, he wondered how he would live the rest of his life without his ma. He wanted freedom, but not without her. Not knowing how to leave Clarissa behind, George Henry gripped her body tighter, cuddled her against his chest and stroked her head. Clarissa's eyelids rose so slowly that they didn't seem to be moving at all. George Henry was startled when she glanced at him through the slits of her eyelids. He shook his head in disbelief as he gathered more of her in his arms, all of her that he could hold on to. When her lips moved, he placed his ear against them.

"Where we be, boy?" Her whisper had no warmth.

"On the other side, Ma."

George Henry sat back on his heels grinning with satisfaction.

Darkies came down the hill chanting in low guttural voices:

> *Let us cheer the weary traveler,*
> *Cheer the weary traveler,*
> *Let us cheer the weary traveler,*
> *Along the heavenly way . . .*

"Dem angels singing. Dey comin' for us, Ma! We's dead! Gone on to the Lawd's world."

"Naw, boy. Dat be freedom."

A group of Negroes appeared from out of a mass of trees, led by Harry, a tall young man with big arms. He placed Clarissa on a thick mat.

"You here now," he said.

The strange voice calmed the turmoil inside George Henry.

Harry bundled Clarissa in blankets. With the help of others, they lifted the four corners of the mat and toted her back to the campfire. George Henry was blanketed, too. He rode piggyback on Junny, who reminded him of the brother that his ma spoke of many times. The rest of the slaves marched behind them, speaking in hushed tones.

Clarissa looked closely at Harry's back and then Junny's. George Henry knew that she wondered if one of them might be her Toby. Harry was near Toby's age and was tall and slim, like she had described him to George Henry. Junny was slim but not as tall as Harry.

At the encampment, Clarissa sat on the frozen ground, resting against the sturdy back of Mag, whose face she couldn't see. Another soul with kind eyes, a broad nose, and gently smiling lips, removed Clarissa's blankets and soaked garments. The woman layered the fragile gal with fire-warmed blankets before she scattered the wet things around the campfire to dry. Afterward, she spoon-fed Clarissa a tepid mush.

George Henry leaned against his ma with his legs stretched beneath the covers tucked around him. He hunkered over a small gourd, gulping steamy pot liquor that had a gamy aroma. He giggled when he thought he saw Sally on the other side of the gourd, waiting her turn to hold it. Between sips, he hummed the tune, "Follow the drinking gourd," just as he had heard his ma do many nights before they ran and often on the trail.

Clarissa's eyes shifted back to Harry. She couldn't clearly see his face or all that she remembered of Toby. In her mind, she was sure that she heard Toby's voice come from Harry, "I be good. I be seein' you again."

"Harry, kin you help me fetch dat bit of twig next to ya?"

When he reached for it, his neck rose up out of his coat. There was no fluttering butterfly and Clarissa didn't see one on Junny's neck. She reverted back to her familiar, void feeling. Clarissa manipulated the twig, wishing it were Toby who handed it to her. She pondered each man's face. None was Lily's Copper Tom either.

"Ma, where's dat train you been tellin' 'bout?" George Henry asked again, as the orange glow of firelight danced on his cheeks and brushed the tip of his nose.

"Don't rightly know, boy."

Luke, one of the campers, was a short, broad-shouldered, ebony man who moved nearer to Clarissa and George Henry. He smelled of earth and burning wood. He leaned closer to George Henry and spoke to him in a private voice.

"You's at dat station now, boy. Dat train be comin' 'round dat mountain. We be dem passengers dat gonna ride on dat train."

Luke flung his arm, pointing in no particular direction.

"When the conductor show up, we be gittin' on board. Goin' on to Jordan. Dat Gloryland be waitin' for us. It ain't far now," Luke said in his baritone voice. He was proud that he could share his knowledge with the woman and her boy.

A cold, icy wind blew over the campers, forcing them closer to the fire. The woman supporting Clarissa's back moved away, allowing Clarissa to stretch out toward the beckoning warmth of the flames. The slaves chanted, prayed, and then slept.

The next morning, the sun came up, pushing a tinge of peach, covered by a gauzy blue tinting, across the bottom of the sky. George Henry sprang from his dreams. He reached for Gran's old quilt drying by the fire, threw it over his back, and tied it at his neck. Exhausted and wobbly, he spun in a lopsided circle, clapping his hands, and dancing a slow jive. When he stopped spinning, he belted out a song he had heard the darkies singing in the fields. "A band of angels comin' after me. Comin' for to carry me home."

The others joined in. They hummed and swayed as if in a stupor. Luke's deep voice radiated from behind the crowd and was heard above their song.

"Don't stop! Pound dem drums! Sing loud as you can! No need for a hush-up! We's free now! Dat long walk's over. We's movin' on from dis here bondage! Ain't gonna be no more massas! No more whips! No more hunger! No more shuckin' and shackles! No more pain or pickin'! Dat freedom train be a comin'. Listen to dem drums. Dey be tellin' you so."

Clarissa smiled as she clung to Effie's coverlet, pushing it to her lips and softly talking into it like it had baby ears.

Miss Effie, you dere? I done got your cover all gathered up to my face so we can talk. Just be wantin' to tell how I knowed you was in dat river wid me. I hear you and Jake callin' to me when dat water rush over my head. I thanks you plenty for savin' me . . . and my boy. I told you we's gonna make it to dis here freedom. We gonna be gittin' on dat train. Miss Effie, I be hearin' somethin'. It be makin' my heart pound'. Ain't Big Bo's hammer neither. Everybody be singin'. Miss Effie, the time done come for us. We goin' on. Goin' on to Jordan. Cain't talk no mo'. Gotta go!

The Negroes rapped on their drums with firm, thudding fingers. Others plucked banjo strings, snapping them with triumph. Gaiety swept through the air, bending and rocking the flames with each beat. A bustling and rustling came from the trees. It tempered the drums and the banjos.

"Be still," Luke whispered.

A rumbling of voices seeped from the tall timbers:

> *Git on board, little chillen,*
> *Git on board, little chillen,*
> *There's room for many a mo'.*

Clarissa grabbed George Henry. She wrapped Petunia's paisley scarf around his neck, intertwining it with the quilt, and then tied Effie's scarf around her waist.

"Dis here be our luck. Take care, boy, don't lose dat scarf. Petunia's prayers be all tied up in it. Miss Effie's prayers be twisted in dis here one I got on me. Dese scarves gonna be keepin' us safe like dey been doin'. Come on, boy. We be gittin' on dat train. Don't gotta wait no mo'."

The End

Epilogue

Clarissa and George Henry joined the Underground Railroad. It took them north to London, Canada, where they lived the rest of their lives. Toby escaped from his owner in Nashville, Tennessee, and traveled to St. Louis, Missouri, where he found his twin sisters, Mary and Molly, who were fifteen years old and lived with a scholar named Dr. Smith. Toby stole them away. He took the girls with him back to Kentucky to find Clarissa and George Henry.

Toby hid the twins in the bush along Cox's Creek, down from the Bloomfield Turnpike that ran across the front of Ben Mullins' farm, where his mother and younger brother had been enslaved. Crossing the road, he followed the sound of the blacksmith's hammer. He saw and spoke with Bo, now the master blacksmith. He told Toby that his mother and brother ran away some time ago. He hadn't heard news of them being caught and didn't know where they were.

Toby and his sisters left Spencer County, Kentucky, and headed to Ripley, Ohio. With the assistance of abolitionists, such as ministers and their wives, Toby and the twins were able to continue on their way to Cincinnati, Ohio. Once there, another abolitionist and his family helped them get to Detroit, where they crossed the Detroit River into Windsor, Ontario, Canada. They traveled northeast until they reached London, Canada, where they established a homesite.

Toby worked as a carpenter and took care of his twin sisters as they continued with their education. One evening, he and his sisters attended a gathering at a Catholic church with the other Negroes living in London. The group assembled once a year to celebrate their freedom. They sang and shared stories of their adventures and escapes on the Underground Railroad. Toby told of how he and his family traveled from Virginia to Kentucky to be sold on the auction block, and how he and his twin sisters were separated from their family. Clarissa, who was among the crowd, realized that the handsome gentleman speaking might be her son and that the young ladies, who were identical and standing next to him, were possibly Mary and Molly.

When she saw the butterfly birthmark on the back of the young man's neck, Clarissa parted the crowd with her cries. She extended her arms, embracing Toby and the girls. George Henry was hesitant to move closer. His only recollections of them were those kept alive by his ma's storytelling.

From that day on, the family resided together. Clarissa tacked the last bird wings, that represented George Henry and herself, onto to Gran's old quilt. She kept the quilt, her auction skirt, and Miss Effie's coverlet locked in a chest that Toby made for her. The girls grew up to become teachers. Toby bought the carpentry shop where he worked, married, had two sons and a daughter, whom he named Alice. George Henry worked with Toby and became a carpenter and a writer. Clarissa retired as a laundress. She cared for her grandchildren until she left her life on earth to join Jake. They believed that he died of old age and a broken hea

Discussion Questions

1.   Why did the author introduce her story with a scene from the auction? What fears did the auction conjure up for slaves? What indignities did they experience?

2.   What would you have done if you had witnessed your family being sold away from you? What were Clarissa thoughts at the auction?

3.   Why was Ben Mullins despised and hated by his slaves? What was the evidence that he had a better side to his character?

4.   Margaret warns Ben Mullins to mind his manners at the lawn party. He falls over a guest and kisses the darkie on the lips. Did his drinking influence his actions or was alcohol an excuse for his behavior?

5.   Social justice is based on the principles of equality and solidarity, and recognizes the values of human rights of every human being. What violations of justice occurred in *The Long Walk: Slavery to Freedom*?

6.   Petunia was troublesome and despised by Margaret. Most owners would have sold her down the river. Aside from being a gift from his aunt, why do you think Ben Mullins insisted on keeping her?

7.   Margaret viciously lashed out at Clarissa. What was the main source of Margaret's anger? What were Clarissa's feelings about the treatment she experienced at Margaret's hands?

8.   How did Copper Tom's character influence the dynamics of the hoedown?

9.   Ben Mullins was a well-to-do farmer with enough slaves to care for his farm's daily needs and could have purchased more if he needed to. Why was he obsessed with capturing Clarissa and George Henry?

10.   Ben Mullins loved Effie and could not bring himself to do her great harm even thought he could quickly draw a master-slave line between them. What element gave their relationship such a strong foundation?

11.   What was the symbolism between the teacup and saucer and the potion that put Margaret to sleep? Did Margaret need to be sedated?

12.   What did Clarissa do to prepare for her escape? What special gifts came her way that helped on her the journey? Was George Henry too young to endure the struggles and challenges of escaping? Explain.

13.   What were your feeling about *The Long Walk: Slavery to Freedom* and the characters that you encountered? What event stood out most and why?

14.   At the end of the story, Hycus, the overseer was uneasy in his saddle and had little to say when he and Ben Mullins were at the river. Why was he troubled about not capturing Clarissa and George Henry?

15.   How would you compare and contrast the dramatic elements of the auction block scene with that of Clarissa and George Henry crossing the Ohio River?

16.   How would you describe the celebration around the campfire on the Indiana side of the Ohio River? What were Clarissa's thoughts as she waited for the Freedom Train?

Suggested Reading

Ball, Edward. *Slaves in the Family*. New York: Farrar, Straus, and Giroux, 1998.

Botkin, B. A., ed. Foreword by Jerrold Hirsch. *Lay My Burden Down: A Folk History of Slavery.* Athens, Georgia: University of Georgia Press, 1973.

Dewolf, Thomas Norman. *Inheriting the Trade: A Northern Family Its Legacy as The Largest Slave Trading Dynasty in U.S. History.* Boston: Beacon Press, 2012.

Dow, Francis George. *Slave Ships and Slaving*. Mineola, New York: Dover Publication, Inc., 2002.

Farrow, Anne, Joel Lang, and Jenifer Frank. *Complicity: How the North Promoted, Prolonged and Profited from Slavery.* New York: Ballatine Books, 2005.

Gates, Louis, and Cynthia Goodman. *Unchained Memories*. Boston: Bulfinch Press, 2002.

Hagedorn, Ann. *Beyond the River: The Story of the Heroes of the Underground Railroad.* New York: Simon & Schuster, 2002.

Jacobs, Harriet A. *Life of a Slave Girl*. 1861. Cambridge, Massachusetts: Harvard University Press, 2007.

King, Wilma. *Stolen Childhood: Slave Youth in Nineteenth-Century American*. Bloomington: Indiana University Press, 1995.

McCutcheon, Marc. *Everyday Life in the 1800s*. Cincinnati, Ohio: Writer's Digest Books, 1993.

Northup, Norman. *Twelve Years a Slave*. Mineola, New York: Dover Publications, Inc., 1970.

Schomburg Library of Nineteenth-Century of Black Women Writers. *Six Women's Slave Narratives*. New York: Oxford University Press, USA, 1988.

Thomas, Huge. *Slave Trade: The Story of the Atlantic Slave Trade 1440–1870*. New York: Touchstone, 1997.

Victor, Metta Victoria Fuller. *Maum Guinea and Her Plantation "Children" or Holiday-week on a Louisiana Estate*. Bedford, Massachusetts: Applewood Books, 1999.

Vlach, John Michael. *Back of the Big House: The Architecture of Plantation Slavery*. Chapel Hill: University of North Caroline Press, 1993.

Weld, Theodore Dwight. *American Slavery As It Is: A Testimony of a Thousand Witnesses*. 1839. New York: Arno Press and the *New York Times*, 1968.

Yetman, Norman R., ed. *Voices From Slavery: 100 Authentic Slave Narratives*. Mineola, New York: Dover Publications, 1970.

———, ed. *When I Was a Slave: Memoirs from the Slave Narrative Collection*. Mineola, New York: Dover Publications, 2002.

About the Author

Judith C. Owens-Lalude is the great-granddaughter of George Henry "Pap" Johnson born in 1850 and enslaved with his

mother, Clarissa. They lived on Ben Miller's 600-acre farm in North Central Kentucky, now less than an hour's drive from Louisville, Kentucky, where Owens-Lalude grew up and resided until 2017. After listening to tales told by her family's closest members about their ancestors, she wanted to know more and visited the farm where her ancestors had been enslaved. She strolled the grounds, reflected at the fireplace hearth where a slave cabin once stood, wandered along the streams and creeks, and photographed the barn and other outbuildings that were a part of her great-grandpa's and his mother's daily world.

Inspired to write a book, Owens-Lalude traveled to her husband's native Nigeria for a better understanding of the history of slavery in the Americas. She wanted to know its impact on other Africans and African Americans, including her family who lived in Nelson and Spencer counties, Kentucky. She was also intrigued by the writings of Harry Smith, *Fifty Years in Slavery in the United States* and Isaac Johnson's *Slavery Days in Old Kentucky.* Both authors were enslaved in Jefferson, Nelson, and Spencer counties where Owens-Lalude's family was also enslaved and later lived as freed people.

From these readings, her research, her travels, and her powerful imagination, Owens-Lalude wrote two compelling novels: *The Long Walk: Slavery to Freedom* and *Miss Lucy: Slave and Civil War Nurse.*

National Park Service, National Underground Railroad Network to Freedom program has applied rigorous scholarship in identifying and awarding membership to more than 400 sites, programs and facilities in thirty-one states and the District of Columbia. Additional members are added twice a year. *The Long Walk: From Slavery to Freedom* (application title) by Judith C. Owens-Lalude was accepted into the Network to Freedom as an program for students and adults in 2007.

www.ingramcontent.com/pod-product-compliance
Lightning Source LLC
Chambersburg PA
CBHW070447120726
47910CB00003B/965